A
Winter
Night

ISBN: 979-8391212836

www.douglaslindsay.com

Podcast: Cold September, on Apple, Spotify and Amazon

A
WINTER
NIGHT

DOUGLAS
LINDSAY

LMP

for Kathryn
always

An Unreliable Narrative

i

This is why we're in the mess we're in. This is why the world, all of it, all of us, all of everything, everywhere all at once, is crashing into a flaming ball of tragic stupidity. This is why nobody fucking loves you.

See what we did there? The everything, everywhere all at once line. We meant that. OK, we'll explain the layers. Some might say that's like explaining a joke. Once you start explaining subtlety, then there goes the subtlety, right? But this is what we're talking about. People and marketing and words and bandwagons and all kinds of shit. People say, oh, this is amazing, and wow, you should see/read/inhale/choke on this, whatever it is, you have to eat there, or you have to cover yourself in this stuff, it's mind-blowing, and then you do the thing, and you're sitting there thinking, what the fuck? Like, what the actual fuck? What are we missing out on? What is it everyone else sees that we don't? Are *we* the stupid ones? Is that it? Or do they just want us to think we're stupid?

Fuck 'em. Fuck 'em all. We're not watching any more than one episode of *Succession*. We just don't like it. We're not watching *House of the Dragon*. We're not reading *The Thursday Murder Club*. We hated *The Banshees of Inisherin*. We're not drinking fucking Strongbow, we're not drinking gin, we're not food-shopping in M&S, we're not travelling around Italy drooling over Stanley Tucci – come on! – we're not buying this year's album for the young middle class, whatever the fuck that is, and we hate Ed Sheerin, Billie Eilish and BTS. And we didn't like *Everything Everywhere All At Once*, we just didn't. But we say it, and it makes us the negative ones. We're the gainsayer, the sourpuss, we're the ones with the chip on our shoulder, the ones who don't like anything, the ones who failed at our own shit, so we begrudge everyone else their success.

We can only attest to our own genius. And we are not that

negative person. We hold no grudge. What we can do, is see through them. See through the lies and the bullshit. We understand. And we are not Internet conspiracy theorists. We are common sense, that's all. It used to be valued. Nothing is valued anymore, unless it brings in money. Only money is valued. We don't do money.

It's about time there was a little payback. The people that brought us this life will die. We don't need to travel very far to know where to start. Then let's see how everyone else deals with a knife in the throat of a corpse dumped in a mash tun. Big that up, you fuckers.

We have got to stop swearing. Like, seriously.

1

January continues to follow December, every damned year. Never changes. Bleak and grim and endless. The only month with seven hundred and fifty-three days.

I'm not sure why Eurosport exists as a television channel. I mean, whose go-to channel for sports is Eurosport? Except, I have it, so that on weekend mornings in January I can watch skiing. I'm not, as it happens, the slightest bit interested in skiing. Sure, it's a sport and people do it, and the people who do it are pretty fucking fearless and they've got to be damned fit – apart from that one old Swiss bloke who looks like his daily training regime consists of dipping a hundred bratwurst in a gallon of molten cheese – but does anyone care who wins?

Yeah, all right, I'm projecting my total lack of interest on to everyone else. But I don't watch for the sport, I watch for the mountains, and the snow, and the beautiful clear air. The days when the sky is an unbelievable Springsteen blue, and the branches of the fir trees are laden with snow, and the mountains above and the valleys below are pristine white, those are the best. Those are the mornings to sit with a cup of coffee and wallow in it.

The days when it's raining, or the cloud is low, or there's little snow, the race run on an artificially snow-enhanced track, I just turn it off, with a strange feeling of loss. Like that game of football you've really been looking forward to getting postponed at the last minute.

As I sit at my desk on a bleak Wednesday morning I'm discussing this with Constable Ritter. She asks why I don't just watch old skiing shows on YouTube, then I could guarantee snow conditions. I tell her that it has to be live. That's the point. That somewhere right now, while I'm sitting here in my average little apartment in the hinterland between Cambuslang and Rutherglen, and the weather outside is just a bleak and grim Glasgow grey, there's a part of Europe that's glorious and beautiful and perfect, and I can at least dream of being there. It

---

still exists, even as the human race piteously destroys everything worthwhile on earth.

Eileen and I took a break to Switzerland once, and that was wonderful. I could do with that again. But somehow there's a distance between us these days, and a trip to Switzerland does not seem very likely.

Why don't you go yourself? asks Constable Ritter, when I say I have no one to go with. It would be good for your mental health, she adds, as her generation likes to talk about mental health.

My generation doesn't do mental health. We do another shot of vodka.

I don't answer, and turn back to the screen, and the report I'm writing on Monday afternoon's arrest. James Watts, forty-seven, known to his pals as Three-Stone. He must weigh at least eighteen stone, so maybe it's a joke. Fuck knows. No biggie, it wasn't like we busted him for assault or a sex crime. Public nuisance, related to repeated playing of loud music. It was that boring. Nevertheless, he's been found guilty of this crime seven times before, and the last time the judge told him that if he got busted again, he could expect a custodial. First thing he says after we've brought him into the station is, I'm a woman now, you have to call me Tracy. I think he's joking, and he hasn't even thought to say it until he's sitting there, but then he probably sees the look on my face, as my will to live seeps hauntingly out of my eyeballs, and he decides to stick with it.

Paperwork ensues.

That's what I'm doing now. Those Swiss mountains seem a lot farther than a thousand miles away.

* * *

'Sergeant,' says Chief Inspector Hawkins as she walks past my desk, nodding in the direction of her office.

I share a quick glance with Ritter, which I suppose is what people do, but I have no idea why I'm being summoned, so there's nothing in the look. Nevertheless, I get the sense of something. Like this is the moment in a Bond novel when 007 gets called in to see M, to be told that Moneypenny has his first class tickets to Jamaica, and that he's only got fourteen hours to save the earth.

I get in there, closing the door behind me. Hawkins is

---

already behind her desk. She's wearing a tight-fitting, high-necked black sweater. I only mention this because she looks absolutely fucking gorgeous, which is the sort of thing you're not really supposed to mention anymore, never mind even think, but the boss looks like she's just about to audition for the part of Emma Peel – sexy as fuck, with the ability to hand you your arse – and I'm here for it.

'Got much on?' she asks.

Jesus, I really am getting a strong Bond vibe. This is *exactly* how Bond movies start.

: *Got much on, 007?*

: *Yesh, but moshtly shagging birdsh. Whatsh up?*

'Sergeant?'

She snaps her fingers.

'Nothing major.' I pause, but have something else to add, and she indicates for me to continue, and I say, 'Not sure there's enough going on to justify my being here at the moment, I'm afraid. We could probably do with someone getting murdered.'

Classic glib Hutton. She doesn't react.

'Did you read about the murder on Islay at the weekend?'

I give the merest pretence of thinking about it, then shake my head.

'Tend to ignore stories not on our patch.'

'We're all one big patch, Sergeant.'

These new, fangled ways of Police Scotland. They'll never be my ways. I keep my mouth shut.

'A fifty-five-year-old man was found dead at his distillery.'

'He owned the distillery, or he just worked there?'

'Joint owner with his brother. It's a new one, Kilcraig, hasn't sent any whisky to market yet. Currently surviving on the gin trade while the whisky matures.' She pauses, then adds, 'Or whatever it is that whisky does.'

'Is it a brothers fell out, family intrigue kind of a thing?'

She takes a moment, then holds her hands out. 'We don't know. It's certainly messy.'

'Families…'

'Yes, families. But also… there seems to be a strong undercurrent of political divide.'

'Uh-oh. Would that be left and right, or the other thing?'

'The other thing. The murdered brother was a strong supporter of independence, the surviving brother a member of the Conservative Party, and a firm unionist. This seems to have affected their working relationship, creating division within the company. It's too early to say if this might have led to the murder.'

'Sounds like fun.'

'Yes, sergeant,' she says drily, 'as murder usually is.'

Elbows on the desk, she entwines her fingers, and rests her chin in her hands for a moment, staring at me, while she contemplates the next part of the James Bond novel.

'Obviously it's a very delicate situation, requiring tact and the utmost restraint, and officers capable of such.'

We stare at each other for a few moments. I find myself wanting to look over my shoulder. Partly as a comedy manoeuvre, partly because it genuinely feels like there ought to be someone else there to whom she's actually speaking. Instead I go for, 'Are you about to ask if I know anyone like that? I mean, Eileen would be pretty decent.'

'Sgt Harrison is not a detective,' she says, mundanely.

'Guess not.'

'What are your views on independence?' she asks.

'Seriously? I mean, if I say one thing or the other do I then get sent on this or not? We're allowing suspects and witnesses to dictate staffing?'

'I'm just curious,' she says, as she relaxes a little, starting to back off from that part of the discussion. 'Whichever way you lean, you might want to keep your affiliations to yourself, that's all.'

'Fortunately, or not,' I say, 'I hate everyone, equally. Thinking of buying some tiny-assed island in Shetland and declaring it independent. I can probably sign a treaty with the Chinese for them to come to my defence if the taxman calls.'

'Yes, that sounds like a plan, Sergeant,' she says, her tone the familiar one of a mother to her incorrigible child.

Then she lifts a hand and indicates her computer screen. 'I'll e-mail you a couple of documents. The story so far. If you could read up on them. You've got a ferry from Kennacraig this evening, and you're booked into the Kilcreggan Guest House on the island. You'll start work tomorrow morning.'

She looks as though she has something else to add, but instead just stares across the desk inviting questions. My first is fairly inevitable.

'Why me?'

She nods, thinking through the answer. It wasn't like that

question wasn't coming.

'Yes,' she says. She looks disapproving. 'Like I say, this was messy, right from the off. An inspector was sent over at the weekend, it very quickly became apparent she was viewed as too establishment.'

'Which establishment?'

'Ha, good. Edinburgh, that one. Like I say, it's messy. On Day Two, HQ acquiesced. They looked around for someone obviously neutral to send, someone with no skin in the Scottish independence game, as one might say,' she says, and sure, if you wanted to use the phrase *skin in the game* which is horribly American, and which normal people can't say out loud without their mouth rejecting it, 'and they settled upon Inspector Kallas.'

Oh boy.

It seems instantly apparent where this is going, but that would be so far into the too-good-to-be-true column my brain doesn't allow me to go there yet. I must remain calm at all times.

'It seems the inspector's partner, DS Lanningham, has recently gone on maternity leave. As in, she just finished working last Friday. Ideal timing, one might think,' she says, though she does not look as though she thinks the time particularly ideal. 'Inspector Kallas has not yet been allocated a replacement officer. She asked that you be sent to Islay to accompany her in the investigation.'

We hold the stare across the desk.

'I'm not sure I entirely approve,' says the chief. 'I know you work well together, and I'm sure Kadri is professional enough to not let whatever it is between the two of you get in the way, but nevertheless... She has been sent to do a job for a period of time away from her family, and she asks that you accompany her. I'm not sure that this is a particularly healthy circumstance for either of you. I am inclined to say that you shouldn't go. However, under the circumstances, it would be extremely harsh of me to refuse.'

That line there – *I'm inclined to say that you shouldn't go* – was like the magnificent goal you've just scored suddenly being sent to VAR, but fortunately the decision to allow the goal to stand came pretty fucking rapidly.

Then the words *under the circumstances* finally worm their way into my head.

'What does that mean?'

'What does what mean?'

7

'Under the circumstances. What circumstances?'

She regards me curiously, then asks the killer question, 'Don't you know?'

Got one of those horrible feelings rising up my gut. Fuck-a-rama. Shake my head. It's all I've got.

'You haven't spoken to Kadri recently?'

I pause, and then have to admit, 'I spoke to her last week. She called. She didn't... there was nothing...'

Think about it, Hutton. You're a fool who survives on gut instinct. You knew there was something she wanted to tell you, you got the sense of it, you could tell she didn't manage to say it, and you didn't force it from her because you knew you were unlikely to like it. *Let's have coffee soon.* That was how it had been left.

'She and her family are moving back to Estonia shortly. I believe she's already arranged her job with the Estonian police force in Tallinn.'

That there is like being hit by the Avanti West Coast 390 as it passes through Cambuslang at a hundred and forty miles an hour.

'Oh,' is all I've got.

You probably wouldn't just say *oh* if you got hit by a train.

The gaze stays as it is across the desk. She'll be reading me now, no question of that, noticing no doubt the oncoming rush of total devastation.

'Maybe I shouldn't have said,' she volunteers, obviously uncomfortable with the silence. 'I expect Kadri intended to tell you soon enough.'

I've got nothing to say to that either. Finally, 'Thanks, boss. I'll read the report, then get my stuff together and head.'

'Your ferry's not until five, so no need to rush. You've been to Kennacraig?'

'Nope.'

'It's by Tarbert, about two and a half hours from here, maybe. You won't need to go until after lunch. Gives you a chance to speak to Emma, sort your desk out, make sure she's on top of everything. Although, hopefully, you and the inspector can wrap this one up fairly quickly, and you shouldn't be away too long. We should probably plan on a few days at least, I would think.'

I stand and I stare. I get a sympathetic smile. I nod, I rummage through the dregs of my brain for something to say.

'Thanks,' is all that comes. 'Send the file through, and I'll take a look.'

She nods.

Fuck it, pull yourself together, Hutton. You can go home and weep or go home and drink copiously, or go home and do *something*, but whatever it is, you're not doing it here.

Drinking copiously would probably be bad, given I've got a two-and-a-half-hour drive to the west coast. I can drink tonight, and be damned.

Maybe one drink before I go. Or two. One or two.

'You look great, by the way.'

There, I said something. Just like a fucking idiot.

She regards me curiously. It wasn't particularly appropriate, and it's not as though I've ever previously told her how good she looks.

'Thank you?' she says.

'It suits you, that's all,' are the words with which I attempt to cover my tracks, and then I turn and leave.

2

There are more distilleries on Islay than there are people, which sounds like it doesn't make sense, but that's just how it is. They're all over the damn place. What it probably doesn't need is another one, but that's where we're headed. Well, it's where I'm headed. The inspector already got there.

The Kilcraig distillery laid down their first batch three years ago. They opened the distillery up to the full visitor experience a year and a half ago, and jumped in, full bore, every money-making opportunity explored to compensate for the length of time it takes to get whisky to market. Since gin has a quicker turnaround – you make gin one day, sell it the next – they're already selling three different varieties. However, it's in whisky that they aim to make their name.

Saturday evening, sometime after seven. Visitor centre closed for the day, distillery floor closed for the day. Nothing doing. One operative making sure everything's ticking over, but since that's mainly ensuring nothing explodes or leaks or does whatever, this is in the hands of the night guard, Bethany. There's no distilling taking place, but there is an earlier part of the process running overnight. Mashing malted barley in the Lauter tun. That's what I read in the report, but that's just a bunch of words to me. I Google Lauter tun, which doesn't entirely help, so I look at the distillery's website, and they have a picture of their equipment. The Lauter tun looks like the top half of a flying saucer. Round, three metres in diameter perhaps. There's a porthole, and what looks like a small, rectangle panel that can be removed in the top. There are pipes and all sorts running in and out of it. Stop me if I get too technical.

Bethany is doing her rounds. The place is low lit by a scattering of fluorescent strip lights. She doesn't waste electricity by turning on all the lighting. In fact, she noted in her statement, she rather likes the quiet half-light. She carries a torch, though there's enough light for her not to have to use it.

She stops, she takes in the quiet. Like all the best suspense movies, things aren't just quiet, they're *too* quiet. She can't hear the Lauter tun working. That seems strange. As she approaches the tun, she starts to get a bad feeling. She starts to think that maybe she should have turned the lights on. She hesitates, she lifts the torch, she shines it on the side of the tun. She really doesn't want to shine the torch inside. She hesitates, the light aimed just to the side of the window. Nevertheless, some of the light finds its way inside, and her eyes are unavoidably drawn there, and she shines the torch fully in through the small window and stares into the frothy, brown liquid, and there's a body and she's consumed by fear, and she's running, and she's not someone who takes anyone's shit, but there's nothing like the fear of the unknown, and she doesn't know what dangers lurk in the night, and she gets to the door, panting and desperate, and throws every light switch on the panel, and turns, fearfully, expecting the shock of the attacker close behind, but there's no one. There's nothing. There's silence.

* * *

'And it was one of the brothers who died?' asks Sgt Harrison.

'Yeah. The SNP-supporting one. The one who wanted a shout at running for parliament. Whatever his long term goals… they ain't happening.'

'Dead now.'

'Yep. Stabbed in the throat, body dumped in this massive, cylindrical urn thing.'

'Floating in whisky?'

'Pre-whisky. It's an early stage of the process, before it's been fermented or distilled.'

'So, what is it?'

'Gloop. There was a word, but I forget.'

'I feel you're bringing me half a thing here.'

'Possibly.'

Me and Eileen, having lunch at the café down in the precinct. We haven't done this in a couple of months. I asked, she seemed a little curious, perhaps unimpressed, but said yes.

'Did they find the knife?'

'It remained in his throat. When the guard found the body, he was floating on his back, the knife sticking straight up.'

'Ooft,' she says. 'That's going to give you a shock.'

'Yeah.'

I take a bite of club sandwich. She does the same. I take a drink of Coke Zero, she takes a drink of water.

Now that the information on the case has been imparted, an uncomfortable silence threatens to return to the table. Eileen and I have done a few uncomfortable silences recently. I don't think this lunch is really likely to help matters, but I felt I had to have it.

'You not drinking Coke anymore?' I say, in some lame-ass attempt to stop the silence settling in.

She can, as ever, see right through me, and she shakes her head.

'I've been reading about the gut microbiome.'

'The what?'

'Everything going on in your gut, the bacteria and the enzymes, the way they interact with each other and the food you eat.' She sounds a little uncomfortable having to explain it to me. 'This stuff, even though it's sugar free, is bad for you.'

I take another drink of Coke Zero.

'Would I be better with wine?'

'Surprisingly, as long as it's in moderation, yes. Particularly red.' A pause, and then she says, 'Too bad you drink white.'

The discomfort between us is enough that even the shortest silence, like the ones that exist between sentences, instantly feels profound, as though threatening to take on physical form.

'This is why you've lost weight,' I say. 'I mean, healthy eating, not giving up Coke Zero.'

She stares blankly across the table. I'm wittering.

'You look good on it.'

Nothing. She takes another bite of sandwich.

'Should you be eating that?' I ask, sort of jokingly, but it doesn't work.

'You can eat anything. It's about balance, and making sure your gut gets the right... wait, why are we talking about this?'

'I don't know, it seems like –'

'You haven't asked me out to lunch in like three months. You don't want to know about the fact I'm drinking kefir first thing.'

'Kefir?'

She gives me the stare.

'I thought you were mad at me,' I say, which is kind of weak, because I didn't really think that.

'You know I'm not *mad* at you, for God's sake. Why are we here, Tom?'

12

How much nuance in that single three-letter name.

Fuck it.

'The reason I got the Islay gig is because Kadri's there and she asked that I get put on it.'

She stares across the table, takes a moment, and then lifts her sandwich and takes another slow, deliberate bite. That is some Al Pacino level shit right there. I love Eileen, but fuck me, that's a balls-out intimidating way to eat a fucking sandwich.

'I know,' she says.

'How do you know?'

'We're one big giant police force, Tom, have been for ten years. We can see what everyone's doing. I heard you'd got the job, and I looked to see who else had been assigned to it.'

I swallow. I'd take a bite of food, but I'm terrible at it compared to her. She's got the screen presence. I'm just a schmuck in a tie, staring blankly across a table.

'You still came to lunch,' I say weakly.

'You asked.'

Another pause. Silence, in its way, quickly pulls out a seat at the table, and joins us.

'Sorry,' finds its way to my lips.

'Jesus,' she more or less snaps, 'you don't have to apologise. We're not a couple. You can go off and solve crime with your pal.'

She stops, takes a breath, a brief closing of her eyes. She's better than that, and she finds that better version of herself very quickly.

'You worked well together when she was here,' she says, managing to expel the tone. 'You'll do a good job. You both will. You complement each other perfectly, in a weird kind of way.'

Now that the pressure has been slightly released, I take another bite of sandwich. Nearly finished.

'She's going back to Estonia next month,' I now let out into the wild.

She stares at me across the top of the bottle of water, which is currently at her lips, as she feeds the thirst of the voracious, living creatures in her gut.

'How d'you mean?'

'She's moving back there with that stupid husband of hers and her three kids.'

'Oh.'

She keeps the stare across the table, although, like the boss earlier, her expression seems to relax a little, becoming more sympathetic.

'You all right?' she asks. 'When did she tell you?'

'The chief just told me this morning.'

'Ouch,' she says, then she shakes it away, a little uncomfortable at using the word. 'So this is kind of a last hurrah?'

I shrug.

'Haven't spoken to Kadri yet. We exchanged a text. We're meeting to discuss the case when I arrive at the guest house this evening, but that's not going to be until, like, eight-thirty or something.'

The thought of Kadri and I being in the same guest house is enough to kick this newer, more sympathetic version of Eileen in the face, and she retreats again. Bottle to her lips, and then another bite of sandwich.

Silence has returned. Silence instantly becomes such a major part of this lunch it has its own sandwich, and it's eating the sandwich with such silent fury, it's taken charge.

I am defeated. I don't know what to say. I put the last of my club on brown in my mouth, and then go on to continue the genocide of the microbes in my gut with some more sugar-free fizz.

3

It's a nice drive up here. Along Lomondside, take a left to Arrochar, up the Rest and Be Thankful, and then round the head of Loch Fyne, and down the other side to the far end to Tarbert, then a short right to the ferry port at Kennacraig. But this is January, the weather is dull and grey, and by the time four o'clock hits, and I'm getting to the scenic part of the drive, it's already dark and the drive is little more than the flashing by of another set of headlights, with occasional snow-topped hills to the left and the right.

Kadri sent more details, and I sit in the small ferry terminal – here an hour early – reading up on the distillery and the information on the crime, such as we have it.

Photographs of the deceased as his body was dumped in the mashing vessel. Presumably they ditched that batch of liquid. Wort, that's the name of what's produced by the process. I mean, there are likely some ghoulish bastards out there who would happily pay even more for a shot of whisky made from it. Whisky is so rank anyway, it's not like a bit of blood is going to be able to mask the taste. Death Whisky, aged in special blood-stained barrels for eighteen years, only a hundred thousand pounds a bottle.

Photographs of the deceased on the slab, before and after he'd been under the pathologist's knife.

And photographs of him in happier times, when he was still with us. Fancied himself, you can see it in his eyes. He was a good-looking bloke, and he knew it 'n all.

Nothing about his corpse to indicate there was a struggle prior to his death. A nice, clean thrust of a knife into his throat. Blood will have spilled. And then his body was dumped in the mash.

There wasn't too much blood around, although enough to indicate the killer hadn't bothered trying to clean it up. Dumping the body in the mash is presumed to be a way of concealing any inadvertently-left DNA of the killer, rather than as an intention to hide the corpse. The machine had been turned off, so the corpse was always going to be discovered. The killer obviously did not want a long, drawn out affair of the missing distillery owner, his body only discovered days or weeks or months later.

At this stage, there are zero suspects, aside from his brother, and his brother is chiefly a suspect because he seems to be a bit of a cunt. Their relationship appears to have been tempestuous, disagreeing fairly violently on just about everything about the business. 'And yet it worked,' someone at the distillery said in their statement.

Well, up to a point.

The reason we find ourselves here – and I mean, Kadri and now me – is that their main bone of contention, the thing from which all other disagreements seemed to stem, was on the matter of independence. It was something on which they'd always disagreed. Caleb, the elder at fifty-seven, was the unionist. John, two years his junior, the victim, the nationalist. Seems like they'd had a couple of decades of fairly amicable disagreement, but then along came the independence referendum to ignite the fire. 2014 came and went, leaving rancour in its wake. Eight and a half years later, they had not recovered. Indeed, they'd got worse as time had passed. It's not as though the debate has gone away after all. And all political debate, everywhere on earth, has slowly descended into the mire as the Internet and falsehoods and disingenuousness have taken hold.

There's a ping overhead, and an announcement about getting to our cars. I push the empty coffee cup away from me, close my phone, slip it into my pocket, and start to think about the bar on the ferry, and whether I can risk having those shots of vodka I managed not to drink when I briefly stopped off at the house to pack a small bag.

4

My mood changes on a sixpence, but here I am, checking in to the guest house all the same. Not sure who chose this, but it looks decent. Perhaps it's just the closest place to the distillery, being only a ten-minute drive away.

Cold out west, a clear night, amazing sky, a gazillion stars, no moon nor light pollution to dull them. When I nearly drove off the road because I'd been driving too fast, possibly because of the four glasses of vodka I'd drunk on the boat, I stopped and got out of the car to take some air. The other guy, the one I swerved to avoid, drove on into the night, perhaps unaware of my near-apocalyptic drama. Nevertheless, I avoided putting my car in a ditch, so there's that. Yet that it happened at all because I'd been drinking, is the sort of thing that fills me with the kind of self-loathing with which I am sadly only too familiar. And here I am, coming to see the woman I love, too. Nearly crashed the car. And even though I didn't, I arrive a little drunk and smelling of booze.

Shameful.

But the stars. Oh, the stars. My God, they are spectacular out here. We never see a night sky like this back home.

I thought that, standing there, neck strained, looking straight up. I found Orion's Belt. That was it. That's like the only thing I know. And the Plough, I guess. I thought, *oh the stars*. Then I giggled at myself for suddenly turning into a nineteenth-century poet, and then I hated myself even more because I was giggling like a drunk asshole. I stopped giggling after that.

Oh the fucking stars.

The landlord is Polish, though he seems happy enough. My view of Poles is that they are mostly miserable, but I'm not sure why I have that view. Their lot, collectively as a country, has been pretty shit, but it's not like I know many of the people. This guy seems quite chipper, however.

'How was the ferry?' he asks.

I stand well back, chewing gum, as though that might make a difference. It certainly won't with Detective Inspector Kallas, and I will make no effort to conceal it. I sat in that bar dreaming about how this might go, she and I alone in a guest house, and all the while I self-sabotaged. I drank, thereby reducing the chances of any intimacy.

Of course, I have no idea about the chances of intimacy. They are all on her. She's the married one. She's the mother of three school-age children. She's the one getting the fuck out of Dodge.

'Smooth,' I say.

I don't feel like speaking, despite his bonhomie.

'It is a beautiful night,' says Janusz, the landlord. 'Particularly beautiful from the ferry. Out on deck, turn your back to the main cabin. If there is a free bench, lie on it. I have spent entire ferry journeys staring at the stars.' He bursts out laughing. 'My wife says I am crazy. You do need a thick coat.'

Well, I sat in the bar drinking Polish vodka, so there's that.

He smiles, but I have nothing to say, having got nowhere near the deck. Presumably used to the full panoply of guests, from effervescent to taciturn, the smile stays on his face as he hands over the key.

'Up this corridor to your left,' he says. 'Your colleague is in the next door room, though I believe she is currently in the lounge. There are only two other guests at the moment, and they are out this evening. She has the lounge to herself, so it is perhaps a better working environment than the room. The lounge is through here.' He indicates a door behind me, through which lies my romantic destiny, then he adds, 'and through the lounge to the left is where we serve breakfast, between seven o'clock and nine o'clock. Do you know when you would like breakfast?'

'Seven,' I say, without thinking. If I was arriving in a better state of mind I might have contemplated a lie in of some sort, but I arrive already feeling like a complete failure, and so I have to at least be present as soon as possible.

'That is good, that is when the inspector is booked into breakfast. You will share a table?'

'Yes.'

'Very good. Is there anything else I can help you with?'

We hold the look across the small counter. A large man, the warm smile still on his face and in his eyes, and me, wrapped up in my hangdog, self-loathing bullshit.

'I'm good. Thanks very much.'

He smiles, he indicates the way to my room, and then also indicates the way to the lounge, and laughs.

I turn away from him, but do not immediately move. I want to go to the room. I want to have a shower. I want to inhale mouthwash. Drink ten glasses of water. Maybe drink a coffee. Arrive in the lounge in half an hour, smelling of anything but alcohol. But she knows me. You can do all that shit, but the stench of it will still be there, and there is fuck all you can do about your eyes. The drink is in your eyes and on your face, and half a gallon of Listerine will do nothing about that.

I head towards the lounge. Down a short corridor, past artworks of familiar Scottish scenes, a small wooden table with a carving of a hare on top. The last painting before the door to the lounge is of the new, local distillery. The Kilcraig. I can see Kadri, her back to the glass door, sitting at a table, a laptop open in front of her. To her left, two armchairs by a roaring fire.

I take a moment to look at the picture of the distillery. There's nothing to see. It could be anywhere, any one of the distilleries on the island, or anywhere in the entire country. Here I am, hesitating before the fall.

Haven't seen her in over two months.

Fuck it. Let out a long sigh, then open the door and walk into the lounge. Hit, immediately, by a glorious, smoky warmth.

Her shoulders straighten, head lifted. She takes a moment, and then she turns. We stare at each other, and then she slowly gets out of the chair and we stand a couple of yards apart, as the glass door swings shut behind me.

Every time I see her, when we haven't met for a while, it's like a pile driver to the face just how beautiful she is. Fuck me. Every damn time.

'Hey,' is all I manage.

I can see in her face that she already knows that I've been drinking. She would've been hoping I hadn't been. Disappointment flashes across her, and then it's parked and placed in the requisite compartment.

'I will make coffee,' she says. 'We will discuss the case and what needs to be done tomorrow.'

* * *

She plays me like a kipper. Nope, not kipper. Fiddle. I mean fiddle.

It wasn't like I arrived ready to jump into bed and spend the next few days having sex, because I arrived in a fog of self-inflicted disgrace, but I certainly did not get here thinking, *let's talk about work!*

But here we are, talking about work, and she's got me focussing on it, rather than on the way she softly bites her bottom lip, or the way the light sweater is resting on her small breasts, or the movement of her fingers as she indicates names on the screen, as she runs me through the personalities in the case, the people she's already spoken to.

We're sitting across from each other, rather than side by side – solid concentrating smarts from the lead investigator there – the laptop in between us.

'No one's jumping off the page?'

'Caleb is the principal character from the Kilcraig distillery who would have motive.'

'But he has a cast-iron alibi.'

'Yes. He could, of course, have paid someone to do the job for him, or an associate of his did it, or someone who was on his side of the argument did it without his knowledge, but I do not feel we are yet ready to go into the whimsical world of gangster-style hit jobs.'

'Whimsical?' I say, unable to keep the smile off my face.

'I mean fantastical. There is no Estonian word for whimsical. I mix it up sometimes. I would like you to speak to Caleb tomorrow. I feel he is a misogynist. He has no respect for me as the lead investigator. Perhaps he is also bigoted, it is hard to tell. I do see it every so often of course.'

'He sounds like an asshole.'

'People have their reasons,' she says, being way too forgiving of this prick. 'However things are with this man, I would like you to interview him. I have arranged for this to take place at eight a.m.' She pauses, and then I get the look from across the table, then the, 'That will be OK?'

Fuck me. Those eyes.

'We're having breakfast together at seven,' I say.

'That is good.' A pause, and then she can't help herself. She is a mother of three, after all. 'You should not drink anymore this evening.'

I've got nothing to say to that, other than, 'I won't.' There's an apology there for having drunk anything at all, but it doesn't get anywhere near my lips.

'After meeting Mr Henderson, you will be shown around the facility by Bethany, the night guard. She has agreed to come in, and she will talk you through Saturday evening, though obviously you are already aware of the details. I will see the lay of the land there, then I have arranged to speak to two nearby distilleries, to begin assessing this producer's competitors, and whether that might impact where the case will lead. As you are aware, there are many whisky producers on the island. However, three years prior to Caleb Henderson's arrival to establish his distillery, the Glendun and Ardbreck distilleries set up in direct competition in the vicinity of the village of Kilcraig. There was some rancour. They both wished to use the name Kilcraig for their whisky, and arrived at a compromise that neither of them would use it. They have been fierce competitors ever since. And then Henderson arrived, and took the name. He does not seem to have cared at all what the others thought. Now, in the three-way battle of new distilleries within such a short distance of one another, there exists an uneasy alliance between Glendun and Ardbreck, with Kilcraig viewed with much resentment.'

'Like the alliance between men and elves against the orcs,' I say.

She stares blankly across the table. I mean, come on, is there one amongst us who can hear the word alliance and not immediately think of *Lord of the Rings*?

'I am not sure if we will need to speak to the other, older distilleries on the island,' she says, pretending I never opened my mouth. 'For the moment I feel this may be a very localised matter.'

'Good to have two cars,' I say, mundanely.

'Yes. I will aim to return to the distillery by eleven a.m. and we can assess our next steps. We have one local officer to help. This is Constable Laird. She seems on top of her brief. She will be an asset to the investigation. Nevertheless, I do need help in speaking to everyone with whom we are required to make contact.'

'You don't have to justify me being here,' I say. 'Not to me, at any rate.'

We share a look that feels wrapped up in a hundred layers, then she continues in her way.

'There is one more thing. The distillery is hosting a Burns Supper on Friday evening. It is the inaugural event of what they intend to become a long-standing tradition. I have, as yet, not determined that it should be cancelled, and neither have they. Some, I believe, think it questionable on their part, but they are currently intending to go ahead. I believe Caleb Henderson has said that it is what his brother would have wanted, although not in my hearing.'

'A Burns Supper?'

'That is correct. We have been invited. You do not look impressed.'

'Are you familiar with Burns Suppers?'

'Yes, I have been to many.'

'Oh my God, why? I mean, the food's nice enough, but you can get nice food anytime. Why ruin it with all that poetry?'

'I have family in the town of Haapsalu in western Estonia. There is a thriving Burns society there. There is a man who has translated all the poet's work into Estonian, and every January they have a Burns Supper. I was familiar with this before I came to Scotland. I liked the people that came to the event from Scotland, as did Anders, which was one of the reasons we decided to come here in the first place. I do not go to Burns Suppers every year now, but I have been to some. You do not like them?'

I'm not used to hearing her say so much in one go, but I didn't really get beyond the fact that there's some diddley-squat little town in Estonia that no one's ever heard of – again, projection, but really, you point it out on a map – that has a Burns society *and* someone who's translated it all into Estonian. Oh my fucking God. Why?

'Aren't there Estonian poets?' is all I can think to say.

For the first time since I arrived she smiles.

I melt.

Yep, fuck it. I love it when she smiles, and I fucking melt, and maybe that makes me the bastard love child of Keats and Shelley, but I don't care.

'Yes, of course,' she says. 'Nevertheless, there is a lot of affection in Estonia for Scotland. Haapsalu's is not the only Burns Supper.'

'Well, I'm not sure I want to visit anymore,' I say, smiling, and she joins me in it. 'I hate them. I hate the speeches, I hate people trying to be funny who aren't, and even if they are funny, I'm too busy expecting them not to be funny that I won't look forward to it, and will just be relieved when it's over. And I hate the poetry. Although, I should add, I hate all poetry.'

She smiles across the table. Well, this is the Hutton she knows and loves. This is the Hutton she's preparing to never see again by returning to her homeland without actually telling me anything about it.

'Maybe someone else will get murdered, and we'll really have to cancel it,' I say.

She smiles again, this time with a small eye roll, and then slowly the smile dies away, and we're back where we began, just the two of us sitting across the table, staring at each other, the horror of a potential Burns Supper on the horizon forgotten.

The width of the table. Two and a half feet, maybe. I could lean across there and place my lips on hers. Just at the thought I feel the shivers course across my skin. And in the silence of a warm room, and the dying light of the fire, she stares back across the table and she swallows.

Time does its standing still thing. Here we are, inevitably, at the moment when the work discussion is over, the end of the night has leapt into view, and we have to face what's next. The pain of separating, and sleeping apart with barely a couple of yards and a bedroom wall between us, or the pain of sleeping together, with all the guilt and potential hurt it would bring.

A movement beyond the glass door, footsteps, and then the door is open and Janusz enters, breezy and smiling and happy to see the detectives at work. He can report back to the rest of the island, if this is the kind of person he is, that we were working at eleven at night, rather than loudly occupying one of the bedrooms.

'The fire is dying. You would like to place another log?'

That'll do nicely, my brain says silently. And get a warm blanket for us to wrap ourselves in as we romantically fuck on the rug in front of the fire. And a bottle of champagne. I think a 1985 Dom Perignon should do the job, the police are getting the tab.

'No, we are done for the evening. I will go to bed now,' says Kallas, and she smiles at him, and Janusz nods approvingly.

'I will put the guard across then,' he says.

Kallas gives me a glance containing all the layers in the world – but not a layer that says *come to my room in ten minutes, clothes optional* – and then closes the laptop.

And the evening is done.

5

Likely I'm getting too old for this shit in all sorts of ways, and one of those ways is eating a full Scottish breakfast. But fuck it, I do it anyway. Kallas has muesli and yogurt and dried fruit, because of course she does. And we drink coffee and orange juice and we talk about the case, and then we go back to our rooms to get ready for the day ahead, and then we're meeting in the car park, and here now, seeing the place in the first light of dawn, I realise how close we are to the sea, and that this island is absolutely stunning.

We're a few hundred yards from the sea, nothing in between here and there except wild grass and a wide beach. Rolling countryside all around, barely any other sign of humanity apart from a few standalone crofts, and one large house away to the right, and then in the distance, snow-covered hills, rising to meet a perfect blue sky.

The air is crisp and cold and clean.

Kallas stands beside me for a moment as I take in the wonder of it, and she nods.

'It is very beautiful,' she says. 'Yesterday, I found myself doing the same as you are doing.'

I don't have any words. I look out to sea, nothing beyond, stretching away into the hazy distance, the sound of the waves carried on the gentle wind.

'I expect it's like this about five days a year.'

Like I'd know. Well, it's Scotland, you have to make certain assumptions.

She stands silently, and then finally accepts that someone has to drag us away from here.

'We should go. There will be other chances to look at the view, although I cannot guarantee the weather.'

* * *

'It's marketing. One hundred per cent marketing. Like

24

everything else on earth. People buy what you tell them to buy. What does the whisky taste like? Let me park that in the bin with all my other shits.' Oh, he's using a variation on that line, is he? I hate this guy. Kallas said I likely would, after all. 'How often in life do you find that the little niche whatever-it-is, the little brewery, the farmhouse cider, the homemade chocolate biscuit, is an intrinsically better product than the well-marketed, big brand? But, quite possibly, that big brand started out small, so how did it get big in the first place? Because it tasted great? I don't think so. Because some corporate whizzball marketed the shit out of it, that's why. You want to know our biggest expense to date? Jeremy, the copywriter. Fuck me, that guy could have you sucking his cock before lunch if he wanted to. He writes like a God. Expensive son-of-a-bitch, but he's already the making of us. I mean, ask the fuck around. We're taking more advance orders for our first release, four years from now, than half the more-established distilleries on the island, and those fuckers are pissed. I mean, why wouldn't they be? No fucker knows what our shit'll taste like, but they're prepared to buy into the promise. That's human nature for you, sergeant. People always want something new, and we're giving it to them. But as long as we hang on to Jeremy, they won't be going anywhere. Just when the whisky-buying public are thinking they might want a change, Jeremy'll write some genius piece of shit to persuade them that *staying the same is the new change*. He'll write words and you're just like, what does that even mean, or, are people actually going to buy that shit, and then ten minutes later you realise the man's a fucking genius. Fucking genius.' He finally pauses, and then tosses in, 'I don't even like whisky.'

'Just in it for the money?'

'Yep. And the investment opportunity. Growing business, ain't going anywhere. Brexit is a shitshow, but people still drink whisky, people everywhere still want to buy whisky, whisky as a major export is only going to keep growing and growing. War in Ukraine? Fuck me, it might be awful, but it's got people drinking more. I mean, why the fuck not? We're all in danger of imminent death, might as well fucking drink ourselves there, and enjoy the journey.'

'What about the people who say the explosion of distilleries now, not producing for another five or ten years, is going to lead to a vast unsold whisky lake like there was in the nineteen-eighties?'

'That notion is predicated on the idea there's a finite number of whisky drinkers. They're wrong. Were there a finite number of coffee drinkers before Starbucks? A finite number of wine drinkers before Napa Valley and the Antipodes decided to start producing a billion bottles a week? You don't meet demand, you *create* demand. There could be double the number of distilleries and we'd still be OK.'

'What did John think about it?'

Well it's been ten minutes, and he's been happy to spout forth, sitting here in his executive office, in the suite of rooms above the factory floor, a window looking back up the glen to the white hills. Whatever financial portfolio they put together before setting out on this operation, a decent amount of the money went on this office.

Having said that, they didn't just spend big on Jeremy the wordmeister. Everything about this place speaks of wealth and elegance and sophistication. This is high end spirits for high end bastards with money to spend.

Now that the name of his brother has finally entered the conversation, Caleb Henderson pauses. I get the stare across the desk. Hands rubbed together, fingers entwined.

'My brother was an idealist. And a bum. I was the businessman. I still am, even if he is no longer much of an idealist. People thought we were a good team, but only those who hadn't worked with us.'

'It was tempestuous?'

'Yes, a good word. I was right, and he was always wrong. The business will benefit from his passing, I must admit, even if no particular individual will.'

'Tell me about him being a bum.'

He scowls.

'Whatever. I asked him up here because he was good at what he did. He could put together a marketing package. He could make money. But he liked to work about an hour and a half a day, and spend the rest of the time indulging in his weird blend of sex, alcohol and organic kombucha. And, for some reason, he seemed to expect that the quality of our product should match the price.' He shakes his head, but he's only pausing long enough to express his distaste with his brother. 'I said, who's defining quality? Well, look, I know who's defining quality, but why should we be paying any attention to them? Why should we pay attention to the business, when the business is not our market? Individuals are our market, so let's aim at individuals. All you have to do with an individual is tell them a good story, tell them they like what they're drinking, or that this thing they're drinking is in fact the best thing they've ever damn well drunk.' He pauses, perhaps to make sure I'm not recording this, and then he says, 'People are stupid. And rich people are rich and stupid. Rich people could prefer the taste of a cheap blended malt from Lidl to an eighteen-year-old Macallan, and they'd still buy the Macallan. You have to be seen to be drinking the right thing. Those are the rules. So here we are, pitching at the right market if we want to make money. Money follows money, oldest and truest saying in the book.'

'Certainly worked for Rangers when they signed Tor André Flo,' I say, bringing in the arcane, twenty-year-old football reference. This fucker has Rangers supporter written all over him, so it's not like he doesn't get it. Another twisted scowl.

'Apart from you, who's pleased to see him out of the picture?' I ask, hitting the fucker over the head with the bluntness of the question.

'Oh, very good, sergeant,' he says. 'I will miss my brother, for all that we disagreed with each other on virtually everything. He brought a sense of balance. I'm sure now, without him, my entrepreneurial hubris will get the better of me. That's certainly what a lot of people are thinking, at any rate.'

'And the independence matter, how did that play out?'

'Oh, God, not another one.'

'At least three people have reported the incident last summer when the two of you literally threw punches on the shop floor.'

Silence. Fucker must have known the question was coming.

'That argument started with a discussion on independence,' I say, pressing the point.

'It had nothing to do with the business, independence continues to have nothing to do with the business. The argument itself was inconsequential, but our relationship was as it was. We always played in the shadowlands of aggression.'

The shadowlands of aggression, eh?

'Whose idea was the Burns Supper?'

'Mine, but John supported it. For different reasons, of course. He saw Burns as the perfect expression of Scottish nationality, the use of language something to aspire to in literature and communication. He thought everyone should be taught old Scots in school.'

'And what makes you favour the Burns Supper then?'

'Ha! I can tell from the way you utter the words you don't like them, Sergeant.'

'Doesn't matter. Why did you want one if your brother saw them as so positively pro-independence?'

'I hate them myself. Never listen to the poetry, don't like haggis, don't like whisky, don't like speeches.' Fuck, I can't stand it when I find myself largely in agreement with some asshole. Of course, the fucker's wrong about haggis. 'But they are the perfect vehicle for the export of Scotland. That's all it represents. It's a safe expression of our nationality, embraced by the world over, including the English. A bit of poetry, plenty of food, maybe someone says something funny, men in skirts, all very ethnic and exportable and non-threatening. The Yanks and the Japs lap it up. Those bastards can't get enough of it. I'm happy to use that all day long.'

God, I hate this fucking guy.

'Has there been any threat made to the distillery?'

He makes the pretence of thinking about it, then shakes his head.

'Who do you think killed your brother?'

'One of the others.'

'One of the other distilleries?'

'Probably. Most likely Glendun or Ardbreck. They're the local start-ups, they have the least credibility on the market, and consequently have the most to lose.'

'What about the infinite number of whisky drinkers you're going to create?'

'Doesn't matter. With start-ups like this, with the three in the same location, there is absolutely going to be a war. It's inevitable. And with every war, there are winners and there are losers.' He leans into the discussion, points a finger at me, even though, when he talks, the words are not aimed at me at all. 'The body in the mash says it perfectly. They fuck with our whisky, they know what that says to suppliers and to buyers. Obviously we'll ditch that batch, but is that it? That's all we do? Do we give the tun a bit of a wash, and get it going again? We might say we'll replace it, but will we actually? Damned expensive bit of kit. And how much does what happens in the tun affect the washbacks and the stills? Well, not at all, as it happens, but the general public don't know that. And you can guaran-fucking-tee

---

28

that soon enough some fucker is going to start spreading that rumour. Entire distillery contaminated by blood-soaked, dead human. You really want to get your whisky from there? Well, sure, there will be some who would, but that, my friend, is a very, very niche market. We are not surviving on that.'

'You have a plan to combat that, since you can see it coming?'

'More than likely, we won't know where it's coming from until it arrives, but we need to be ready to firefight. We'll have plans in place. Let's see if this thing has played out yet.'

'You think there might be another murder?'

He answers with a slight movement of the shoulders, then, 'People die for all sorts of reasons, sergeant.'

And I don't know whether it's just because he's a brutish, if wealthy, asshole, but he manages to make it sound like a threat.

* * *

'Have you ever seen a dead body?' asks Bethany Wright.

I give her a sideways glance, which is odd, given that we're sitting directly opposite each other at a desk.

'God, what am I talking about,' she says, 'you're a police officer in Glasgow. You probably see them every weekend.'

'Well, I'm not actually in Glasgow, and it's not every weekend, but I've seen my share.'

She looks discomfited by this, although I'm not so sure the look on her face would be any different if she'd just discovered a bit of blue mould as she was getting to the end of her piece 'n jam, then she says, 'What's that like?'

I stare across the table. Not often you get asked that question, to be honest. But here's a woman who's come across her first corpse, she's understandably traumatised by it, and looking for context. Or maybe she's just curious, as plenty of people would be. Either way, I have a sudden urge to tell her.

'There was a woman last year,' I say. 'Last summer. She was involved in a case I was investigating.'

Bethany Wright's eyes widen a little, instantly drawn into the narrative. I should probably shut up, but the words are just tumbling out.

'I slept with her. I mean, that was bad.'

Bethany Wright swallows, her eyes widen even more. She

---

looks like Kate Winslet. She looks so much like Kate Winslet, it feels like I'm talking to Kate Winslet. Maybe that's why I just introduced sex into the conversation. I mean, despite being me, I'm not looking to have sex with Bethany Wright. Nor, in fact, Kate Winslet. But I saw that movie Kate Winslet made with the Irish lassie about the fossils, and while there was stuff about fossils in the fossil movie, and there may have been a broader message about the place of women in society and their struggle to get recognition in a male-dominated world, which has parallels to this day, its main attraction was the banger of a lesbian scene. I mean, come on, it doesn't matter what your movie's about, you put those two women in bed together, and you get them to do as close to a porn movie lesbian scene as you're going to get in mainstream cinema, people just aren't going to be talking about fossils.

I've had a lot of respect for both actresses ever since.

Yeah, I know, shallow as fuck, but that's why we're all here.

'Wait,' says Bethany Wright, 'so not only is this story about death, it also has sex?'

'I suppose.'

'You had sex with a dead body?'

'No, she was still alive when we had sex.'

She lets out a low whistle.

'Well, that's good.'

'Isn't it?'

'So, you slept with a woman who was involved in an investigation. That sounds like, you know, you probably shouldn't have done that.'

I nod, and do that confirmatory *oh yes* face that people do.

'So, what happened next?'

'It turned out the person we were looking for, the person who'd already committed two murders, or maybe three, I forget, wasn't this woman's husband, as we'd been presuming...'

'Wait,' says Bethany Wright, 'just wait.' Her brow furrows, she takes a drink of tea, she sets the cup back down. 'You had sex with a triple murder suspect's wife? Like, what were you thinking?'

This conversation is going too far, I know. But you know what this is? This is clearly a confessional. This is me spewing out the demons of my past. If I don't put a sock in it, I'm liable to still be here this time on Monday. On the other hand, we're getting shit out on the table. We're opening this thing up. I'm being honest and giving, and as a result, Bethany Wright will be too.

That's the plan.

I mean, it's not a plan. Obviously it's not a plan. But it might happen anyway.

'It was a thing that happened.'

'Sounds like it.' She takes another drink of tea. I should probably get to the point, then we can move on to the part of the conversation where she tells me stuff.

'So the killer turned out not to be the woman's husband after all.'

'Well, that is good. Although he must've been pissed off that you'd shagged his missus.'

'He never found out. The actual killer was a butcher, and so had certain skills. She used them to decapitate both the presumed suspect, and his wife.'

Bethany Wright stares blankly across the table. Her lips part, her brow creases even more, her eyes are getting to the Disney princess stage.

'What the fuck?' she finally manages. 'That never happened.'

I nod, but as I've spoken, my enthusiasm for the discussion has gradually drained away. Turns out I don't like talking about the past so much, after all. Just as we all knew.

'Where were these heads? Like on a platter, like you see in, you know, classical art? Or wait, did you come across the killer holding the heads by the hair? Wow.'

'One was in a fridge, and the other was in a box.'

'Wow.'

Yeah, wow.

'Wait,' she says, 'You're making that up. It would've been in the news. I don't really look at the news, but I would've heard about that.'

'The murders were in the news, the details were kept out. Hasn't come to trial yet, but it will. I mean, she's pleading guilty, there's not going to be some massive, endless thing, but these things take time all the same. When she's in court, then the papers will have it.'

'Wow. And this was in Scotland?'

I nod, lift my coffee, take a sip. Rats, waited too long, coffee's cooled too much.

'Holy shit. We're a hard bunch of fuckers, ain't we?'

'She was Polish.'

'Polish? Wow.'

'Anyway,' I say, 'so yes, I have seen death.'

'There are more?'

'Some.' *Lots!* 'But, you know, it happens, and you have to deal with it.'

'How do you deal with it?'

'I get by.' No, I fucking don't. 'So, how are you doing? You sleeping OK?'

She takes some more tea, settling the cup back down on the table.

'Are we done talking about these decapitated heads?'

'Yes,' I say. 'I'm afraid I've got a busy day ahead of me, so we should get on.'

'Aye.'

'You're doing all right?'

She kind of shrugs, then says, 'Not really. Took me five hours to get to sleep last night, then I woke up, jumped awake, with, like, I could see John's body was falling from the ceiling, right down on top of me, and the knife was buried in his throat, and the blood was dripping, and he was screaming in terror.' She stares blankly across the office, her eyes haunted. 'I mean, I was dreaming, so there was that. But, fuck me...'

'You need to find someone to talk to,' I say. 'We'll get you trauma risk assessed.'

'What's that?'

'It's where the mental well-being of witnesses is established to decide whether they're going to need counselling or not.'

'Right.' She's staring across the office as she thinks about this, then she says, 'I think I might need counselling.'

'Did you know Mr Henderson well?'

She continues to stare blankly for a while, and then she finally turns back, conjuring up the question from the ether, and nods.

'Aye. John was always around here. I mean, he was the marketing guy, right. Head of marketing. He was completely on the business side, rather than the whisky side, you know, but he was always coming into the still, always talking to the staff.'

'He talked a lot?'

'Aye. Quite flirtatious.'

She's staring off across the office again, and now a smile comes to her face at some memory or other.

'Very flirtatious. Oh, we all liked John. Except Caleb, I suppose, the two of them didn't seem to get on so well. But still,' and now she returns to the present, dispatching whatever memory had brought the smile, 'must've worked, right? We're crushing the opposition.'

'Did you ever sleep with him?'

'John?' she asks.

'Yes,' I say.

She laughs. I stare blankly across the desk.

'You serious?' she asks.

'Yes.'

'Oh. Well, all right, sure. Of course I slept with him. John slept with everyone.'

6

Not that there was any reason to come and see the corpse, but I chose to do it anyway.

Kallas and I stand side-by-side looking down at the cold, blue body. Dr Stevens, who carried out the post-mortem, has joined us. Slow day on the island, I guess. Perhaps she's enjoying the unexpected bruhaha.

'You read the report, Sergeant?'

'Yep.'

'I'm not sure there's going to be anything further to add. As you can see, however...' Oh, I love that. There's nothing to add, but I'm going to keep talking anyway. It's an Estonian in the Upside Down. 'Mr Henderson was a strongly built man. He worked out.'

'An hour every morning, right?' I say, and Kallas nods.

'Well, there's your evidence. To get the knife in the throat like that,' and she pauses to mimic the thrust of the weapon, 'suggests he was taken by surprise. Either his killer came out of nowhere, or it was someone he knew.'

'Not necessarily,' I throw in, and then at her raised eyebrow, I add, 'I mean, I don't know you, but you're still going to surprise the shit out of me if you suddenly stabbed me in the throat.'

She laughs, the sound loud in the small room.

'You make a good point, sergeant, I'll give you that. I can confidently say, however, that he was not killed in the middle of some brutal argument with his brother, which descended into violence. Indeed, although they were known to have exchanged blows in the past, there's nothing here to indicate he's been in any kind of altercation in recent weeks.'

We stand and stare at the stiff. Silence returns. Complete stillness, bar the low, background hum of whatever electrical equipment is keeping this place running.

I'm coming to enjoy the silences. Not so much the awkward ones with Eileen and Kadri, I suppose. Just the general silences, when no one's talking at me, and so I don't have to listen.

'Did your internal examinations reveal anything further?' asks Kallas, who probably enjoys a silence herself, but who is obviously more minded to crack the fuck on with this thing.

'Heavy drinker. This is a man who got into making whisky because he liked it so much.'

'That is confirmed by his wife, and several others.'

'Did his wife say that he was drunk most nights?'

'No.'

'Hmm.' Stevens gives it a little thought, factoring that in to whatever else she's learned about him, and then she indicates the corpse with a sweep of the hand. 'He drank a lot, but sure, maybe he could hold it. Maybe he drank more than anyone realised. But it's interesting that he exercised the way he did. And also, he looked after his gut, *alcohol aside*. He had the gut biome of a hardened kimchi eater.'

Gut biome. Fuck me. Funny how you can go your entire life never hearing a phrase, and then suddenly up it pops twice in a couple of days. I'll need to tell Eileen, except I'm not sure we have those kinds of casual, flippant, what-the-fuck-is-going-on conversations anymore.

'So, we're in live hard, die hard territory. He drank to excess, but perhaps attempted to counter it with healthy eating and plenty of exercise. I guess we can tell the latter just by looking at his corpse. Perhaps his wife will be more forthcoming.'

'Had he been drinking prior to his death?' I ask, playing my part.

If I was a lead actor in a drama, I'd never be one to argue for more lines. I'd be like, nah, it's fine, let Billy Bob say that line, I'm good. I'd be Nicolas Cage in *Willie's Wonderland*.

'He had been drinking all day, every day. If you've looked through his office, I expect you've found a decent stash of Scotch.'

'Yes,' says Kallas. 'Of course, given the business he was in, it was not unusual for him to have whisky in his office. Nevertheless, it sounds as though he will have had a higher turnover than perhaps others knew about.'

'I'd say. This man's liver was toast. Would've been dead in a year or two, under normal circumstances, but then, you never can tell. Some people just have the constitutions to keep on

---

35

keeping on. He might've been one of them.'

Kallas is nodding, and I get the sense that this is her doing the wrap-up. Time to go and speak to Mrs Henderson. There only is one current Mrs Henderson, as Caleb is divorced. Three times divorced, one should note. I can relate.

'He drank heavily, and countered that by exercising regularly and eating healthily,' says Kallas. 'Anything further?'

'Got the usual tests to run, so you never know. There was a classic hair beneath the fingertips, but, to be honest, in my experience those hairs usually end up belonging to the deceased. So, that's where we are. If anything else comes up, I'll let you know.'

Stevens nods to herself as she takes, what might be for her, a last look along the length of the corpse, and then she says, 'Hopefully you won't have anything else for me.'

She smiles. Kallas nods, says, 'Thank you, doctor,' and then she includes me in the short nod, and turns away.

* * *

Mrs Finola Henderson laughs.

It's just after eleven in the morning, and she's drinking gin. I know it's gin because we watched her pour the glass. Neat fucking gin, by the way. That's bold. She poured what was probably about four measures over two ice cubes, sat down at the kitchen table and said, 'So, I'm drinking gin before lunch. Bite me.'

She's twenty-six. John Henderson cradle snatched the shit out of this relationship. He was married to his first wife for twenty-two years. Twenty-two years, three kids. They're still in Somerset.

'We met at a parents' evening. Seems like forever ago. Jesus.'

She stares grimly across the room. We're in another one of those amazing kitchens that people don't have in real life apart from – in my experience – when someone in their family gets murdered. Kallas and I on one side of the table with coffee, her on the other with her family-brand hooch. I stopped myself asking if there was vodka or wine. The model professional.

I occasionally glance at Kallas, but when I do I just think about the fact that she's leaving the country soon, and I'll likely never see her again, and that neither of us has mentioned this

---

36

thing since I got here, and the thought of it is like a brutal, poisonous hand reaching into my guts and squeezing until they explode, so really, I should probably try to concentrate on this dumbass murder case instead.

Dumbass? Yes, it is. All murder is dumbass, after all. All pointless, all a stupid fucking waste. Of life, of time, of potential, of everything, for the victim and their killer.

'You were a teacher?'

'Ha.' She takes a swig of gin. 'I was a pupil. In the same year as John's eldest. Not that his kid and I really knew each other or anything. You know what upper sixth's like, and that place, Millfield, it's huge. And there are so many, like, famous actors and the like there, so many famous kids, so many sports people that are about to win Olympic medals or grand prix or open the batting for England or whatever, and if you're just a regular kid like I was, no one gives a hoot about you. And then there was this completely random guy, a parent, looking at the art I'd done and he was like, holy shit, this is amazing. *You can really paint.* He was the first person to say that to me.'

Another drink, she looks between the two of us. She's about the same age as my daughter, so it feels in a way like interviewing a kid, rather than a woman who's already been married for six years.

'He said he wanted to buy one of my pieces.' She laughs again. 'He always said he liked them, but really, he just wanted my eighteen-year-old tits.'

She looks at Kallas, attempting to bring her into the sisterhood. Those kind of attempts usually fail, to be honest.

'Did you insist on him marrying you before he got them?' I rather indelicately ask.

'God, no. I mean, you'll have seen him. He was fit, he was good looking. At that place, there was a lot of DILFs, right? Nic Cage, Brosnan, one of the Beckham kids was there, there were attractive, famous parents coming out of the walls. But there was something about John, and he still managed to stand out. Jeez... I had him in the back of his car, first chance we had.'

'Back of his car?'

'More space in a Porsche than you think there's going to be. He took me to a castle in Devon the next time. Left his wife after about six months. Her fault, she wasn't putting out anymore. The man needed to fuck. We got married, then Caleb talked him into coming up here and joining his whisky start-up.

37

And here we are.'

She laughs again, bitterly this time.

'Will you stay here?'

'Are you kidding me? Not a chance. Waiting for his estate to clear probate, and boom, I'm gone. I'll likely get the fuck out of Dodge early on in any case, and go down and stay with my parents for a while. Mum'll be delighted. She can bring me breakfast and do my laundry and fulfil all her maternal needs, while castigating me for doing nothing with my education, and advising me on where best to start looking for a job.'

'Your husband was a heavy drinker?' says Kallas, getting back on track. My question about remaining on the island might not have been particularly pertinent, but let's not pretend that the twenty-six-year-old ain't a suspect.

Finola looks pointedly across the table and takes a slug of gin, leaves the glass by her lips for a moment, and then places it deliberately on the table.

'He drank whisky all his life. Started at Oxford. Got in with the whisky-drinking crowd. Expensive single malts, obviously. They thought it set them apart. You can imagine. There are pictures of him in his early thirties when he's overweight. Downright fat. He said his wife nagged the shit out of him, and he finally cracked. Started doing health. Never stopped drinking whisky though.' A pause, and then, 'I can't stand it, could never stand the smell of it off him. That got old very quickly.'

'So, it wasn't you who got him to work out and eat fermented cabbage?' I ask.

At the words fermented cabbage she does, what I call with my daughter, her banana face. The tortured, childlike grimace at the mention of a food she hates.

'Ugh, god no. I mean, don't get me wrong, I loved that he was fit. And big, right? I mean, I've seen shows, I know how this works. You've already seen him naked, right? Well, I'll be honest, I didn't have a lot of prior experience, but he was all man compared to Olly and Hugo, that's for sure. But there was no way I was touching any of that awful stuff he ate.'

'You know why anyone would want to kill him?' I throw in, suddenly broadening the scope of the questioning. Her eyes widen briefly, she retreats behind the gin glass, then says, 'I answered that yesterday,' and makes a small gesture towards Kallas.

'I'm catching up,' I say.

'You two don't speak to each other?'

We stare at her across the table. She looks between the two of us. She can't stop herself smiling.

'You're pretty gorgeous for a detective,' she says to Kallas. 'I mean, you've got your funny accent and everything, but you're nice. Are you two, you know?' and she makes a crude shagging gesture, quite unbecoming of the deep, tortured romance of the relationship between Kadri and I.

'No,' says Kallas bluntly. 'Will you answer the Sergeant's question?'

Finola smiles knowingly, although obviously she knows about as much as that bearded, *Game of Thrones* zombie prick Jon Snow, then she turns back to me. 'What was it again?'

'You know why anyone would want to kill him?'

'Right.'

She nods, takes another drink, the fun of teasing the detectives seems to leave her, faced with thinking about her husband's murder, and then she's looking at the table, and she finally, for the first time since we got in here, seems to be hit by the weight of it. Husband dead, police in her house, murder investigation sweeping across the island, with the widow at the centre of the maelstrom.

'Either Caleb or one of the competition, presumably. John complained about both on a regular basis.'

'He was argumentative?'

'No, not John. Caleb's the fighter. John would argue with him, but left to their own devices, Caleb would argue with someone who just happened to pass him in the street, while John would happily drink whisky and flirt with any woman he could get hold of. Caleb was the only one who made him angry. As he did with me and everyone else.'

'So what about the competition?'

'Well, you should speak to them. I don't mean, you know, the big distilleries down by Bowmore and around there. The start-ups near here.'

'Glendun and Ardbreck?'

'Yeah, them. They were always nipping at John's ears, as though they had a monopoly on being a new thing. It was like... they seemed to treat it like it was zero sum, you know. Like only one of them could survive, while the other two went to the wall. Those two were enemies, and then Caleb and John turned up, and suddenly Glendun and Ardbreck were in league against the newbies. It was only Caleb who could get John really riled up and shouting, but it wasn't like those two fuckers didn't piss him off. He did cold fury with them, however. He hated some of those guys.'

She looks between us, and I get the feeling from the look in those young eyes, that she knows full well she's pointing a finger, and she's more than happy to do it.

7

Kallas and I split up again. So far it's been all business. No mention of the elephant. The thing that's completely fucking with my id. The thing which I know I will allow myself to be devastated by, using it as an excuse to retreat full bore to the off licence. All your vodka, please, shopkeep, and at least fifty per cent of your white wine!

Anyway, here I am, walking into reception of the Glendun Distillery, a sparkling new addition to the Islay single malt scene. That's how it's described on their website. *A sparkling new addition* seems kind of mundane. Obviously they haven't spent the big bucks on the high end marketing talent the way Kilcraig has. Not that I've read anything from this Jeremy character to make me think he's worth his salt.

Show my ID to the receptionist, she takes the time to read it, she studies the photograph and then my face to make sure everything matches up, then I get, 'How can we help you, Sgt Hutton?' delivered like a sharp slap to a bare arse.

* * *

'They didn't have to come here, that's all. I mean, have you seen Scotland?' This is Terry, the Chief Operating Officer. Strangely thin, with an ugly moustache. 'Have you seen how much space there is, how many rivers there are, how much land there is free, and how much of that land is for sale? They could have had their pick. Gone anywhere. Damn it, they could have gone to the north of England. Why not? If their marketing is going to be so terrific, go there, start selling English whisky. Those two bastards wouldn't have cared, would they? It's just about money to them, and if they're so shit hot, they could have made their money anywhere. But they come here to look, and look, I don't mind saying, and often enough Margaret tells me we brought this on ourselves, but as soon as that Caleb turned up, we told him he could fuck off. This corner of Islay was taken. End of. It

---

41

was bad enough having Ardbreck move in at the same time, but at least they're small. Smaller than us, at any rate. But then that bastard pitches up here with his money and his investments. And you know,' and here he leans conspiratorially across the desk, 'a tonne of it comes from Russia. I'm serious, I really am. That's where his money originates. Same as every other fucking Tory. No one wants to talk about that, though, do they? When Ukraine started, there was all this bluster and bullshit about sanctions, but those bastards down there, they are up to their necks in Russian money, and everything they did, *everything*, it was all for show. Doubt they did anything that they hadn't negotiated with their Russian overlords before they did it. And that Johnson character jetting off to Ukraine every five damned minutes. Something going on there too, I'm telling you that for nothing. When it comes out, when the exact relationship between Johnson and Putin and the FSB comes out, it'll be so scandalous and such a giant fucking turdburger, no one will believe it, and the BBC won't touch it with a stick. Fucking Kuenssberg. It'll just be those in the know, the few good souls sidelined as Internet conspiracy theorist nutjobs, who will know and believe the truth. No one else will want to believe it. Too mind blowing. People can't cope with the big stuff. So, you know, I wouldn't be surprised if this whole thing, this murder you're all here talking about, wouldn't be surprised if this is related to Russia-Ukraine in some way. There's weird shit going on all over, why should it be any different out here?'

* * *

Well, my meeting with Terry, the Chief Operating Officer rather quickly descended into conspiracy theory nutjobbery, right enough.

On some matters, however, he obviously had a point or two to make. I really doubt that Caleb Henderson came here out of badness because someone he'd never met before was pissing him off, but at the same time, if he genuinely could have gone anywhere – and we know that the decision to invest in whisky certainly preceded the decision to buy the land – then whoever he set up next to was always going to be cheesed off. Only way to do it without stepping on toes would be to go to an island with no established stills, or maybe to the heart of some scheme in Glasgow. I guess Garrowhill Single Malt probably isn't going to cut it in the international, high-end whisky stakes.

Now I'm in with the Factory Manager, Rosalind Mann, and she seems a little more measured. I have a cup of tea, as I was offered, and I thought it about time. I really wanted alcohol, and if she'd offered whisky I would one hundred per cent have taken it, even though I hate the damn stuff, but here we are. I got offered Scottish breakfast or Darjeeling, and so I took the breakfast and I'm lumping it. In a sign of quality, however, it came with a small piece of tasty shortbread on the side.

I've just been putting some of the points made by Terry, and Mann has regarded me warily throughout.

'Well, I don't think there's any actual evidence of Russian money,' she says, 'and even if there was, I'm not sure what difference it makes. Yes, no doubt there's still rather a lot of Russian money swilling around in British and EU business. But I really don't know where Terry, and indeed Mr Bridge, got this information. Nevertheless, they're happy to disseminate it, and there are some who are happy to believe it.'

'Maybe they just made it up,' I suggest.

She naturally has nothing to say to that. Mr Bridge is the founder and owner of the distillery. Currently posted as absent. He came, he set up a business, he fucked off back to Edinburgh. He was around long enough, however, to see the arrival of the Hendersons, realise the potential impact, and to kick off the handbags at dawn. It was Bridge to whom Terry, the COO was referring when he said they'd told the Hendersons to fuck off. It was a negotiation that did not end well.

'When did Mr Bridge leave the island?' I ask, having taken a drink of tea and made the appropriate *decent* gesture.

'He stopped living here at least two years ago, but he returns the first working Monday of every second month. So we last saw him three weeks ago.'

'And how were things then?'

'*Things* were just fine, Sergeant. There is no doubt that the closer Kilcraig gets to full output, and the more they put into their gin brands, the greater the impact upon us. Nevertheless, we will survive, of that I have no doubt. Collectively, it's our job to make sure we go beyond surviving, to thriving.'

Nice line.

'Was there any contact between Glendun and Kilcraig while Mr Bridge was in town?'

'During this last visit?'

'Yes.'

'Mr Bridge has not, to my knowledge, had any contact with them in over a year. There's no need. We're competitors, not housemates.'

'Did you ever have a cost analysis done on the impact of Kilcraig's arrival?'

I get another cold look across the desk. That was obviously a decent question.

There's something, albeit not much, of the Sandra Bullock about her. If you imagine one of those movies where Sandra Bullock plays a hard-nosed business executive who takes no one's shit. No obvious sign of light relief beneath the frosted-over outer layer, however.

'Look,' she says finally, and shit, don't we all just love answers that begin with 'look', 'I'm not sure what you're implying here. That, perhaps, Mr Henderson's murder is related to us? Seriously? Yes, we were disadvantaged by them coming, yes Mr Bridge had his disagreements and that perhaps spilled over into arguments between other members of staff. But the Hendersons, as I'm sure you're already well aware, are a quite dreadful pair of men. Angry, spiteful, bitter. We are far from the only people who will be glad to be shot of John Henderson, but since the lead executive is his brother, I don't see how it makes much difference to us in any case.'

A fine defence. Not that she answered the question.

'Did you have a cost analysis done on the impact of Kilcraig's arrival?'

She takes another drink of tea, then sets the mug back down so sharply some of it spills.

'Yes,' finally squeezes from her lips.

'And how did that look?'

Another harsh stare across the table. This is Sandra Bullock in one of those movies where she plays a psychopath who kills people with her eyes. To be fair, I haven't seen that movie.

'It's business confidential,' she says eventually.

* * *

'He was a man,' says Myrna Berschweiler, the chief distiller. 'I had no idea who he was, just some guy in a bar one night. He was gorgeous, he wore skinny jeans, T-shirt tucked in, ripped abs.' She says all this with utter disdain, although I think it's mainly at herself for having been sucked in by it. 'He could talk too. I'm pretty well-educated, pretty broad-minded, you know, I can talk about anything really. I enjoy it. Enjoy sitting in a bar of an evening, talking about sport and politics and history. From the Sybarites to the Arsenal, I can do pretty much anything. And then here was this good looking guy, and he matched me every step of the way. It was like he fell into my lap. That'll be right.' More disdain for the self. I can associate. 'We had dinner, we had sex, he talked about his investment portfolio, I talked about the distillery. He was fascinated, he asked all about it, I ended up showing him around. No idea who he was.' She pauses, she stares across the desk, she shakes her head at herself, a movement that indicates an acceptance that she might as well spit it all out. 'We had sex down there. I mean, down on the distillery floor. Late at night, no one else about, obviously. And we had sex in here. There was a lot of sex. And I mean, this lasted like all of three days, but I guess that was all it took for him to find out everything he needed to know. And you know how he broke it off, this glorious little romance of ours? Told me the truth. He had a twenty-three-year-old wife. Oh my God, that was a punch in the face. So off he goes, fully armed with all the information he'd set out to gather.'

'You really had no idea he was Caleb Henderson's brother?'

'Why would I have? He didn't live here yet. This was his first visit. He didn't stay with his brother, he stayed in a hotel and played the island. Slipped in under cover, gathered all the information he could, and left. Never said a word about the distillery or who his brother was.' She taps the side of her head. 'Even when he ditched me, he didn't say anything about that, just told me about his little wife. Doubt she'll last much longer up here now, will she?'

* * *

'Aye, they came in here and bought up one of everything in the shop. I had no idea who was doing that at the time. Seemed really weird.'

'Why didn't they just take photographs?'

'You're not in retail, Sergeant, I see.'

The man behind the shop counter. In charge of his domain. I expect he gets his staff to call him Commander or Captain perhaps. I can see this guy getting played by Tom Wilkinson in a particular mood of pompous twattery. *Behold my dominion, for it is the finest shop in all the land.*

'Good spot,' I say, drily, 'I'm not in retail.'

'You have to understand quality. The meaning of quality.'

He looks around, deciding ultimately to lift the closest thing to him. A small, white bowl, a blue etching of their building inside, the words Glendun Distillery beneath it.

'You see a photograph of this, and what is it? Is it handmade in Scotland? Is it China? Or is it cheap junk manufactured by a five-year-old slave labourer in a Guangdong sweat shop? You see what I'm saying?'

'And which is it?' I ask. Like I care.

'Sadly, the latter, but that's who we are. We can aim high, but you can't get to the top of the ladder without starting at the bottom.'

'Nice analogy. How does that apply to the Hendersons?'

'They bought the ladder.'

I laugh. He's not trying to be funny, but I can't help it.

'I'm glad you're amused. They came in here with the intention of measuring themselves against every single thing we do. Did the same with Ardbreck. Exactly the same playbook. Bought up the shop, and off they went. Established who our suppliers were, and then made sure they spent more on everything. Have you been into their shop?'

'I passed through. Didn't browse.'

'Well, if you look at their prices, they're obviously running some loss leaders. But that won't matter to them. For them it's about crushing the opposition. They're not even at market yet, and they're already ahead of us in terms of sales. They'll grow faster than us, and if they can... if they can, they will run us into the wall. I've no doubt that's the intention here.'

He pauses, he surveys his realm of single malt whiskies, augmented by tea towels, coasters, tumblers, keyrings and mugs.

'That man is a cunt. I have no idea why someone murdered his brother and not him.'

8

I received a text from Kallas while I was wrapping up my conversations at the distillery.

Taking half an hour break to go for swim at Mallaibh beach before the sun goes down.

Hmm...

So, she's going swimming in the, well, North Atlantic I guess, in January. We've been here before. She's Estonian. She used to swim every day, year round, in the Baltic. She's kept this up by swimming in the *not quite so cold but still insane to swim in* Clyde. I've seen this first hand. Troon beach in October. She swam naked. Probably the most glorious thing I've ever witnessed in my life.

However, that was impromptu. Here, she's on an island running an investigation, she knew she was coming for a few days, she will have come prepared. I'm kind of guessing she won't be naked.

There's also the matter that she told me where she was going and what she was doing, but didn't actually ask me to join her. Shall we take it as implicit in the text?

Too right we shall.

And so I drive down to the beach. There are three cars in the carpark, which is disappointing, as it means we won't be alone. And while I'd logically talked myself out of the hope she'd be naked, this pretty much confirms it. Any talk of butt-naked swimming detectives will travel round an island faster than syphilis, and will not help in the respect category.

She's already swimming by the time I arrive. It's a long beach. Away to the left, far away, someone with two dogs. I don't see the owner of the third car.

I stand at the edge of the sea and look out over the flat calm that stretches towards the setting sun. The sky is a rich blue, as the darkness encroaches from the east. The air is still, the breeze in off the sea almost non-existent. Cold though. And crisp. A beautiful afternoon, the thermometer in the car exalting a solid four degrees. Kallas might well find this balmy.

I stand beside her small pile of clothes on the beach. I note the bag and the towel. Unlikely to be naked in there. Oh well, whatever she's wearing, even if she gets out of the sea dressed in Victorian swimwear, covered from head to foot, she'll look sensational anyway.

Her head is above the water, hair up, making sure not to get too much of it wet. She swims out to sea for a certain amount of time, and then turns back, so that she is now swimming straight towards me. The sun is directly behind her.

I watch her slow approach. Take a glance along the beach to see if there's anyone else around, but the dog walker at the far end has disappeared, and there's no one else in sight, then I turn back to my siren in the sea.

Fuck's sake, listen to yourself.

Her movement changes as she reaches the shallows, she takes a moment, and then she stands, the chill water pouring off her. She shakes the top half of her body, and then walks towards me. She's wearing a tiny, maroon bikini. She looks freezing. Fuck me, these Estonians are bonkers.

When she's a few yards away, I finally manage to snap out of my stupor, and pick up her towel, so that I'm holding it towards her as she approaches.

'Thank you,' she says, and she takes the towel, and starts dabbing water from herself, as though drying off in the heat of a warm Mediterranean summer.

'How was that?' I ask mundanely.

'Fresh.'

She kind of smiles.

And so she dries herself off, and I stand a couple of yards away, and neither of us has anything to say.

'How did you find things at Glendun?' she asks finally, now mostly dry, holding the towel to her side.

Her nipples are obvious through the thin fabric. Don't stare. Don't stare. Don't be that guy.

I stare.

I look away, down the beach. The dog walker has appeared again in the far distance.

'There's a lot of resentment,' I say. 'The leap from resentment to murder is a pretty big one, of course, but it's a start.'

I look back at her, try to look her in the eye.

———

48

'I'll write it up,' I add.

She smiles.

'I do not mind you looking, Tom. It is nothing you have not seen before.'

OK, we're good, everything's good. But at least try not to say anything too drippy. You'll be getting expelled from the cool alcoholics club. And then, 'You look amazing,' is out of my mouth before I can do anything about it, and all the cool alcoholics are turning in their graves.

'Thank you,' she says. 'Do you mind if I change? There is no one around, you do not have to look away.'

I swallow, and make a small gesture to indicate her clothes. If all I'm capable of in such times is banal drivel like *you look amazing*, probably best if I just communicate in small hand gestures.

She removes her bikini in a familiar, understated way, dries herself off, then neatly lays down the towel on the dry sand and, sad to report, starts getting dressed.

I love that Dylan line in *Mississippi*: *I'm gonna look at you 'til my eyes go blind.* I think of that pretty much every time I see her, even when she's not naked. When she's naked, multiply it by two thousand, three hundred and fifty-six.

And then she's dressed, and she's slipping on her shoes and putting on her coat, taking the towel to the end of her hair, and then neatly folding the bikini and putting it into her bag.

'There is also much resentment at the Ardbreck distillery. I agree about the leap to murder, but as you say, it is a starting point. We do not yet narrow it down.'

'We should also consider,' I say, as the fun is wrapped up for the day and we turn away from the water's edge and begin to walk back up the beach, 'that this could be his old life catching up with him. Everything that's going on here could be a distraction, and someone from down south has chosen their moment. He'll have upset a lot of people when he ran off with a schoolgirl.' A pause, and then, 'Who knows, maybe one of his own kids finally got old enough and thought, bugger it, time for dad to get his comeuppance.'

'The family's whereabouts have all been identified, they were all in Somerset when the news was passed to them by the police there. However, there could be others.' She pauses, she weighs the question, and then she says, 'Would you say that someone who is willing to betray their spouse and walk out on

---

49

their family, may be more inclined to betray a business partner, to walk out on a deal?'

She sounds apologetic as she asks. I am a wife betrayer after all, although I didn't so much walk out on my family, as leave under a cloud of mutual enthusiasm. No one wanted me there by the end.

'Sorry,' she says, when I don't immediately answer. 'I do not mean to judge.'

She may well, of course, be considering her own infidelity.

'No, that's OK, I was just thinking about it, rather than being silently offended. And I'm not sure. Everyone's different, everyone's motivations are different. But, as you may have learned at Ardbreck, he basically came to Glendun undercover, like as an accidental tourist, seduced the distiller, found out everything he could about the organisation, and then scarpered when he had what he needed. Seemed entirely relaxed about being a heartbreaker.'

'I learned the same thing. He bought up everything in the shop, he had an affair with the distiller, he did not disclose his attachment to Kilcraig.'

'That's our boy,' I say. 'So, really, we get a good picture of who he is and the methods he's happy to employ. Very easy to imagine him pissing people off in his previous business life down south, and then... Well, perhaps someone bides their time.'

'Yes.'

We arrive at the cars, then we both turn back to the setting sun, the merest tip of the circle now evident above the horizon, in a blaze of orange.

We watch in silence for a while, standing side by side. It feels natural to slip my hand in to hers, but I can't do that without looking to see if anyone's watching us, and I don't want to break this moment by even turning my head, so we stand there together, unmoving, until the sun has disappeared.

'We should go to the local police station,' she says. 'I will introduce you to Constable Laird. There is still much to do today.'

We stare from that painful distance of a couple of feet, and then she nods, turns, and gets into her car.

9

'I'll be blunt,' says Constable Laird.

We're standing in a small office at the local police station in the village. This, presumably, will be a room where suspects come for interview. Although, I'm not sure how many suspects will ever actually be interviewed here. A one-woman station, in place to clear up the detritus of small town life. Should anything of consequence come along, it will very quickly find its way to the metropolitan heart of the island, Bowmore, population seven hundred and nothing.

There are two whiteboards on the wall, and the Constable has put something of an investigation-so-far narrative in place. Pictures of the deceased, photographs of the three distilleries, lists of all the other distilleries on the island, names and dates and places and faces such as we know them. A state of play.

'I've been at this station for twenty-three years now, and I've never made up a situation board before. Never had to. This isn't that kind of station. So, really, I will not be bothered if you want to completely scrub everything I've done and start again. I won't lie, I've done this largely based on the kind of thing you'd get on TV.'

She's staring at the board with her hands on her hips, like she's Howard Keel and is about to burst into song about how amazing the fields looked this morning.

'Not from around here, are you?' I can't help myself saying, narrowly heading Kallas off at the pass as she was likely just about to say that the boards are fine, and there's no need to change anything. Because they are and there isn't.

'Possilpark,' says Laird, turning back. 'Spent the first five years working out of Anderston. Centre of town...' She shakes her head, and I nod.

'A little different from around here, then.'

'Fucking brutal. The weekends were just an absolute shitshow. I mean, don't get me wrong, the city can scrub up reasonably well, it can look good for visitors, but that's not

---

51

where we work, is it? We work in the margins, and we get the drugs and the alcohol and the domestics. And we get Old Firm weekends. Fuck me, if I'd had to visit one more battered wife on an Old Firm weekend, I'd have topped myself. Couldn't hack it, I won't lie. This job came up, and I thought, worth a shot. I assumed someone local would get it, then it transpired no one local wanted it. They'd all buggered off to Glasgow.' A pause, and then the perfectly dry, 'I hope they're still happy.'

'This looks great,' I say, and Laird turns back at the board.

'Thank you. You guys want to take it over, or d'you want me to –'

'No, you have done a good job,' says Kallas, 'I would be grateful if you could continue to update the board as and when we gather information. If you are still OK to be involved, I am happy for you to be just as much a part of the team as either the sergeant or myself.'

'Not doing anything else,' says Laird. She embraces us both with a smile. 'Not so different from the past twenty-three years, to be honest. I mean, don't get me wrong, there's plenty to do, but just not a lot of actual crime. A murder is a bit of a head explosion.'

She makes a one-handed head explosion gesture. I can't help smiling with her.

The smiles go, we all turn back to the boards.

A small windowless room, a table and two chairs. A couple of regulation police information posters on the walls. We may need this, the collation of everything we know into one easy-to-use area, but I can't imagine I'm going to be spending much time in here. It would suck the life out of anyone.

'Did you ever have dealings with either of the Hendersons previously?' I ask.

'Not exactly.'

We both turn and give her the look that statement demands.

'You've heard about John Henderson's first visit to the island?' she says. 'Pretty much came incognito, infiltrated both the Glendun and Ardbreck distilleries, slept with women at both places, gathered intel and left.'

Kallas and I both nodding.

'Have you spoken to Jean Forsythe over at Ardbreck?'

'Yes, of course,' says Kallas. Their chief distiller, the one who fell for John Henderson's abs.

'When John Henderson arrived that first time and did what

---

he did, she came to me to complain about it. Myrna over at Glendun didn't, but Jean did. Her exact complaint was that he'd seduced her with malicious intent.'

'How'd that go?' I ask. Can't keep the smile out of the question.

'Not so well. The more I said there was nothing I could do about it, the more detail she gave. I mean,' and she hesitates, and then accepts that we're all grown-ups here, and we're all in the police and so therefore have seen and heard of much, much weirder shit than this, 'I got a lot of detail about sexual positions. Like, she genuinely thought she had a complaint against him in the law because she allowed him to *rear end* her over her desk.' She lets out a low whistle. I almost laugh at the way she says rear end, but manage to keep it together. 'She seemed annoyed at me at the time, though you'd be surprised how annoyed people can get at the police, particularly when there's not much going on.' Another pause, and then she waves away that last remark. 'Of course you wouldn't be surprised, you know exactly what they're like. I suggested she could possibly consider a civil suit, and she stomped off saying that's exactly what she was going to do, but I've heard nothing since. I presume that if she did talk to a lawyer, the lawyer wasn't interested. And given the kind of things lawyers will get interested in, that pretty much shows you.'

'How did you find her?' I ask Kallas.

'She did not mention previously speaking to the police. She was not at all concerned about John Henderson, certainly. Unconcerned to the point of callousness. She was also happy to share with me the reasons why she remained annoyed at him. I presume from your description that you never spoke to Mr Henderson at the time?'

'Never,' says Laird. 'And I never had any other cause to. I saw him at the Black Sheep quite often. He usually drank on his own. A couple of times he got involved in shot drinking competitions, but that didn't last. As soon as people realised he could likely hold a gallon of whisky more than anyone else on the island, they tended to steer well clear of him.'

Silence returns, and we all stand and look at the information. Speaking for myself, though, I'm not really reading it. I'm just kind of vaguely staring in its direction, and thinking about what will come next. I'm thinking what should come next is Kallas and I sharing a bottle of wine over dinner back at the guest house, before we quietly slip off to my room.

'Thank you,' says Kallas. 'These boards are very useful.'

She nods at Laird, and then turns to me.

'There are two pubs in the area. I suggest we split up and go to one each. I do not suggest that we covertly try to gather information. Any such opportunity is long gone. Nevertheless, pubs are good places to talk and listen, and we never know what's likely to come our way.'

That's not part of the plan.

'Are you free for the evening?' Kallas asks Laird, and Laird lets out a great belly laugh.

'You're new to island life,' she says, then, when the smile has left her face, she adds, 'it's January. I'm free for the evening.'

'Would you mind accompanying Tom? It will be useful for him to get completely up to speed with the island and the various characters involved.'

'Sure,' she says. 'The sergeant and I take the Sheep, you can do the Thistle?'

'That will be fine,' says Kallas.

She gives me a quick look. Nothing in it, of course, nothing for anyone else to read, but that there's a look that says, we're not spending the evening getting romantic, there's work to do, we need to split up to gather as much information as quickly as possible, and although I'm saying nothing to the constable, you and I both know that I've asked her to accompany you so that you are not left alone to drink. So, please, do not push it, do not keep drinking after she's gone, do not get drunk, do not do anything stupid.

She may also silently add that she wants me sober so we can meet again back at my room at eleven, though I may be reading too much into it.

'Boss,' I say, nodding.

'Thank you,' says Kallas. 'We will get something to eat at these pubs?' she directs at Laird.

'The menu's pretty much the same in both, but sure.'

'Then I think we are done here for this evening, and we should go about our business,' says Kallas with wonderful Estonian formality, given that we're going out on the lash, rather than setting up a NATO Working Group on weapons system interoperability.

54

10

Sitting in a bar in the Hebrides and some fucker pulls a fiddle out their arse is pretty much island pub 101. If there's a list of clichés to be written about these establishments, that's got to be at the top.

The constable and I are eating fish suppers – she has a pint of some rustic ale, and I, the southern sophisticate, am drinking a delicate pinot grigio – and the guy has just started playing. No idea what the tune is. I mean, they're all the same, right? There only is one fiddle tune, just played at different speeds. And don't get me wrong, I'm sounding dismissive, but I love it. *Desire* is one of my favourite Dylan records, and that's got fiddle on every track.

'Feels like we've walked onto the set of a movie,' I say, glibly, after a mouthful of wine. I ordered the large glass, rather than a bottle, aiming to make it last at least through to the end of the food. That's fifty-fifty at the moment.

'You're not wrong,' she says, and she makes a small movement of her fork, indicating the bar. There are currently seven customers, and two staff. 'Malcolm never used to play the fiddle in here, then he watched the *Banshees of Inisherin* and he thought, oh, I play the fiddle, I can do that.' She pauses to take a mouthful of food, then adds, 'People seem happy enough with it. You like it?'

'Sure. Very ethnic,' I add glibly, knowing I'm with one of my own from down south, and she laughs.

Laird has removed her sweater, given our proximity to the roaring fire, and is now wearing just a low-cut T-shirt. With the jumper gone, she's all breasts. I'm doing my best not to stare, but there's no danger of me doing something stupid anyway. Not with DI Kallas in town, having asked me here in the first place.

'I hate that movie,' I say.

'Really, how come? I loved it.'

I stab a couple of chips, then correct myself.

'OK, I'll rephrase. That movie was like cats. I don't –'

'You mean *Cats* the movie, or cats, you know, the pets.'

'Cats the pets.'

'OK, I'm with you,' she says, indicating with her fork for me to go on.

'I don't hate cats. I mean they do their thing. They kill shit, and good luck to them. What I hate is cat owners, who treat their cats like the cats have two fucks to give about them. Cats are only friendly to their owners because they feed them. Don't feed them, they'll fuck off next door at the rustle of a packet of biscuits.'

She's nodding by the time I'm finished.

'I have a cat, and that's exactly what happens when I forget to feed the little bastard.'

'But owners who anthropomorphise their cats, that drives me nuts. They're killing machines. That's it. They just don't kill you, Marjorie, because you're too big.'

She's laughing, she speers a couple of chips, and says through the food, 'All right then, Sergeant, dial round to the *Banshees of Inisherin* now.'

'I don't hate the film. It was just a movie. Wasn't awful, but you know, it's kind of fucking bleak, by the way. And it is one hundred per cent not a black comedy. Zero comedy. And not a comedy in some grand theatrical way, in which the word comedy might be getting used in some higher sense. That fucker was just a depressing-ass movie, period. And the finger thing? That was just stupid. But people talk about it in hushed voices, like it's the *Godfather* multiplied by *Toy Story* or something.'

She laughs loudly, in her way.

'Now that's a movie I'd watch.'

'And you read these reviews stating how extraordinary it is, and you're thinking, what did I miss? Wait, is it me? Am I stupid? Did I not understand it? And you end up feeling you've been gaslighted. But the movie's just a movie, and it's the people that are the problem.' A pause, and then, 'They just need to shut up.'

'Hmm,' she says, and she kind of shrugs. A big shrug, and I try not to look at the movement of her breasts. 'I know what you mean. I felt a bit like that about *Manchester-by-the-Sea*.'

'Oh, I loved that.'

She laughs again.

'Maybe you don't like the Irish, have you thought about that? I take it you're from the Rangers half of town.'

She's still laughing as she says it. She laughs a lot. I wonder if she laughed when she was called to the distillery on the discovery of the corpse.

'I'm from the Partick Thistle side of town, and anyway, I loved *In Bruges*, so there's that.'

'Ah, that explains it,' she says. 'There's hardly any swearing in *Inisherin*.'

'Aye, if only Mad-Eye Moody had told Colin Farrell he didn't want to be his pal 'cause he was a cunt, infinite improvement right there.'

Another laugh, and a great shaking of her bosom.

The fiddle tune comes to an end. I pause, ready to pounce on the applause like an unfettered eagle, but no one else claps, so obviously I don't. Seems rude not to, but I don't know the pub etiquette, and anyway, the old guy doesn't care, and soon enough he kicks off another tune. Or possibly the same tune with a couple of notes missing. Hard to tell.

'So, what's with you and the inspector?' she asks.

'I don't know, what does that mean?'

I lift my delicate pinot grigio to my lips.

'Seems like there's a bit of fizz between you. You a couple?'

'Nope.'

'You used to be a couple?'

She's shaking her head as she says it.

'She's married with three children, so no couple,' I say.

She stares into my eyes across my carefully placed, face-concealing wine glass, and nods.

'I see. I shall pry no further.'

Probably for the best.

'Are you going to this Burns Supper tomorrow?' I ask, to quickly move the conversation along. Obviously, I'd quite happily talk about Kallas all night, but this is definitely not the appropriate company. Not sure anyone other than Eileen would be the appropriate company, and now it turns out that even Eileen isn't either.

Maybe I could talk to Anders. I could invite him out for a drink, and we could have a manly chat about which one of us would be better for his wife. Anders, mid-forties, high-flying, multi-lingual consultancy executive, and the father to her three children, or me, late-fifties, alcoholic, bottom-feeding, cave dwelling, serial philanderer, possessing a liver with a shelf-life

---

of no more than about a month and a half?

Tricky decision for any woman.

'Everyone's going. I mean, literally everyone in the village and the surrounding area. Well, at least, everyone's invited, but I can't imagine many will miss it.'

'Even the folk working for Glendun and Ardbreck?'

'Those people will be knocking the doors down to get in. They want to see what's going on, get the full scope of what they're up against. As if they don't already know. You're coming?'

'I'm hoping we get everything solved and wrapped up in the next twelve hours, then we can go home tomorrow afternoon, thus avoiding it,' I say, and she laughs again. 'But sadly, since we don't anticipate doing that, I think the inspector is looking for us to attend. We know who's making the speeches?'

'Well, Caleb Henderson is the compere, or the host, whatever you call it. It's his thing. He's a good talker, I'll give him that, though of course most people hate him. John would've been addressing the haggis, and I've no idea who they've got coming on as substitute. The Immortal Memory, and the addresses to the lads and lassies, no one knows. Surprise guests, apparently. Rumour is he's got, you know, actual stars coming in on a paid, speaking fee type of affair.'

'Oh,' I say, tucking into the last piece of fish. Unusually, for this stage of a fish supper, I'm not stuffed. 'Well, that's a positive. At least they'll be professionals.'

She nods, then I feel the need to correct myself.

'Of course, people pay Liz Truss to speak, and this guy's a Tory, so you never know. If she's on the bill, I'm volunteering to take the dirk instead of the haggis.'

'Ha! I'll fight you for it.'

'Is there dancing?'

'Oh, aye, there's dancing. But not until after the speeches, obviously, so don't be expecting to get out onto the floor until after midnight.'

Fuck me.

Last chip, and with it, the last of my glass of wine. Amiable though this evening has been, I'm not sure it's getting us very far. I might as well have been with Kallas, and I'm already wondering how long I have to leave it, how long I have to sit here having good-natured conversation, before I head back to the guest house, hoping she'll already be there, or to sit in the lounge awaiting her return.

'Tell me about John Henderson swanning in here seducing women,' I say, it being about time we properly talked about work.

'That was certainly something he did. The ladies in question don't seem to mind owning up to it.'

'Weren't people talking about it after the first one, so that the second woman might well have known what was coming?'

'Nah, he was much more sleekit than that. He met Myrna in the Thistle, I think, but I doubt anyone else thought there was much to it. Thereafter, they kept themselves to themselves. However, when he ended it, the way I understand it, he kind of left it open. She makes it sound like a brutal guillotine now, but I think at the time he left her hanging for a while. Meanwhile, he's pulling the same manoeuvre over at Ardbreck. Finally fessed up to the two of them on the same evening, and then vanished. Came back a couple of months later, pretty young wife in tow.'

'Finola.'

'The glamorous Finola.'

'She must've come to hear about the sex, though, surely?'

'Oh, I think she's heard about *all* the sex.' She smiles. 'There's been a lot of sex. It was kind of John Henderson's brand. If he could've been said to have a brand.'

'Which d'you think is more likely? He was killed because of business rivalries, because of arguments within his own business, or by a spurned lover or jealous husband, or his own wife for that matter?'

She drains her pint and sets the glass back down on the table.

'Hmm, tricky. It's not good when one considers just how many different reasons there might be to kill a man is it?'

'Nope. You didn't answer the question.'

She laughs. Her breasts shake intoxicatingly.

Yeah, whatever.

'OK, I'd say internal argument seems slim. He's going to have pissed people off within the company, but to dump him in the tun? I don't see it. Business rivalry with either Ardbreck or Glendun? Now that seems more likely, but still, since we're talking about brands, does not seem on brand for either of those guys. Those businesses, I mean. They're kind of being crushed, but I don't see them resorting to murder. And, overall, I'm not sure a body in a vat of wort actually does anyone on the island any good, you know? I don't think ultimately it's just going to be Kilcraig that suffers.'

She lifts her pint, seems to notice that she's already finished it, tips the dregs into her mouth, and then pushes her chair back.

'Which leaves the sex.' She smiles, lifts her glass to ask if I'd like another, I accept that I really have to stay long enough to have one more, then she says, 'And you can never rule out sex when it comes to murder, can you?'

And she turns away, and I think that she's probably right. But then, you can never rule out money either.

11

Inevitably, I arrive back at the guest house before Kallas. I sit in the lounge, and manage not to ask Janusz for more wine, instead taking a cup of tea and a couple of pieces of shortbread. There's a fire going, and while I overlap with a German couple, and we exchange a word or two, my presence works mainly to drive them out prematurely, and soon enough I'm on my own.

I text Kallas to let her know I'm back here. She replies that she will be back at some point in the future, with zero clue as to whether it will be imminently or in the middle of the night.

I get a notebook out, and start making lists of names. People I've spoken to, people I know about, connections between companies and groups of friends. Look at me, working and not drinking at nine-forty-five in the evening. Have turned, for likely one evening only, into a try-hard, because I want to impress my crush. Very shallow.

Currently the list of people who might have wanted John Henderson dead is limited to everyone who ever met him. So not limited in any way whatsoever.

He slept around, he used people, he exploited people, he surreptitiously, if metaphorically, castrated people. It would hardly be a surprise if it turns out we're in a *Murder On The Orient Express*-type situation, and that everyone in the village got together to dump the fucker into the mash.

For now, though, we likely have to work towards a more mundane explanation, which means starting with alibis. Someone dumped that body, so it has to be someone whose whereabouts are not known for the evening. The person who claims to have been driving to the other side of the island, or walking the dog, or sitting alone watching television.

So, we have people at the three distilleries, and we have people known to have been lovers of John Henderson. Plus the untitled, unknown group, who could be made up of literally anyone, because this is the group with a motive of which we are so far unaware.

I need to speak to the widow again. We didn't really get into talking to her about lovers, but that there was a woman who did not look particularly bothered about being a new widow.

I should go to see her in the morning, on my own. Not sure what that will do, but it'll be worthwhile to attack the interview from a different angle. And I should get round to Ardbreck and speak to their people, make my own impressions. A familiar kind of mixed bag of personalities at Glendun, but naturally, no one leaping off the page. When people do, it often enough means they're not guilty.

I start to make a plan for tomorrow. Kallas is the boss, of course, and she might have other ideas, but I should put something together, for her as well as me. Look willing. Look switched on. I've only had two glasses of wine, so I'm not even remotely drunk. I can try to carry off the part of competent police officer, and maybe she'll sleep with me.

Because that's how it works.

* * *

She returns to the guest house about an hour after I do. She enters the lounge, she nods, she assesses the situation, she says, 'I will make coffee, would you like one?' and I – so full of relief that she's finally turned up and hasn't just immediately retreated to her bedroom – say, 'Sure, thank you,' even though I usually don't drink coffee at this time of night. I'm just doing it because she is. And yes, if she jumped in the Clyde, I too would jump in the fucking Clyde.

And then we're sitting in a small room, the fire is still going – Janusz arrived to toss another log into the dying flames a while ago – and there's a wonderful, low-lit, smoky warmth.

Neither of us says anything for a while. We stare at each other. I guess that might be weird with some people, but it feels entirely natural for Kadri and I. Like we're having the conversation without having to say anything.

Trouble with that kind of conversation is that it does leave open the possibility of a certain amount of misinterpretation.

'How did you get on?' she asks eventually.

I hide my disappointment that the first words are about work, but I suppose we need to get them over with.

'It was OK. Nothing major, although I don't suppose either of us was expecting that. I made a plan for the morning. You can take a look.'

I lift the notebook that I'd laid on the small table beside me when she entered the room.

'It is OK,' she says, 'I shall look at it at breakfast.'

And that's that for work. I don't ask her how she got on. I mean, I mostly don't care, but she's given me the excuse by more or less parking everything until the morning.

'Why didn't you tell me you were going to Estonia?'

Words just out of my mouth. Nothing I could do about it. Hadn't been intending to ask. I mean, I'd silently had the conversation in my head a few times on my drive to the island yesterday, and it never went well. It never ended with her saying, fair enough, I won't go, I'll stay and we can move in together and make love every night. So, don't ask, I'd been thinking. Let her tell you. But now, fucking blabbermouth, couldn't keep it shut, could you?

'I am sorry. That was why I called you last week.' She pauses. Silence threatens to sweep in and take over. I think of that conversation, and how, at the time, I'd known she was leaving something unsaid, but ultimately, when she didn't really say anything at all, and a few days passed without me hearing from her, I'd forgotten about it. Funny that I hadn't had some awful premonition.

'I called to tell you, or else I called to say that I would come and see you, and in the end I did neither. I should just have turned up at your apartment, but I could not do that either.' A pause, but this one with words hanging just at the end of it, then she says, 'I do not want to break your heart.'

'You don't owe me anything.'

'And neither do you owe me, but my heart is still breaking.'

Fuck me.

She can sound so... robotic. So put together, so in control. Even now, when saying this, there is something functional in her tone.

But this is me, and I can't stand it. I can't stand the intensity, and I crack in a familiar way.

'Well, what we need to do is run away to Iceland,' I say, smiling, and she can't help herself smiling with me. 'I can get my pension, and you can probably join a local police force. I mean, if the novels are anything to go by, there must be like five or six hundred murders a year in Reykjavik. We can get a little cottage outside the city, and when you're at work solving all those brutal sex crimes, I can do the garden and grow... whatever it is that grows in Iceland.'

She's laughing by the end of it, and she comes out of the laugh with a slow-fading, sad smile.

'Then I would break Anders' heart, and I would break my daughters' hearts, and I cannot do that.'

Classic Estonian. She didn't have to take the Iceland idea seriously. Even though it's a fucking great idea, by the way. And with the daughters thrown in at the end there. That was good, because I was probably not so far removed from some cavalier cry of *Fuck Anders!*, that wouldn't have played well with the audience.

We go back to the staring. I know she's torn. I should be bigger than this situation. I should take myself out of the game. I should walk away. I mean, I can't walk away from this investigation, but I should be the one to bring the tough love to the party, I should be the one to stand up, and say good night. See you in the morning. Let's get the crime solved, and let's get back to our lives. You'll need to start packing.

But the words aren't there. My legs won't move. I have no great romantic tragi-gesture to make this easier for us both.

Silence takes hold. Sure, the fire crackles in the hearth, and somewhere there's the sound of movement in the house, but those noises, those trivial sounds, are lost to this. This silence between us crushes sound.

A tear trickles slowly down her cheek, and the feel of it on her skin seems to rouse her from the moment. She shakes her head, wipes away the tear, lifts her cooling cup of coffee, and takes a drink. She stares at the carpet, and then turns with a far more positive air about her than she's shown since she arrived back here this evening. My heart begins to sink at what is coming, as she's obviously found within herself what I was unable to.

'We cannot sit here all night, Tom,' she says. 'But we are trapped in this moment nevertheless.'

I find a nod from somewhere.

'I need to speak to Anders,' she says, 'but if it is OK, I will come to your room afterwards.'

That's so unexpected, that I just kind of sit there like a lemon. I mean, that's probably better than my more natural response, which would be to leap off the sofa and literally explode in a firework of enthusiasm. No one wants to see that in a fifty-seven-year-old man. So, fortunately, I don't need to tell myself to calm the fuck down, as I'm so surprised, I've remained calm throughout.

'Are you sure?'

'Yes. I will be a while, but I will come. If that is OK.'

'I'd love you too.'

Another long gaze, and then she nods, gets to her feet, turns away from the fireplace and leaves the room.

* * *

I don't believe it will happen until there's a knock at the door. That's the trouble with going our separate ways, particularly when the woman in the relationship is going to call her husband. God knows what level of guilt that conversation will leave her with. And then, there are all the other things that can go wrong in the short period of time between the decision to have sex and the actual sex. Something's happened to one of her kids; someone else in this whisky-flavoured investigation gets murdered; there's a fire; the Ukraine conflict descends into all-out, global nuclear war. I mean, let's face it, when that happens, and it's coming eventually, there's going to be someone, somewhere, just about to have amazing sex, and then, ruh-roh, no, you're not.

I don't rush, as I don't want to sit with nothing to do, waiting for the knock at the door. I go back to the room. I brush my teeth, and take a shower. I put on those M&S pyjama shorts and T-shirt that I wear to bed these days. I contemplate putting on the TV, and then instead, sit in the chair by the desk.

Having done everything I need to do, now worry starts to encroach. I look at my phone, I work out how long it is since we parted. Forty-seven minutes. I wonder if she's coming. I look at sport on my phone, and then at the news, and then at something, anything, quickly accepting I've run out of things to look at on my phone. I don't need or want my phone. I put down the phone, aware that I dread the ping, as she texts that she's changed her mind.

There's a knock at the door. I let her in, and she enters, wearing the white robe of the guest house. I close the door behind her. Now, alone in the room, we do not hesitate. No need for words. She is in my arms, our lips meet, we press against

65

each other. Her hands run over my hair and my face, and then she loosens the tie on her robe, shrugs it off, and she is naked in my arms.

This is what any of us live for.

An Unreliable Narrative

ii

People are so fucked up. We shouldn't be surprised, of course.
We know they're fucked up. We wouldn't be here if they
weren't.

We dumped the body of that asshole in the mash. You'd
think that would be enough to put people off. *People.* You'd
think that might throw Jeremy off his game. Lil' Jeremy, the
copywriter, making the big bucks. But makes no difference to
him. No fucks to give, just doing his job. What have you got for
me to work with today? A corpse in the whisky? No problemo.
For one section of the market, we'll pretend it never happened:
for another, it'll be a selling point. There are going to be a lot of
people who didn't know we existed last week, and now, boom
time. No such thing as bad publicity, particularly when you
don't need to worry about the Child Abuse exception to the rule.

Fuck Jeremy. Jeremy is just going to have to cope with an
escalation. Hey, Jeremy! How d'you like this?

Jeremy's time is at hand anyway. He loved, he left, he'll
get what's coming. We've decided. So none of it really matters.
But, it's true what they say. You stab one fucker in the throat
with a knife, and you kind of get the hankering to do it again. To
do *something* again. But like we said, an escalation.

When was the last time you saw a decapitated head on a
spike? And we don't mean, in a movie. Probably never, right?
We've certainly never seen one IRL, that's for sure. We like the
idea of the spike, but it's not so practical. Not much of an
audience for the head on a spike. As soon as one person sees it,
the spectacle is over. So, we need something a little more
audience friendly *than a spike*.

Shouldn't be too hard.

Whose head? There are a lot of women to choose from, but
we think we know who makes the most sense. Pretty sure death

will become her. And the weird thing is, she'll let us walk happily in through the front door.

12

Don't ask what it's supposed to be.

Friday morning. The day of the Burns Supper. The village is buzzing. There was a queue of trucks through town, on the way to the Kilcraig distillery to set up for the bash. There's no building hereabouts big enough to meet the scope of Caleb Henderson's vision, and so a giant marquee is being erected in the grounds. A marquee? In January? Aye, that's the size of it. But this is a solid-ass bit of kit, they have large, free-standing gas burners coming, for inside the marquee and out, and it's as if Caleb has dominion over the weather. It's due to be cold, and there may be a little snow, but those are both vastly preferable to wind and rain, and neither of those is forecast.

'It's like a grand ball in a Jane Austen novel,' Janusz said to us this morning at breakfast. Despite not getting much of a reaction from Kallas or me, he remained in excited good humour. He's got the catering contract for desserts, and is looking forward to his busy day.

I wanted to say, you're in the wrong story, my friend. You should be in a Hallmark Christmas movie. This is a six-part, brutal murder drama. You need to calm the fuck down.

But that would've been mean. I kept my mouth shut.

Now, I'm executing the first part of my plan, having come back to see the widow, Finola Henderson. I guess there are a fuck-tonne of wives and mums and divorcees and widows and women with all kinds of life experiences by the time they're twenty-six, but there's still something about her reminding me of my kid Rebecca. Perhaps it's for the best that her asshole, philandering husband is dead, and she can go back to her family and live some sort of normal, young woman's life.

Maybe her life won't be so different.

I'm in her studio, at the rear of the large house, which is on the side of a hill, out of sight of the distillery, looking down over a field of sheep, to the beach and the sea. It is at the end of the beach where I watched Kallas go swimming, and I realise now that this is the house I could see in the far distance. I also note the large telescope in the corner, and I'm glad the inspector and I did not choose that moment for our first embrace on this trip.

Finola has just shown me her latest painting. I have no idea how to describe what I'm looking at. It certainly doesn't look like anything, existing somewhere in that giant region that occupies the space between the ordered simplicity of Rothko and the utter frenetic shitshow of Jackson Pollock.

'It's called *The Sorcerer's Lament.*'

She pauses. She's probably reflecting that art, like humour, loses something when you have to explain it.

'Who's the sorcerer?' I ask.

'I am.' She reaches out and runs a soft finger down the side of the painting.

I stare at it. There's probably something going on with that title. I mean, presumably artists usually have something going on with titles. Not sure why she would refer to herself as the sorcerer rather than sorceress, although I suppose *The Sorceress's Lament* is a little clumsy. But gender-related titles are a minefield now, and my intention is to die without ever going anywhere near the mines.

I know, rank coward. Don't care.

'You don't have a lot of arrangements to make following John's death?' I throw into the conversation.

She lifts her coffee and takes a slurp. And it really is a slurp. That's an entitled, posh English school for you, no one to tell them to mind their fucking manners. Yes, clearly, I'm just going to let my prejudices spew forth.

'Caleb is insisting on taking care of everything. The funeral, the burial, the wake, or whatever it is they call it up here.'

She turns, managing to drag herself away from her latest magnificent work of art, and looks at me curiously.

'Do you call it a wake?'

Put on the spot like this, I'm not sure. I feel like we call it a cup of tea and a sausage roll. Like Cup of Tea And A Sausage Roll is the official title of the event.

'Yes,' I say, as I can't think of anything else.

'So, that, and everything else, really. The will, the insurance, the sale of this place, the removal when it comes to it. You've spoken to Caleb?'

'Of course.'

'He does everything. Or he has people who do everything. Surrounds himself with people who get things done. He's one of those types. He needs to be in control. I like him, despite all the arguments they used to have.'

I take a moment to consider how indelicately to put the next question, and she heads me off at the pass, a rueful smile on her face.

'Of course, John having died without giving me a son, according to Deuteronomy, Chapter 25, I should now marry Caleb. What d'you think about that?'

'Probably best not to live your life by the Old Testament. Anyway, since your husband already had kids, I'm not sure Deuteronomy applies.'

'Oh, right. Well, that's a relief.'

She laughs lightly, head shaking.

'These Bible nuts really show their prejudices, don't they?' she says. 'Marriage is between a man and a woman, it says so in the Bible. Wait, it also says in the Bible you should be executed for working on the Sabbath. And stoned to death for committing adultery and calling your dad a prick. Hmm, maybe not those ones. But the marriage is between a man and a woman one, let's stick with that, that's a good one... Assholes.'

'I've heard talk about your husband's infidelity,' I say, Leviticus, or whoever the fuck it was, giving me the opportunity to jump into the question headfirst.

She looks at me again with a smile, then bursts out laughing.

'Infidelity? Nice way to put it, sergeant.'

'Seems appropriate.'

'I suppose. I used to call it his shagging around, but I suppose you felt you couldn't be so vulgar when talking to the demure widow.'

She laughs again, slurps at her coffee, then lays down the cup.

'I'm going to have toast. Would you like some? Sourdough, baked yesterday. It makes the most amazing toast. I've got raspberry or strawberry jam. Oh, and marmalade.'

'I'm good, thanks.'

'Of course, you'll have had one of Janusz's breakfasts, they're divine.'

There is, naturally, a kitchen area at the back of the studio with a kettle and a coffee machine and a toaster, and she goes about the business of making the toast, which may or may not be a distraction tactic, given I've just asked her about her husband's adultery. I look at a few more of her artworks – which we'll be kind and call abstract, rather than just plain pish – then stand at the window and look out at the sea, beneath a light grey sky.

'What have you heard?' she asks, coming to stand beside me.

'That's not how this works,' I say. 'Tell me about John's infidelity.'

'Really, it is perfectly OK to call it shagging around, I don't mind.'

I ask the question again with a bit of an open-handed gesture, inviting her to talk.

'John was the kind of man who lived life to the extremes. He drank too much, he ate ridiculous food, he exercised compulsively, he had a lot of lovers. Lived his life at a hundred miles an hour. He didn't really do drugs, but then every now and again, if the opportunity arose, he'd snort cocaine until his heart exploded. We went to New Zealand, and he spent two weeks acting like a twenty-year-old. Paragliding, sky-diving, bungee, white water rafting, on and on.' She pauses, then adds, 'I sat on the balcony drinking a selection of crisp New Zealand whites.'

'Sounds like a holiday.' I don't say that I'd have been on the balcony with her.

'When he asked me to marry him he said he would never leave me, but he couldn't promise to always be faithful. Well, that was one way of putting it...'

I consider the next question, but we're here now, and she does not seem like a bereaved widow, so might as well get the fuck on with it.

'It's easy enough to be bold and calm and whatever and talk about infidelity like you're too cool to care, but what did you really think about it? Didn't it bother you? Didn't it hurt? You're waiting for him to come home, he's late, and you know, every time, it's not because he's talking to New York on some business matter, it's because there's a new girl working at the shop and he's taking her over the desk.'

The toaster pops, there's the sound of a piece of sourdough flying up and out and landing on the counter. She swallows, looks at me, gives me a many-layered gaze, and then turns and walks to the back of the studio.

'I made two slices,' she says, 'you sure you don't want

one?'

'I'm good, thanks.'

I turn and watch her as she goes about the domestic business of making toast. Butter, jam, all very careful and precise, then she pours herself another cup of coffee, and returns to our spot by the window, laying the cup down on the small table that's there for this very purpose.

'It was humiliating at first,' she says. 'Everyone knew, of course. So, there was that. I realised soon enough when I got here, and sure, I felt the shame of it then. I didn't understand. Barely knew him, really. I mean, he'd told me he'd fuck around, it was practically written in the pre-nup, but I thought, I don't know, maybe it wouldn't start for a while. Maybe it would take some time before he got tired of my young, perfect tits. But nope, he never stopped. You know that bit in the *Godfather* when James Caan fucks whoever during his own wedding reception?'

'You've seen the *Godfather*?' I can't stop myself blurting out, like that's what the moment needs.

'A-Level Film Studies. Anyway, I'm not saying John actually did that. Well, I know he didn't, 'cause he fucked me during our wedding reception, but he certainly had that level of male entitlement.'

'So why did he marry you?'

Her brow furrows, as though this is the first time she's ever considered this question, then she shakes her head and shrugs.

'I don't know. I guess he needed sex on tap. I mean, even for fit guys, I suppose it's not always readily available. And especially since he was already talking about coming away up here, to the outer rim of the galaxy. He said when his wife was approaching the menopause she was absolutely desperate for sex. Like, permanently horny. He was like, sure thing, I'm here for that. Sex at least twice a day. I mean, like, she was in her late forties, and she was taking him on the kitchen table. And then, boom, peri-menopause ends, the menopause kicks in, and she could barely look at him.' She laughs ruefully at the weirdness of the female body. 'I am not looking forward to that shit, I'll say that. Anyhoo, that coincided with him meeting me. I was happy to have him three or four times a day if he wanted it. Anytime, anywhere. I mean, that shit didn't last, but it survived long enough for us to get married.'

'And you signed a pre-nup?'

'Not unreasonable. You meet so many rich, middle-aged guys brought low by divorce lawyers, right?'

'How does the pre-nup look now that he's died?'

'Oh, you know, I think a bit better for me.'

She finally crunches loudly into a piece of toast, then suggestively licks the side of her mouth. Right, I wasn't thinking straight. I'm standing here looking at her like she's my daughter or something, but she's fresh off her marriage to a guy who wasn't all that much younger than me. She thinks she can flirt.

Whatever.

To be fair, there would have been times when she could've done.

She smiles. 'You thinking that maybe I killed him for the dosh?'

'Did you?'

She laughs and takes another loud bite of toast.

'Nope. Never even thought about it, to be honest.'

'Not even when he was humiliating you?'

'Nope. I mean murder's pretty extreme. I thought about leaving, but Jesus, my mother would have loved that, wouldn't she? She would have loved that admission of my humiliation. So I stuck it out. I got him to build me this place. This is a nice spot. So I got this as a trade for him being a duplicitous asshole. Murder was not required.'

'So, who d'you think killed him?'

Another smile, another bite of toast, the next few minutes of the interview to be conducted to a crunching accompaniment.

'I wasn't really in on all the business stuff, so I can imagine he pissed some people off, but I don't know. There were a few angry husbands around the island, though, so maybe you want to start there. I can give you some names, if you like. But not sure if they're really more likely to be the killer, or whether that's just based on my own experiences and prejudices.'

'You give me the names, I decide what to do about them,' I say.

'Fine. You got a pen and paper?'

13

The trouble with approaching some guy – we'll call him Mr Z – and saying, *so this bloke banged your wife, how did you feel about that, and did you kill him*, is that, just because the widow Henderson knows her husband slept with Mrs Z, it doesn't mean Mr Z knows. He might be blissfully unaware. The two of them might be quite happily married, the sex with John Henderson just a thing that happened. Perhaps Mrs Z has guilt, perhaps not. Either way, I show up with my size-eleven galumphers and lob a hand grenade into their marriage, and suddenly everyone's fucked. Lives ruined, kids are crying, and Mr Z is standing on the rocks, looking wistfully to the horizon, contemplating a quick divorce and a life at sea. Plus, there's always the possibility that the widow is wrong, or that her husband lied to her.

Delicacy is called for.

Yep, that's why I'm here.

Finola Henderson gave me a list of seven names, while implying there were many more she didn't know. Five married women, one of whom is married to a woman, and two others in on-going relationships, who'd had sex with her husband in the past few years. And now I'm at the police station with Constable Laird, and she's looking over the list, while we eat doughnuts and drink tea. Not sure where DI Kallas is at the moment, but it's not like there's a shortage of places to go and people to talk to.

'OK, straight off you can get rid of Iain,' she says, and she puts a red line through a name in the middle of the list. 'That one's very well known. He cried a lot, everyone in the village got to share in his experience. There was a lot of counselling, they got through it. I mean, maybe it happened again that we don't know about, but Shona found Jesus afterwards, and has lived her penance pretty much every day.'

To me you only definitely put a line through someone's name if you have eyes on them when the murder was committed, but I'm not going to argue.

'Jack works in Aberdeen, and has been off the island for the past fortnight. Due back later today for this evening's bash, but as a potential killer, he's a no. Tom and Clare have been on holiday since last Thursday. Fuerteventura. They're all over Instagram. Hmm, Janice and Sandra?' and she makes an interested face at the inclusion of the lesbian couple. 'So, Finola said that her husband had slept with Janice?'

Having a mouthful of doughnut, I answer with a *well, she's on the list* gesture.

'Hmm, I would not have seen that coming. Janice? You're sure she said Janice?'

'Yep,' I finally manage to get out.

'Well, I have no idea what they were doing at the weekend. You might have to speak to Janice.'

I get another look, and then, 'You'll be delicate, right? I mean, I don't think Sandra is going to see this coming.'

'It's a small village,' I say. 'Anyone we interview, we can easily say that we're speaking to everyone, asking everyone the same questions.'

'Martin, we've already spoken to. He and Jill spent the evening with friends, so there's nothing to see here.' She takes a moment, softly tapping the other two names, while lifting the doughnut and taking a large bite. 'Think you might have to speak to these last two, if you can. I don't know this guy, actually. Pretty sure he's not in the village. Is he still on the island?'

'Not sure.'

'OK, well, I guess the same rules apply as with talking to Janice and Sandra.'

'I shall tread carefully.'

'Thank you.'

I'm sitting across the desk from her, and we both sit back a little, still staring at the list. My back is to the window, a bright day, despite the uniform covering of light grey cloud.

'There's something else I find a bit odd,' I say, and she invites me to continue, the tea at her lips. 'The reason the inspector is here, and as a result the reason I'm here, is because the previous officer dispatched from the mainland was sent packing because of her views on independence.'

'That's correct.'

'No one's mentioned independence to us. I spoke to the

inspector about it this morning. There's been nothing.'

She takes another long drink of tea, nodding her way through it.

'Sounds about right,' she says. 'Generally, there's a conspiracy of silence. It's coming on ten years of non-stop talking about it, and everyone's views are well known. It's like a truce. Then Inspector Watkin arrived from Edinburgh, and she obviously started asking questions about it. She, at least in the estimation of Caleb Henderson, had a chip on her shoulder about Westminster. Caleb felt threatened. He pulled some strings.'

'The Tories have strings to pull in Edinburgh?'

She kinds of shrugs, then says, 'Different sides of the same coin, and all that. It's just a game they play, right?'

'I guess so.'

'If Caleb hasn't tried to get either you or Inspector Kallas sent home, it's only because neither of you has made too much about independence, and if either of you have mentioned it, it must've been on neutral terms. Or, in fact, given we're talking about Caleb here, in pro-Westminster terms.'

'Oh, that definitely won't have happened.'

She smiles, she looks back at the list, she turns it back around and pushes it across the desk towards me.

'I wish you luck, sergeant. Try not to end too many marriages while you're about it.'

* * *

I find the bottom name on the list of seven, Mhairi Andrews, part of the crew erecting the marquee at the distillery. Well, the name on the list is Ruaridh Andrews, but I decide to speak to the wife first, to get the lay of the land before blundering into conversation with her husband.

It's a cold day, but she's wearing a tight, white T-shirt, slim jeans, boots and a pair of robust gloves. She sees me waiting for her while she's in the middle of erecting a pole, she finishes what she's doing, while the investigating sergeant scrupulously avoids paying attention to the tight fabric of the top against her breasts, and then she approaches me, wiping her brow with her wrist, just like she would have been told to do by the director of the Hallmark movie she's appearing in.

Do Hallmark make murder movies? Maybe they do. Maybe there's this whole raft of syrupy serial killer films, that still manage to have a happy ending, even though seven women have been locked in a basement, skinned alive, and then left screaming, while their flesh gets eaten by rats and maggots.

That's probably not a movie, to be fair.

'You're the policeman over from Glasgow?' she says. Lovely island accent. Wow, feels like just about the first one I've heard. Most people seem to be English, or soft, imperialist lowlanders. Like me.

'Sgt Hutton,' I say, and I produce my ID, which she doesn't bother looking at.

'What can I do for you?'

I don't need to worry about discretion here. There's a lot of noise, a lot of bustle, no one paying much attention. The inspector and I are questioning a broad spectrum of people, and over the course of the next few days, assuming we don't get a quick result, we're liable to speak to just about everyone who lives hereabouts.

'I heard you'd had an affair with the deceased.'

Not sure what she was expecting, but it wasn't that. One can see the colour start to drain from her face, which has previously been showing the flush of exercise on a cold morning.

'Who told you that?'

I'm happy to give my source, the widow being entirely blasé about the idea, but I won't play my hand so quickly.

'Doesn't matter. You had an affair with the deceased?'

She swallows, she looks around to make sure we're not being overheard. There's a loud clang from the other side of the square, a cry of *Fuck!* and then a burst of laughter. I don't turn, but I'm guessing nobody died.

'People don't know about that,' she says.

'People?'

'People don't know about it. Ruaridh doesn't know about it.'

'I'm about to go and speak to him,' I say, and before the words have travelled from my lips to her ears, she's reaching out to grab my arm. Proving that fear is faster than the speed of sound.

'Oh, God, please don't. He doesn't know. I mean, it happened twice, it wasn't an affair. It scratched an itch, for me and for John. That was it. Seriously, twice. Neither even lasted very long. Please…'

'How d'you know Ruaridh doesn't know?'

She laughs awkwardly, the kind of laugh that might be about to lead to tears.

'Oh my God, really? He would not have kept that to himself. Ruaridh does not keep things to himself. There are no silences.' Having removed her hand, she now squeezes my arm again. 'Please, you cannot say anything. It'll be awful.'

'For you or him?'

'Both of us!'

'What was he doing last Saturday? And you might want to stop squeezing my arm, people are going to be asking what's going on.'

I mean, normally, I'm perfectly happy for women to squeeze any part of my body. Just thinking about Mhairi here, that's all.

She pulls her hand away, her face still showing the fear.

'What was he doing last Saturday?' I repeat.

'Why? Why does it matter? What does it have to do with what John and I did six months ago?'

'Because someone killed him, and we've no idea whether it was business or personal.' Like someone's reasons for travelling on easyJet. Is it business or personal? And would you like travel insurance, more bags, a better seat, a car on arrival, a hotel, and to make a £50 green levy payment to offset your carbon footprint?

My mind still wanders.

'You think I might have killed John? Oh, wait, no, you think Ruaridh might have killed John? Seriously? Have you met Ruaridh?'

I manage to stop myself smiling. Interviewee bingo. Rank incredulity at the police officer asking questions.

'I haven't met Ruaridh, and I don't think he might have killed John. But then, we have no idea who did kill John, and we can't just go excluding people we've never met without first at least having a word with them.'

'Why would he do it?'

I say *he had a motive* with my face. She shakes her head.

'He doesn't know!'

'How can you be so sure?'

'I said. He would have killed me! Wait, damn, I don't mean that. That was just an expression. There's no way he wouldn't have had something to say about it. Just no way.'

'So, tell me what he was doing last Saturday evening. If he's covered and has a clear and obvious alibi, then we can move on. That's all I'm looking for. The more people I can rule out, the better.'

Silence. She holds my gaze for a short while, but eventually her eyes fall. Not so much, I think, at not being able to provide him with an alibi, more about the fact that it means I'm going to have to talk to him.

'He goes night fishing,' she says. 'Sometimes one of his friends joins him, but he was alone on Saturday.'

She lifts her eyes, she kind of shrugs.

'He came in on Sunday morning. He was pretty wet. Said he'd slipped in off the rocks.'

'Had he ever had any dealings with Mr Henderson?'

She shakes her head.

'OK. Well, I'll need to speak to him, but don't worry, I'm not going to mention the sex.' That's a lie. I'm going to *try* to not mention the sex, but let's not get carried away with my abilities with tact. 'I'll say that I've spoken to you, and that I'm talking to everyone who lives within the vicinity who doesn't have an alibi.'

'That sounds a little thin.'

I kind of shrug.

'I'll do my best.'

'How'd you hear about me and John anyway? I could really do with hearing who already knows about it. So I can, you know, manage the situation.' A pause, and then she looks hopelessly lost and adds, 'Sorry, that came out wrong as well. That sounded like, I don't know, Jason Statham saying he was going to manage a situation.'

'I don't think you've anything to worry about,' I say.

* * *

I stop off to see Janice first as she's closer. Janice is sitting in a small workshop making wreaths that are going to be placed in the centre of each table at tonight's event. This really is an all hands on deck type of affair. And, despite the high-price speaking talent the man is bringing in, good on him for spreading the business around. Or else, one can see it as the rich guy using his money to court favour.

'Who told you that?' asks Janice, without looking up.

Janice is someone's idea of a lesbian. Just not mine. Let's say that Janice would easily take me in a fight, and leave it at that. And she's definitely not, from what I've seen so far, John Henderson's usual flavour profile.

'Doesn't matter.'

'Finola, I suppose. I don't believe her husband shied away from telling her how things were. Liked to keep her in her place.'

She finally looks up. She looks tired, rather than angry and pissed off, which is kind of how she sounds.

'Anyway, Sandra knows, so I'm not sure we're going to be of much use to you. I expect you're looking for people with motive to kill John, and spurned lovers and cuckolds will fit the bill, but that's not us. Don't get me wrong, if I was with another woman, Sandra would lose her shit. But cock? She was just looking at me like, what the fuck d'you do that for?'

'What did the two of you do last Saturday?'

She holds my stare, obviously has to think back on the evening, and then sighs.

'Oh my fucking God, this is so lame. We sat in, binge-watching *Killing Eve*. Just like every other lesbian couple on earth, only two years after everyone else.'

'And then you went to bed together, presumably.' And just to be clear, I'm asking to make sure she wasn't alone, rather than, you know, looking for titillating information on her sex life.

She looks at me in a particular way, but I'm not fifteen and I don't care, so she soon enough removes the look from her face and says, 'We went to bed. Neither of us went anywhere. For what it's worth, Sandra isn't capable of hurting a fly, so motive or no, I'm pretty sure you can strike her from your list.'

'What did you mean by John liking to keep Finola in her place?'

'He was an alpha. He liked to be in charge. Odd… yeah, Sandra and I have talked about this. Odd that he came up here to get involved in a business his brother was setting up. That doesn't really tie in with who he was, how he came across. Sandra told me a story about Finola and John having a stand-up in the supermarket down in Bowmore. Nothing to do with shopping, everything to do with John being John. She witnessed it. A Saturday afternoon. Nothing got broken, Finola was mad, close to shouting, which is odd for such a stuck-up, repressed,

English bitch. Sandra said that John never raised his voice, barely said anything, but... he was terrifying. Cold, you know. Cold like the coldest, most brutal killer you could imagine. Cold like the guard in a death camp who has no qualms about ushering the children into the flames.

'I presume you must have spoken to Finola, probably more than once already, and I presume she will be able to list off every single one of John's lovers, because he would have been quite happy to let her know.' She pauses, then adds, 'That'll keep you busy, sergeant.'

* * *

Sandra is the local vet, so naturally when I come to speak to her, she conducts the interview with her arm buried elbow-deep up a cow's arse.

I'm just generalising. That's what you think's going to happen. In fact, she's sitting in her office doing paperwork.

'It's been hellish since we left the EU,' she says, head shaking. 'The things I couldn't do to these charlatans and mountebanks.'

Mountebanks? Nice. I might use that one a little more often myself when talking about the Tories. If I can remember not to call them cunts.

'You OK to answer a few questions?'

'Of course.'

She's tapping quickly at a keyboard, she presses send, then turns. Everything about her says that she doesn't have much time.

'I'm investigating the murder of John Henderson.'

'Of course.'

'Throwing a wide net, at the moment.'

'Well, fair enough. Mr Henderson had sex with my wife, and I guess that means I've got motive. And,' and she makes a general gesture to indicate the veterinary practice, 'it's not like I'm not over-burdened with means to commit murder.' A pause, and then, 'I didn't do it.'

'Where were you on Saturday evening?'

'We stayed in. We watched *Killing Eve*, which I can say without thinking, because we've been watching two or three episodes a night for the past week. I've been arguing with my niece about whether this constitutes binge watching. She says eight episodes in one night would be binge watching. We're amateurs, apparently.'

'There are lots of definitions which change as we get older,' I say, and she smiles for the first time.

'Look, I understand why you're here. Given the size of the community, I wouldn't be surprised if you ended up talking to *everyone*, but you certainly have reason to talk to me. I really don't know what Jan was thinking. I'm particularly confused about what she was thinking the second time. But people do the strangest things, I'm sure you know that well in your line of work. We are, of course, just animals. We've invented chess and worked out how to make ice cream, but in many, many ways, we're not that far advanced from the primates. Certainly, we still like to fuck and eat, and there's an awful lot of shit in the world as a result.'

'Both metaphorical and actual,' I say, and she laughs.

The laughter goes, she lowers her eyes, she takes the time to address the issue. Maybe this is her talking to someone about it other than Jan for the first time. Maybe all sorts of things.

'I was upset. Between you and me, and I don't know why I say that, because you don't owe me anything, but if we *can* have a private conversation, I was devastated. I couldn't believe it. I mean, what was she thinking?' She looks up now, an earnestness in her eyes. 'She's gay. *She's gay.* There's never been a bisexual bone in her body. What the fuck was she doing?' A long, exasperated sigh, the accompanying head shake. 'I don't know. I didn't hold anything against Henderson. I mean, like zero per cent annoyed at the man. It wasn't *who* Jan had sex with. The who of it was of no importance whatsoever. It was all about Jan, and the fact that she did it at all. But… but I didn't want to lose her. I still don't. So, I let her away with it. What else can I say? I acted like it didn't really matter. Acted like, you know, I'd rather you didn't do that again, but at least it wasn't pussy, so we're good…'

She shakes her head, shaking away the emotion, trying not to get taken by it, although she's currently losing the battle. 'We're not good,' she says eventually.

I'm sold. I need to get out of here and let Sandra McIntosh put that emotion back in the compartment it just oozed out of, or else she'll be taking it home with her this evening.

* * *

———

'I don't get why you're talking to me.'

Ruaridh Andrews is the weediest looking guy on the block. I mean, you probably can't call people weedy anymore. Like it's rude to weeds or something, but this guy has nothing about him. Zilch. No muscle, no shoulders, no backbone. Terrible posture, and an ill-fitting head. At least, to be fair, he's not butt ugly, but you can see why his wife would've been attracted to the muscle of John Henderson. Sure, that's playing to some stereotype of women wanting a manly man, some bullshit like that, but this is just the way it is. Henderson was ripped, this guy needs help opening a can of Coke.

'We're going to end up getting around everyone, Mr Andrews.' I affect a tone of tiredness, although to be honest, that hardly requires a Michelle Williams *Manchester-by-the-Sea* level performance. Second full day, not making much progress, and getting a bit fed up speaking to people. I need lunch. I need to see Kallas to catch up. 'It's a small community. I was at the distillery this morning. I spoke to your wife. I asked her, as I'm asking everyone, if she had an alibi for last Saturday, and she said she didn't, because you weren't there. It's not much, and it hardly makes you a person of interest, but nevertheless it bumps you up the list, so we get round to talking to you more quickly than some others, who may well be more deserving, but we don't know that yet.'

He looks resentful, looks like he wants to continue the argument, but he's too dumb to pick holes in it. And so he turns back to the television.

He's watching live darts. I've no idea why live television darts even exists, but obviously some people enjoy it.

'Tell me about Saturday night,' I say.

He lifts his can of Tennent's, takes a drink, sets the can back down. Jesus, the impression I got of this guy from the way his wife talked about him was so wrong.

'Went fishing,' he says.

'Whereabouts?'

He settles in to taking his time before answering each question.

'Over by Crow's Point, if you know where that is.'

'Nope. Will I find it on a map?'

'You will if it's the right map.'

'Who'd you go with?'

'Usually go with Sam, but Sam's in hospital in Glasgow. Crushed his leg out on his scooter, you know that diddy old, pink vespa he's been riding around on for the past fifteen years, not a kid's scooter. Got taken in for, like, a night or two, then he picked up Covid, then he picked up MRSA, then he picked up all sorts of shit. Went into hospital for two nights maximum, and he's still there two months later. God knows what state he'll be in when he gets out. *If* he gets out.'

'So you went fishing yourself?'

His eyes move to look at me, his head barely turning. A literal side-eye.

'Aye, I went fishing myself.'

'Did you catch anything?'

He holds my look for a while, then says, 'Nope. Slow night.'

'Too bad there's no proof, then,' I can't help myself saying, and he scowls like a movie villain in response.

* * *

'Fuck off.'

That's more like it. That's the kind of attitude towards the police we know and love.

'Nope.'

'I've got nothing to say.'

'Tell me where you were on Saturday evening?'

'Tell me why you're asking.'

'It's a small village, we're asking everyone.'

'Oh, really?'

He's fixing up a temporary fence, presumably about to put some sheep into this field of weird turnip-looking things. Dressed for the cold weather, bobble hat and industrial gloves, heavy wax jacket. The last guy off the list presented to me by Finola Henderson.

'That's it,' I say.

'Not including kids, there are over a hundred and fifty people in the village. Add in the neighbouring, whatever you want to call them, hamlets and farms and you know,' and he turns and points in the direction of a hill, 'that little development over the other side of there, that fucking carbuncle of an eyesore down by the loch, add it all, there are near enough four hundred adults around here. And you're talking to everyone, are you?

You and Margaret and that foreign detective lassie?' He holds my look, his eyes full of contempt, then he says, 'I don't believe you. Tell me why you're asking, or you can fuck off.'

He waits, I try to think of something other than the real reason why I'm here. I don't have it. He shrugs, he looks bored and turns away. Puts his tools back in their heavy bag, and dumps the bag back on the quadbike he came here on. He wants to have total contempt, to just drive away without saying anything further, but he can't quite pull it off. He sits on the bike, he hesitates before starting the engine, and then he turns to face me.

'So, what?'

'Finola Henderson told me her husband had sex with Alison Mackie.'

I get a cold stare.

'Which would give you a motive for taking Mr Henderson's life.'

The stare does not change. Cold and harsh, attempting to burrow into my head. I'm way too fucked up for that to work, but he can give it a go. You have to respect the effort.

'You think?'

'Wouldn't be the first time.'

'If someone had been going to kill that cunt for sleeping with their wife or girlfriend, it would've happened a long time before now.'

He spits the words out through gritted teeth. Very impressive display of anger and vitriol, except for one thing.

'That doesn't make sense,' I say, my tone becoming even more glib than normal in the face of his surly annoyance.

'What?'

'It's not Mr Henderson who's the subject of the murder. He's the object. You're the subject. So, the fact that many other people previously chose not to kill him for his infidelity, does not have any effect whatsoever on the fact that it happened now. The fact that your girlfriend slept with him just before Christmas would do, however... How are you coping, by the way?'

He looks like he wants to chib me, then he finally finds the balls to leave without saying anything further. He starts the bike and is gone.

I stand and watch him for a few moments, and then, when the sound has faded, and the silence of the islands in low wind has returned, I look away across the land, to the sea in the

———

86

distance. The same low cloud as there's been all day, light slowly beginning to fade, and the first hint of snow in the air.

My phone pings. DI Kallas.

Meet me at Dr Stevens' office.

I reply in the affirmative, giving myself ten minutes to get there, and then turn back to the car.

14

'Well, potentially your assailant, your murderer, did not manage to pull this off,' says Stevens. 'I mean, dumping the body in a vat of mash as a means to evidence eradication. The small hair beneath the fingernail I mentioned previously turns out, against the odds, to not have belonged to Mr Henderson.'

'And you say potentially, because of course, he could've picked that hair up from anywhere,' I say.

'Yes. But I'd say it's a starting point. As we discussed, there are no marks on his body, so he wasn't in a struggle, but you never know. You get a knife in the throat, you're automatically going to lash out. Your time is going to be limited, though. So, if we can get an ID on the hair, it would hardly be a clincher, but it'd certainly make up part of your case.'

'You are not going to know whose DNA it is though, presumably,' says Kallas.

'Sadly, no, we don't. It is a woman, we have that much. It's already been run through the required database, so anyone on the island who's had their DNA officially recorded, for whatever reason, is in the clear.'

She looks at the short report that's lying on the desk in front of her. Purses her lips, looks up from one of us to the other.

'Hmm, sorry, maybe this wasn't quite worth your time both coming in here. I guess this is me trying to inveigle my way into the drama. Been watching too many shows.'

'That is OK,' says Kallas. 'Neither of us have come far.'

'I always hope you're going to be able to say, I don't know, thirty-seven-year-old, female, blue eyes, red hair, scar on her right shoulder,' I say, feeling that a little of my trademark facetiousness is what's required. 'That kind of thing.'

'I don't even think you get that on shows, sergeant,' says Stevens.

She taps a finger on the report, her lips do a contemplative thing – contemplative lips are an actual term in human physiology – and so I say, 'What are you thinking?' so we can cut to that part, and she says, 'This feels a little odd. I mean, it's not like I've got a lot of experience since I arrived here, you know, of sending DNA samples back to the mainland. A few unexplained deaths, one murder. That was a sad and tawdry affair. But in my experience here, you send a DNA sample to the lab in Glasgow, and you wait, what…? Twenty to thirty days? The tests themselves take some time, but mainly you're stuck in a queue. You guys will know what it's like. It's public sector, no one has any money. And yet this one I get back in two working days. Seems odd, that's all.'

I nod. I mean, we've all waited for DNA results before, and we know how it works. If they come back quickly, it's because some suit somewhere has picked up a phone.

Kallas says nothing, because that's who she is. I expect it's the same in Estonia, as it will be the world over. Stevens takes this, however, as a measure of complicity, and I can see the thought process playing out. The first detective sent over was quickly removed, obviously on the instructions of the centre, and now DNA results are being turned around in record time. There's something fishy going on, and Stevens has no idea who's part of it.

'Well, there you have it,' she says, to move things along. 'If I get anything else, although I think my part in this is more or less done, I'll give you a call.'

'Thank you,' says Kallas, she gives me a glance to see if I have anything to add, and then we're taking our leave and heading for the car park.

Standing outside by the cars, Kallas says, 'We should catch up, so we are not running duplicate investigations.'

'Sure. Shall we head back to the station?'

She looks a little non-plussed for a moment, as though she hadn't thought of that, then she says, 'I thought we could have coffee, but you are right, we should go to the station.'

'Let's do both,' I say. 'Coffee first, then we'll check in with the constable. I need the break.'

Her lips form their familiar smile.

* * *

'I hope you enjoyed last night,' she says.

Two coffees. No food for the boss, a frangipane for me. Not sure what happened there, I guess it just looked decent. And it is. I still retain the latent ability to judge a tart.

There's an unexpected neediness in her tone, a reminder that she is weirdly as much in my thrall as I am in hers.

'It was wonderful,' I say. 'I'd do it again tonight.'

'Oh, yes,' she says, and she laughs lightly at her own unexpected enthusiasm.

We stare drippily across the table by the window of the café, like a couple of hack actors in that Hallmark Christmas movie everyone keeps talking about, before we finally manage to pull ourselves together, snap the fuck out of it, and get back to work.

'We need to park the romance in favour of the day job,' I say.

'Yes.'

She nods, she takes a drink of coffee, she looks out of the window at the quiet waters of the bay. This is weirdly calm weather for January in the far west of Scotland.

'You think we're getting anywhere?' I ask. 'I got a list of potential angry cuckolds from Finola, but I'm not sure any of them really jumped off the page.'

'You spoke to some of them?'

'All of them. At least, all of them who were in a position to commit the murder. Nothing's tugging at my gut instinct, though. Not even the last angry asshole guy. How about you?'

'I have spent the day so far on the curious matter of Scottish independence. At least, it is curious that I have been asked to come as a neutral, and yet no one seems concerned about it.'

I'm nodding by the time she's finished.

'I said the same thing to Constable Laird. She says there's a kind of strange truce fallen over the land.'

'Such truces are not to be trusted,' says Kallas. 'More than one person has said this to me. It is odd. It seems to me there are three possible reasons for the murder of Mr Henderson. He was killed due to his Machiavellian business practices; targeted because he upset a lot of people with his philandering; or because of his hard line, and it would appear, vitriolic stance on independence. People seem very open to talking about the first two issues. The fraught disagreements between the whisky companies are clearly open for discussion. Mr Henderson's sexual endeavours are similarly openly discussed. And yet no one wants to talk of politics. They have all shut down, as though coming to some sort of peculiar agreement to disagree.'

'Which could make it more likely it was the reason he was killed, or else… it's not being discussed for a reason. i.e. it's just not relevant.'

She takes some time to think, placing the cup precisely in front of her, in a way she often does. Her eyes are out on the bay, but she's not looking at anything.

'I find the two most interesting players to be Myrna Berschweiler and Jean Forsythe. You have spoken to them both?'

'Just the former.'

'You should find the time to speak to Ms Forsythe.' She glances at her watch, then looks back out at the day. The grey light is beginning to fade. 'You are unlikely to have time before this evening, given that everyone seems to be involved in the Burns supper. I am not sure we will get much more done today in terms of interviewing. But we should certainly attend tonight, and hope that guards are dropped, and perhaps information is more forthcoming.'

'You were saying about Berschweiler and Forsythe?'

'Yes, they seem to me to be at the centre of things. For each company, they are the main distillers. The creators of the whisky flavours. The artisans. Not unsurprisingly then, they were also the two women targeted by Mr Henderson when he came to the island on his clandestine intelligence gathering operation. Their views on independence do not seem so polarising, but they are certainly at a crossover of the first two touchstone points.'

'Sex and money,' I say.

'A toxic combination, regardless of whether one is in the heart of a capital city, or in a small island in the furthest reaches.'

'Given Henderson's prodigious sexual activities, and the fact that most people employed hereabouts are at one of the distilleries, should we really be singling out anyone?'

She takes a long drink of coffee, setting the cup down on the table with a finality that suggests our time here is done. And she's right, we need to crack the fuck on, particularly since there's not much of the afternoon left, and the evening is already swallowed up.

'I do not disagree, yet I have a feeling. Whether the answer lies elsewhere or not, these two women are at the heart of this, and have been since the very first time the victim came to the island. I am unsure how seating arrangements are planned for this evening, but I will try to be as close to Ms Berschweiler as possible, and perhaps you could do likewise with Ms Forsythe.'

'This evening's getting better and better,' I say.

'You will find her an attractive woman,' says Kallas.

She smiles as she says it, and so I give her my best innocent face and an accompanying shrug.

'I have no idea why you think that makes any difference.'

She lifts her cup, drains it, and then gets to her feet.

'Sergeant,' she says formally, 'we must go.'

An Unreliable Narrative

iii

Oh my fucking God, what a rush. Heart is still going like, oh my God, like we've never felt. We thought it would burst from our chest like the alien bursting from John Hurt's stomach.

And it wasn't the hunt that did it. We were fine, we really were. Don't worry about us. We were a little nervous, but as we thought, Rhona let us in happily enough. She almost seemed pleased to see us. That was a mistake. Back turned, and whack. We were a little nervous about that. We've seen shows on TV, people get whacked over the head and they're down and out, and we were just a little worried, you know, what if it doesn't work like that in real life. But we were fine. We hit her with a rolling pin, and she dropped *like a stone*. All things fall at the same rate, we learned that in school. We mean, in a vacuum, obviously. It's science. Rhona might as well have been in a vacuum. She fell. Smacked her face off the edge of the table as she went. Did that ruin the aesthetic of the decapitated head? We can't decide. We'll need to wait for the reviews in the papers. Oh, we laugh at that thought.

But the buzz of the decapitation. That was *electric*. We tied her hands and feet just in case she woke up while we were about it. She didn't wake up anyway, though we saw her eyes flicker like she might. We pierced the trachea first, to go for the kill. Was that pusillanimous? Was it? We didn't care. We mustn't get ahead of ourselves. Know one's own limitations. We don't know ours yet, so better safe than sorry. Sharp point of the steak knife into the throat. A little pressure, then the pop and the give and the gargle of fluid and blood and air, and then we cut through the pipe, and that was when there was the eye flicker, and then we presumed she was dead. But there was no relaxing, not as we continued to cut through the flesh. Oh my fuck, the buzz of it. Shit, we keep using that word, but it's the right fucking word!

Buzz! It felt *so* good. Then the bone at the back. God, that was awesome. We tried the steak knife, but it wasn't cutting it.

That was word play. We like that. The knife wasn't cutting it. Now we raided her knife rack. And we knew, of course, we knew there'd be something that would work. She was in the food and drink business, so of course she had the most amazing kitchen. Her largest knife didn't quite have the weight required for a quick execution of the task, but we managed to do the job.

When it was done, when the head was lying to the side, the decapitated body slumped on the ground, we were buzzing. Wait, too much to use the buzz word again?

Buzz word. That was kind of word play as well, though we didn't plan that one, so maybe not.

We were so turned on, that when it was done we stood over the corpse and masturbated. But we had to be careful not to leave anything of ourselves behind.

But we have to cut someone else's head off now. You should try it. Be careful, but definitely try it. What a thrill. We are still *on fire*.

15

I arrive at the Burns Supper to discover a piece of poetry placed
on each table, with the instruction that the table should select
someone to read it out when the time comes. I look around the
marquee and count. There are twenty-two tables. I search for the
camera to look into, so that I can express my horror. I mean,
what the fuck? Not just speeches, not just the address to the
dinner, but twenty-two other poems? And sure, this one here on
our table is only a couple of verses, but can we guarantee that
the deranged psychopath who thought this was in any way a
good idea will have had the sense to make sure they're all short?
What if some of these things are, I don't know, the full eight
hundred pages that Burns wrote? I mean, some of those narrative
poems of his are literally longer than *Lord of the Rings*. Oh my
fucking God. I really ought to just grab Kadri, whisk her back to
the guest house, and aim to resume the investigation in the
morning.

'Hey.'

I turn. There's a woman standing next to me, hand
extended. I don't know who she is, but when the movie gets
made of this sordid little drama of sex, poetry, whisky and
murder, she's getting played by Charlize Theron. I'm not
fucking kidding by the way. She is hot as fuck. Fortunately,
while still capable of recognising attractiveness in other women,
I'm currently too beholden to my Estonian siren, for me to be
making my usual dick of myself over someone this good
looking.

'Hello.'

We shake hands. Firm grip, cool hand.

'Jean Forsythe.'

'Tom Hutton.'

'I wondered if it might by you. I've only spoken to your
inspector so far.'

'You definitely got the better of us,' I say, and she smiles.

We hold a look for a moment, but I guess neither of us

major in small talk, and she looks down at the table, notices the piece of paper, and picks it up. *A Winter Night*, by Rabbie Burns. A familiar word salad. *When biting Boreas, fell and doure, Sharp shivers thro' the leafless bow'r; When Phoebus gies a short-liv'd glow'r, Far south the lift, Dim-dark'ning thro' the flaky show'r, Or whirling drift.*

We silently read that first verse together, then look at each other.

'Any ideas?' she says.

'I'm guessing it means it's cold, but then I'm mostly getting that from the title.'

'And Phoebus?'

'He was the left-midfielder Motherwell signed from one of those wee Latvian teams, like Riga Cornflakes 1750.'

Oh, there I go, making one of my regulation jokes. Good thing she's never met me before. I need some new material. I once spent ten years doing the same gags I'd picked up from Groucho in *Night in Casablanca*, until I made the mistake of watching the movie with my second wife, and she was like, wait, this is where you got your lines? To be fair, she'd seen through me, on all sorts of fronts, way before then.

You can't notice it unless you're looking for a plate of soup, that was one. *Speaks excellent German*, that was another. Neither really works without context.

'You thinking what I'm thinking?' she says, after she's politely smiled at my inadequate Motherwell left-midfielder gag.

'I am.'

'Wow. This is going to be some evening. You fancy blowing this place off and getting dinner at the Sheep? It'll be quiet in there tonight.'

Bugger me. I mean, did I used to get invitations from women who look like this when I was available? I don't think so. And, of course, in general I'm available, just not right now. On this trip. Maybe once Kadri's gone, and I've stopped excessively misery drinking and got over myself – whenever the fuck that will actually be – I could come back here and be casually available to Charlize, see if she's still interested.

'Work to do, sorry,' I say mundanely.

'Too bad. You like a Burns Supper?'

'Special kind of hell,' I say. 'You?'

'Ditto.'

'I have no choice, I'm under the instruction of the Chief

96

Constable of all Scotland. What's your excuse?'

She laughs, and points vaguely in the direction of a rotund man in a kilt on the other side of the room, holding forth to a small group of his kin.

'Mr Gordon,' she says. 'You've spoken to him?'

'I haven't spoken to anyone from your place,' I say. 'You're on the list, although the inspector seems to be on top of it.'

'Mr Gordon is the owner. We're here on a three-line whip. No one's entirely sure why we've all been invited, but here we are, on this table, and there are Glendun on that table over there, while the Kilcraig collective appear to be scattered throughout, a fine little diaspora. It's their show, I suppose, they can do what they like.'

She lifts her glass of champagne, takes a drink and nods to herself.

'You ever read a book called *The Aosawa Murders*?' she asks.

'Nope.'

'Japanese crime novel.'

'I haven't read any Japanese crime novels,' I say. Or, in fact, any crime novels in any language, or any Japanese novels on any other subject, but let us not linger on such things.

'It's a cold case. And you know what Japanese fiction's like, the narrative structure is slightly bonkers. They don't do narrative the way we do.'

'Sure,' I say, hating myself for the disingenuousness of that one syllable.

'But the set-up, the basic plot, is about a birthday party, and there's a large drinks order delivered, the drinks are spiked, most people die. If not, they're very seriously ill. The only person unaffected is an eleven-year-old blind girl. Anyway...'

'The eleven-year-old blind girl did it?'

'I won't ruin it for you. Anyway, I'm standing here thinking, uh-oh. Are we in an *Aosawa Murders* kind of situation?'

I glance at her, and then we both look at the glasses of champagne we have in our hands.

'Might be tricky with his own people spread throughout.'

'There are none on our table, and none on Glendun's table.'

'Revenge for the murder of his brother, which he suspects was done by one or other of you?'

'Exactly.'

She takes another drink.

'Still, tastes OK so far.'

I manage to stop myself taking a drink, despite the fucker being right there in my hands. There's going to be a lot of alcohol, though fortunately much of it whisky, and I can't be getting completely hammered when I'm on the job. I mean, obviously, I've been completely hammered and on the job many, many times in the past, but this is pretty fucking public.

'Or maybe we'll have a Red Wedding type of affair,' she says, then she winces at the thought.

'Seems unlikely.'

'I don't know, Scotland can be pretty tribal these days.'

Having run out of cultural mass slaughter references, we take a moment to look around the tent. There's a small stage at one end, on which there's currently a fiddle player and an accordionist. Not too loud, not too energetic, rather beautiful, really. A nice introduction to the evening. I'd be happy for them to play throughout, and for no one to speak. The tables are slowly beginning to fill up as the evening gets underway. Twenty-two tables, ten places on each, the maths do themselves.

In each corner of the marquee, and at four other strategic points inside, there are gas burners, giving the place an unexpected warmth on what is turning out to be a cold, winter's night. Outside, the snow is falling lightly, although it is not forecast to get too heavy. It's picture perfect snow, painting a beautiful layer of white over the land, but not making travel difficult. Pissarro would've painted the shit out of this. Phoebus on the other hand? That fucker would be crawling back under his duvet.

Finola Henderson is here, standing by the top table, where she will presumably be sitting. One could be surprised that she's present, but having met her, I'm really not. Suitably she's wearing black, but she's not the only one, and it is that kind of evening after all. Not that she had to wear the black that she's wearing. Short dress, low cut. There will be tit tape involved. She must have had confidence in those burners being effective, coming dressed like this for a marquee event on a cold winter's night. Still, two hundred people in a tent will warm things up quickly enough.

She's currently talking to Caleb Henderson, a smile on her face, the look of someone without a care in the world. Perhaps she's relieved. She can leave this island, she can go back down south with her head held high. She didn't have to leave her husband and admit she'd made a mistake. And, presumably, she will come out of the marriage in a favourable financial position. This has been a win-win for her. Unless she had a part in it, in which case the ace crime-fighting duo on the job will make sure she gets locked up.

And now I look at Kallas, just as she's turning from having been looking at Finola to look at me, and we stare across the crowded room, and the look holds us there, silently, for a moment. Somewhere Bob Dylan is singing *Some Enchanted Evening*. (Yes, Bob Dylan.) Kadri looks beautiful and sad and lonely, and I want to go over there, take her hand, and lead her out of this place. This nest of vipers, wherein there might well lie a killer. But that is exactly why we have to stay. A look, a nod, the hold is broken, and we turn away.

I look back around the room, paying attention to the players, plenty more of whom I recognise.

'Wow,' says Charlize Theron, and I turn distractedly back to her, to see what she's wowing at this time. The evening promises rather a lot of wow moments, though many of them will be of the ironic kind. Turns out she's looking at me.

'That's some connection you two have,' she says.

I stand like a speechless tube for one second into the next, then finally manage to pull a change of conversation out my arse.

'You spend any time with Myrna Berschweiler?' I ask.

'Don't want to talk about your detective friend, then?'

'I'm good, thanks.'

'That explains not wanting to head to the Sheep.'

Well, even at my drunken, wasted worst, I'd likely still feel the pull of duty to be here, but it's not like Kallas isn't the main reason.

'You spend any time with Myrna Berschweiler?' I ask again, and Charlize smiles.

'Determined to talk about that, huh? I guess you're working this evening, and what can we say? The Glendun lot and us must be prime suspects. Sure, there will be no end of people who wanted John dead, but the body in the mash... Ouch. That's kind of defining. Doesn't matter that the first batch they set down was three years ago, first time anyone tastes it, the gags will be coming straight out. Smoky, with hints of

---

99

chocolate, honey, mustard and human flesh. Wait, wait, I'm also getting three-day unwashed testicles on the palate.'

I can't help smiling, but being currently sober, with greater plans for the evening, I manage to stay focussed.

'Are you avoiding talking about Myrna Berschweiler?' I say. 'I mean, I'm the investigating officer, that's the kind of thing that could make me suspicious.'

She takes another drink, the smile on her face the same vaguely flirtatious one she's had since we started talking. This woman is hot as fuck, by the way. Despite everything, I can feel an act of grand stupidity coming on. I mean, that would be entirely on brand, right? Sure, this thing that's happening right now with Kadri and I can't last. At best it's got a week, and I doubt we'll be here that long. Given the levers being pulled in Edinburgh, I feel we've maybe got another couple of days, and then we're getting yanked off the field and the subs bench will get spewed forth to close out the game. Or else, at the very least, reinforcements will arrive, and that will make it much more difficult for Kadri and I. Nevertheless, brief though it will be, no one would bet against my ability to fuck even that up. There is, after all, literally no situation on all the earth that I can't ruin.

I take another drink.

'Fine,' says Charlize. 'I fucking hate Myrna. First met her, like, fifteen years ago. We were on the same whisky distilling introductory course in Edinburgh.'

'There's a course?'

'There are courses for everything. Have you never done courses?'

'Fair point.'

'Myrna was the try-hard that everyone hates. The grown-up, the suck-up, top of the class, the one who pretty much already knew what she was doing before she'd arrived. I mean, she barely has an accent anymore, but God, she's got that humourless German efficiency thing nailed. And it could've been OK, I guess, there's always someone like that, and sometimes it makes it easier. There's someone at the front unafraid to point things out, unafraid to ask questions, doing whatever. But then there was some teamwork involved – and this was a three-month, full-time course, I should add – and she and I were on the same team. And man, she drove me nuts. I could not stand Myrna.

'And then, when we were done, well, we both ended up

working at Glenfiddich. Small world, whisky. Didn't last too long, but our paths crossed every now and again, and then I took this job at Ardbreck, and I get here, and guess who's already here, making her mark?' A rueful head shake, another swallow of champagne, and then, 'And no surprise that when I got nailed by John Henderson, he'd already had Myrna first. Jeez.'

She finishes her drink.

'There hasn't been any kind of rapprochement since the arrival of Kilcraig?'

'Not between me and her certainly. Not even sure there's been much between the boys at the top. They act like they're fighting the same enemy, but they're both wondering how they can use it to their advantage, so that they survive, while the other gets crushed. This really is a three-way fight.'

'Someone said the whisky business was all very supportive of each other.'

She drains her glass of its dregs, looking around the room for a waiter with a tray of replacements.

'People say all sorts of things,' she says.

16

The evening progresses. There's a bad feeling growing in my gut. For all my manifest failings as a police officer, my guts aren't usually too bad.

This feels like watching a drama on TV where there's a big event taking place, and you know some cataclysmic piece of shit is about to happen. But the filmmakers are wary of just out of the blue cascading cataclysmic shit down on everyone, so they let you know it's coming by the slow introduction of music. A sinister undercurrent. A wave of strings that might begin with a major chord, but then the discordant minor chord arrives. Menace is heralded. The people enjoying themselves on screen have no idea but we, the audience, we know everything's about to fall apart.

Sitting here, there's no TV soundtrack, of course. Or if there is, it's just in my head. And I can't work out where the ill feeling is coming from. I don't really think we're in for a Red Wedding rehash, and the mass poisoning seems unlikely. Perhaps it's got nothing to do with this case and this grand Jane Austenesque ball, and instead it's entirely related to me. Perhaps all my guts are telling me is that my late evening plans with Kadri are going to get torpedoed. Or they're going to be self-torpedoed, something I'm more than capable of.

Yet, I don't feel that that's what's happening here. Something's amiss, and the major chord is flipping to the minor.

The tune being played by the competent accordion/fiddle duo comes to an end, then there's the noise everyone dreads during any such event – the high-pitched clink of the glass, heralding the speeches – and then the place quietens down, and we're all looking at Caleb Henderson, who's standing at the head of the main table. Kilt, jabot and cuffs, puffed out cheeks and all the airs of the privately educated Tory wanker.

'Ladies and gentlemen,' he says, voice filled with the grandeur of the moment, 'thank you all for coming. And what a perfect, beautiful night for it. As our wonderful bard wrote,

When biting Boreas, fell and doure, Sharp shivers thro' the leafless bow'r...'

Hang the fuck on, mate, those are our lines. Don't be stealing our poetry, you cheeky fucker. Fortunately, he leaves it there, as he talks on about what an amazing occasion this is, the first of many, thanks to the amazing guest speakers, et cetera. The usual kind of bumph. Looks like they didn't manage to get Ewan McGregor and JK Rowling. The speakers are beside him at the top table, and I don't recognise them, or their names. Not that that means much. I am to popular culture what nuance, balanced thinking is to modern political discourse.

As he talks, the waiting staff begin to gather at the sides, appearing en masse as if by magic. Uh-oh. This has the feel of a scene in a movie when enemy forces line up for the kill. Albeit, they're armed with trays of whisky, so there's that. It could be a Red Wedding/mass poisoning combo.

'... And so I am delighted, this evening, to offer you this wonderful surprise. A first public taste of an unexpected early release. A limited edition Kilcraig, which will be officially launched this coming May...'

He continues to talk as the staff move around, a small tumbler of whisky distributed to every guest in less than a minute, with unexpected ruthless efficiency. The prick in the kilt is obviously expecting everyone to wait to try it, so that he can make a toast, and it'll be a thing, and those folk he has moving around with their phones can capture the moment for social media, but more than one person in the room immediately lifts the glass and starts the process of breaking down the drink.

Charlize is not alone at our table in doing so. The breathing in of the aroma, rolling the drink around in the cup, burrowing her noise as far as the small tumbler will allow. More rolling of the liquid, more inhaling of the scent. I look across at the Glendun table, and it's the same there. Kallas is looking my way, and we exchange a glance, then turn back to our fellow guests.

There's a look between Charlize and a couple of others, then in unison they take their first taste. They keep staring at each other as they allow the liquid to sit in their mouths, and then they swallow and wait.

Charlize, the distiller-in-chief, is the first to scowl. Head bowed, teeth clenched, she looks at Gordon, the owner, shakes her head and says, 'Fuck it.' A pause, and then, 'Fuck it,' again, and she lifts the glass and downs the rest of it in one.

She doesn't look at me. There goes that flirtatious good humour she's been employing all evening as she tries in vain, in my head at least, to lure me to bed.

'I presume it's decent, then,' I say, trying to at least play to the mood of the crowd, and keep the don't-give-a-fuck tone from my voice.

'Yep,' she says. 'That is... dammit, that is gorgeous. How the fuck did she manage that?'

'Who?'

'Rhona, their chief distiller. Jesus, she's good.'

'I haven't met Rhona yet,' I say. 'Missed her yesterday.'

'A lot nicer, and I mean, *a lot* nicer than Myrna. And nicer than most of those hard-nosed assholes she works with at that place. I keep saying to her, what the hell are you even doing there? You're brilliant. Get a job with someone who deserves to have you.'

'And in reply she shows you her wage slip?'

'Ha. More or less.'

'Ladies and gentlemen,' booms the unionist-supporting kilt from the head table, 'it's time. Will you please be upstanding. And as the haggis is brought to the table, piped in by Colonel Malcolm, will you please raise your glasses for the first taste of the very first batch of Kilcraig single malt. Ladies and gentlemen!'

The drone of the pipes start up, we're all on our feet, the host downs his glass in one, inviting us all to do the same, and then the diners join him in the toast as the piper marches into the tent, followed by a man with a glamorous silver tray, on which sits a silver cover atop the immortal haggis. Or whatever the fuck the haggis is. It's not the haggis that's immortal, is it?

I take a sip of whisky, as Charlize tips her glass and drains the dregs. The look of jealous annoyance has not left her. I do not share her admiration for the drink, it must be said, but us vodka drinkers are hardly the target audience. Or perhaps we are, as they try to lure us away.

I take another sip. Nope, still don't like it. I appreciate the smokiness, but you can get that from a bag of crisps.

People are clapping in time, though none at the Ardbreck table. This lot are already talking about this damnable whisky they've all just tasted, and curses are being tossed around like its Old Firm weekend in Govan.

The piper fills his boots, the sound fills the marquee, the stamping of feet, the clapping of hands, all familiar and enthusiastic and rousing, and somewhere in my head that discordant note is getting louder and louder and I have absolutely no idea where it's coming from, because so far, no one seems to be dropping dead from the whisky.

The piper finishes, the place bursts into spontaneous applause and loud cheering, the bulk of those in attendance possibly lifted by the high quality of the new whisky, rather than cowed by it, as the Glendun and Ardbreck lot will be. And then the oaf in a kilt up front there, Caleb Henderson, with the pomp and circumstance of the Last Night of the Proms, lifts his arms, glories in the cheers as though they're aimed at him rather than the piper and the spicy sheep offal and oats, and then he finally waves for everyone to haud their wheesht.

Silence quickly descends upon the room, to Henderson's loud cries of, 'Ladies and gentlemen, ladies and gentlemen!' and that silent, menacing orchestral chord is warping into all sorts of dissonant harbingers of evil, and I'm looking around the room and I have no idea where this is coming from, but all of a sudden my stomach is crawling with fear, and I look at Kadri because I don't really care what happens to anyone else but I can't let anything happen to her, but she is standing still, the small tumbler in her hand, watching the proceedings at the head of the marquee.

'Ladies and gentlemen!' he booms again, even though the place has quietened down and he no longer needs to boom, 'we come to it at last! The great haggis of our times!'

Oh great, he's sub-quoting Gandalf. And I almost laugh bitterly at or with him, I don't even know, but my stomach is twisting and I wish I knew where it was coming from, and then with the practiced flourish of the showman, Henderson steps forward, takes hold of the large silver dome, and lifts it dramatically into the air.

Silence.

Oh, fuck.

Someone sitting at a table near the front screams. Henderson really ought to put the dome back down, but he is completely emasculated by the moment, and then the need to do something *right now* hits Kallas and I at the same time, and we're dashing to the front of the tent, as the cacophony rises and all hell breaks loose.

17

On the plus side, we didn't have to listen to any of the poetry, so we'll count that as a win.

That particular thought will stay in my head. I shan't even share it with Kadri, though I know I'd say it, and indeed likely will in the future, to Eileen.

Instead of poetry, the audience was greeted with a scene that will at least live far longer in their memories than ruddy Burns. A scene that has been depicted many times in classical art, usually with that poor bastard John the Baptist on the receiving end.

The silver bowl was whipped away to reveal the haggis, and there was no haggis. No veg, no food of any description. Here, instead, we had the Kilcraig chief distiller, Rhona Campbell, severed head delivered on a silver platter.

Fuck me.

A severed head combined with a crowd of over two hundred is a bad combination. If the responsible party is amongst the guests, and there's a fair chance they will be, it'll be easy enough for them to get the fuck out of Dodge. Sure, we've issued the *naebody-move* directive, we've put the bat signal into the sky to call for reinforcements, we've tried to calm everybody the fuck down, requisitioned an office in the distillery building to use as a temporary HQ, and put everything else in place that can be done under the circumstances at this time of a Friday night on an island in the Inner Hebrides.

Along with Kadri and I, there were three other officers in attendance, with Laird, and Constables Whitelaw and McKay up from Bowmore for the event. I think Whitelaw may be Laird's shag, but that's entirely incidental. The three constables have been put on crowd control. Little chance anyone is getting anywhere near the kitchen until it's been dusted for everything, top to bottom, but at least there's plenty of alcohol out there, even if most of it's whisky, and the folk duo seem happy enough to work for their money. If the called-for reinforcements don't arrive from the mainland in the next hour or two, however, we're going to need to start letting those people go.

Kadri and I in the makeshift office HQ. Caleb Henderson is here, as is the head chef for the evening, Chris McDonald. The kitchen staff are his crew from a local restaurant, not the first time Henderson has hired them to cater a meal on the premises. This one was, however, by far the biggest.

We've already discovered the actual haggis, sitting serenely in a storeroom on an identical silver platter covered by an identical silver hood. The haggis was switched out for the head at the last minute.

The head is back in a storeroom, a room that was cleared of all other food. Caleb didn't want any of that food to go to waste, he didn't want it sitting alongside 'human body detritus.' Classy guy. Not sure when he thinks this food is going to get eaten. When Burns Suppers have been interrupted by a severed head, they're not just postponed until the next day. Pretty much an unwritten rule.

Dr Stevens, another guest at the bash, is with the head, and has already delivered her initial verdict. Dead at least three hours. All the staff at the distillery had been given the afternoon off prior to the engagement – as attendance was required, whether one wanted to listen to poetry or not – and so Campbell had been at home, as far as anyone knew. We need to get round to her house, but that can likely wait until daylight. She did, at least, live alone, and so we don't have to worry about something happening to any non-combatants at her place.

This, of course, is not the first severed head Kadri and I have had on a case. The only thing to say to that is, what the fuck, man? I mean, can't people just kill people anymore? Why does any fucker have to sever any other fucker's head? Everything's at the extremes now, right? Political debate, the size of coffee cups, giant SUVs for taking your solitary, tiny kid to school, and the nature of crime. Everyone wants their own fucking Netflix documentary.

Chris McDonald looks properly traumatised by the event. The man did just carry a decapitated head into a crowded room, after all. That kind of thing's going to fuck you up. Caleb, not so traumatised. Already considering the consequences. The body in the mash was bad enough. A severed head is a whole other ball game. That lad of theirs, Jeremy, is going to have to copyright the shit out of this.

'I laid the tray down on the counter by the door. I was ahead of the game, I was waiting, I was just standing there. I meant to wait. Kind of needed to pee, of course, but I thought, just grow a pair and hang on. Then Danny shouted that I had a text from Mr Henderson. He brings me the phone, I read it, it says I should go to the back galley area immediately.'

He looks at Henderson, Henderson shakes his head.

'Wasn't me.'

'Aye, it didn't make sense, as you were speechifying at the time, but I thought, you must've like texted while you were talking. Some people can do that.'

'The number showed up on your phone as being Mr Henderson?' asks Kallas.

'Aye.'

Henderson, looking bored with this narrative line, takes his phone from his pocket, flicks it open, and hands it to Kallas.

'You can check the message log. I haven't texted chef since this morning.'

'You could have deleted it,' says Kallas, and she hands him his phone straight back. 'Check the number that sent the message, chef,' and McDonald opens his phone, checks the number attached to the name Caleb Henderson and says, 'Ends in three-one-six.'

Henderson shakes his head. 'Not mine. I mean, you can take the phone away to check to be sure if you like.'

'Can I?' I ask, looking at the chef.

McDonald hands me his phone. I check the contacts list, there's only one Caleb Henderson, which means whoever's been in to manipulate his phone, deleted the original number. Then I press call and wait. A few seconds, and the dead signal comes back. Henderson lifts his phone to emphasise the point that it's not ringing.

'OK, chef,' I say, 'so someone got hold of your phone, and changed Mr Henderson's number. This gives us two things. Who had access to your phone? Who was in a position to be able to know that you were just about to emerge, to cut you off and distract you, and then to make the switch?'

McDonald looks disturbed and unhappy, something which sits easily on his face, given his haunted look since we came in here.

'Anyone.'

'Anyone?'

'I don't have a code on it,' he says. 'And I leave it sitting around the kitchen.'

'Why would you do that?' asks Kallas, marginally beating me to it.

'Never thought I needed a code. Ask anyone. It's a sleepy place, no one ever steals anything, no one ever does anything daft. And it's not like I'm looking at anything on it that I wouldn't want anyone to see. I just watch porn 'n that on the laptop at home,' he adds. What could've been a comic line is delivered with such desolation that any trace of humour is expelled.

'Chef, I could give you a lecture on phone security, but now is not the time. May I have your phone for a period so that we can get it examined? It is apparent that the killer, or someone working with the killer, has had access to it, more than likely this afternoon.'

'Did you two text each other often?' I ask.

They stare at each other, McDonald obviously deferring to Henderson to do the answering.

'Given the size and scope of tonight's event, we have talked frequently this week.'

'So, whoever made the number switch, likely did it as close to the time required as possible.'

McDonald and Henderson kind of nod in unison.

'When was the last time you were in possession of the phone?' asks Kallas.

He thinks about it, he stares at the door as though that helps him look back out into the kitchen, then he shakes his head.

'I didn't have it all afternoon. The kitchen was full-on, you know, so the phone was just lying on that shelf over by, where it usually sits.'

'What happened when it pinged?'

'Danny saw the message, and he brings me my phone. I look at the message, I'm not sure what's going on, but it sounded pretty urgent, and I thought, maybe there's some last minute change of plan. I head back there, there's no one there, I slip the phone into my pocket, and come back. Got there just in time.'

'And the haggis had been switched,' I say, and McDonald shrugs.

'Looks like it. I mean, I guess I kind of knew it felt a little different, you know. Heavier. But, by then, there was no time to look. I didn't know what to think about it being heavier, so I just didn't. Think, I mean. Then I took it out.'

'How many people were working in the kitchen at the time?' asks Kallas.

'Ten, not including the coming and going of the waiting staff. But that spot, by the exit... It's in a small alcove area, you know a spot we'll use to pile dishes if there's been a big dinner we've been catering up here. Someone could have made the switch without necessarily being seen.' He pauses, then feels the need to add the obvious, 'You'll need to ask the kitchen crew.'

'Did you see anyone in the kitchen who shouldn't have been there?' asks Kallas. 'Or who you were surprised was there? Were there any of your staff not where they were supposed to have been?'

'What, aye?' he says, which is an odd way to answer, but I think that last question posed by Kallas threw him a little, then he comes out with the entirely pedestrian and predictable, 'Are you suggesting one of my crew did the head thing?'

'I do not suggest anything,' says Kallas, just as I was about to say, *well, they're going to know how to use a knife*. 'There was obviously someone in the kitchen who should not have been there, or someone who should have been elsewhere who was not, that is all. Did you see anything untoward?'

He shakes his head.

'It was so busy, you know. There were people all over the place. And this waiting staff, who were in and out...' He looks at Henderson as though he might personally know all the waiting staff. 'There were people new to me there, certainly not all from down by.'

'As you'll have seen, there are a lot of staff on duty,' says Henderson. 'From all over the island. I'm afraid the kitchen would have been something of a perfect storm. A lot of coming and going, a lot of organised chaos.'

'We will speak to the head of the waiting staff,' says Kallas. 'And we will need to speak to everyone who was in the kitchen. While it is unlikely that this number will include the person who we seek for the decollation of Rhona Campbell, perhaps someone saw something that will help us.'

Decollation? God, she is so fucking sexy.

'So, we'll need to speak to all your people, chef,' I say.

'And everyone else present at the supper,' says Henderson, and it's not entirely clear whether he's trying to comically

---

110

exaggerate, or whether he's just stating a fact. Because we will. And that is a lot of people.

I check the time. A little after eight-thirty p.m. That is a fuck tonne of work to do this evening. We really are going to need the cavalry to turn up pretty quickly. That lot out there are not going to want to hang around much longer.

Still, it may have been a horrible murder, and there may be a long, dark evening of crime investigation and witness interrogation stretching ahead, but as previously noted, that's still better than having to listen to poetry.

Kadri's phone rings and she answers without stepping away. Her face is impassive at whatever news is imparted to her, she listens silently, as is her way, and then she says very formally, 'Thank you very much for your call,' and she hangs up, slipping the phone back into her pocket.

She looks at me, and then at Henderson and McDonald.

'Chef, thank you very much for your help. You are excused for the moment, but please do not go far. Indeed, it would be useful if you would stay with the rest of your crew.'

McDonald nods at her, then at Henderson and I in turn, and then he's gone, the door closed behind him.

'That was Campbelltown,' says Kallas, getting straight to it. 'There are an additional ten officers on their way. They should be here shortly. There is a space for a helicopter to land?'

'There are currently cars parked on it, but we can get them moved,' says Henderson.

'I would be grateful if you could see to that. And, please Mr Henderson, I do not want people leaving once they've moved their vehicles. They need to park elsewhere, and then come back into the marquee. I will go and speak to everyone shortly. Once the additional officers arrive, we should be able to get everybody processed more quickly.'

'These ten additional officers,' says Henderson. 'We do need the numbers, but are we also getting a higher level of authority? No offence, but this has turned into a major incident, we need it sorted out as quickly as possible, and we need power on the ground. We need someone people are going to be cowed by. Bluntly, you're a young, slight, attractive woman, which may be fine in certain circumstances, but I'm not sure that's what's required in this situation. Here, on this island, right now, we need someone that people are going to respect. Fear, in fact. You're not that person.'

'We don't need your blunt bullshit, you Tory fu –'

'It is OK, Tom,' says Kallas, cutting off my vitriol. 'You will get your wish, Mr Henderson. There will be a detective chief inspector arriving from Edinburgh in the morning with his own team. He will take charge of the investigation.'

Henderson is looking daggers at me while she talks, then he turns back to her.

'What's his name?'

His name, eh? Presumptuous twat. Sadly, his presumptions turn out to be right.

'DCI Allan Montgomery,' says Kallas. 'He's a very experienced officer. I am familiar with his career.'

Montgomery? Hang on a second.

Dear fuck. There's a name from the past. And now, standing in a small office with DI Kallas and this awful, hard-nosed Tory scumbag, I'm catapulted back more years than I care to think about, all the way to the start of that fucking awful Plague of Crows business. The thing that still haunts me, the man that still haunts me, come rushing back, the gates flung open.

Fucking Montgomery. He was the copper sent in from Edinburgh because Taylor and I and DI Gostkowski and the rest of the team failed to solve the crime quickly enough. You know, fair enough, the Plague of Crows was a massive cunt, and we spent a long time, many, many months, completely bamboozled. But it didn't mean Montgomery had to be a prick about it. And he was. Right to the last, even though it was Taylor, Gostkowski and I – completely inadvertently on my part, it has to be said – who solved the crime. Even then, largely because of Montgomery's twatery, the main culprit behind the Crows murders, Alan Clayton, got away, to return a couple of years later with the shittiest follow-up since *Highlander 2*, the Bob Dylan Murders. Fortunately, these days, Clayton spends his days in HMP Shotts. Last I heard, anyway. I try – unsuccessfully sometimes – to not think about him. Maybe he's changed his name to Big Bertha, and been moved to Cornton Vale. Maybe he used his people skills to persuade a parole board he was a reformed citizen, and in future would use his free time to rescue puppies. Fuck knows. Maybe, if we're lucky, he'll have been chibbed, although I think I might have heard about that.

This isn't about him, though. This is nothing to do with Michael Clayton. This is about Montgomery, a man who, I must admit, I've given absolutely no thought to since way back then. He was a prick, he came into our investigative lives and acted according to his prick status, then he fucked off, never to be heard of again.

If I had given him any thought, it would've been to hope he'd been caught stealing drugs out the lock-up, then been photographed snorting them off his wife's sister's breasts. But it's been a long time since I thought about him.

And, now he's back. Like the worst STD you could imagine.

'Tom?'

Kallas looks concerned.

'I know him,' I say.

I think about adding some rah-rah positivity about how good he is, but I can't bring myself to do it. Sure, the decapitated head is a bit of a blight on this romantic holiday that Kadri and I are enjoying, but it's nothing compared to the arrival of that fucker.

'It'll be good to get some proper authority in here,' says Henderson.

He gives Kallas another look, she gives him her best blank Estonian stare, he crumbles immediately and says, 'Sorry, but no offence, inspector,' gets nothing in reply, then says, 'I'll go and see to the car situation. The helipad is to the east of the main distillery building, if you want to let your people know.'

'Thank you,' says Kallas, which is more than he deserves, and he's gone.

A flurry of sound and talk and action, and then the door is closed, and once again, for the millionth time in our couple of years together, Kadri and I are alone in a room in silence. We have the capacity to stand here like this, trapped in the wilderness that exists between awkwardness and lust, for several hours, but now's not the time. At least, it's not the time for Kadri, what with her being in charge of the situation.

'Are you all right?' she asks.

I contemplate doing the British thing of saying yes, of course, then the words, 'Not really,' are out of my mouth. One look into those eyes and I cannot lie. 'You remember the Plague of Crows business?'

'Of course.'

I let her work it out for herself, which she does instantly, what with her being a good detective, 'n all.

'DCI Montgomery was the officer called in from Edinburgh,' she says, and I nod. 'I am familiar with his career, but I was not aware that that particular investigation was part of his resumé.'

'Given that he achieved absolutely nothing, other than getting in the way of DCI Taylor, I'm not surprised he doesn't want to talk about it.'

'You and he did not see eye to eye?'

I smile, but the smile quickly fades, and the troubled look sweeps back across my face.

Fuck it.

She reaches out, taking hold of my hand.

'We will need to wait and see how this plays out in the morning, Tom. It may well be that both you and I are sent home. DCI Montgomery is, as I said to Mr Henderson, bringing his own team. It is unlikely he will want us to remain, once we have passed on all the information we've gathered over the last couple of days.' She squeezes my fingers. 'We must do a good job. We must process the interviews with the guests as quickly as possible, we must try to bring as much focus to our findings as we can, before handing them over to the DCI in the morning.'

'What time will he be here?'

'We do not yet know.'

Another hand squeeze, then she steps a little more closely towards me.

'Are you OK?'

I swallow. Nope. I'm really not. I can't lie, so I just don't say anything.

She kisses me softly, then pulls away, withdrawing her hand.

'We must compartmentalise, Tom, beginning right now. We will do our jobs, and when we get back to the guest house, however early in the morning that will be, we will talk.' A pause, and then, 'We will do more than talk.' And then, being Estonian and plain speaking 'n all, she can't help herself saying, 'It may be the last chance we get.'

That sound? That's not a heart breaking. That's a heart being crushed and pulverised, its every fragment obliterated.

On the plus side, there will be alcohol at the end. There's always alcohol.

18

Well, there's a sight to take your mind off your own narcissistic, indulgent, self-pity.

A severed head. Roughly cut around the neck, hair frankly a bit of a mess – can't believe the victim went out looking like that – green eyes open and staring lifelessly upon the world. It's probably quite important that the eyes are lifeless, because if they weren't, then this is a whole other kind of thing going on. At the very least we'd be in Scooby Doo territory, but more than likely something scarier.

Mind all over the place. Mainly my mind is saying, *Wine! Vodka! Now!*

I don't have the shakes, so at least there's that.

I wonder if it would be enough of a distraction if Kadri dragged me off to bed right now, or if I'd be lying there, wrapped in her arms, thinking about the contents of the mini-bar.

The rooms don't have a mini-bar.

'It's usually men who get decapitated in art, isn't it?' I say.

Stevens, who's standing with her arms folded staring at the head, with all the blasé confidence of a doctor staring at a minor lesion she won't even have to stitch, turns to look at me, gives it some thought, and then nods.

'I guess,' she says. 'And it's invariably women cutting the heads off. Or, you know, with that John the Baptist guy, it was a guy who did the act, but at the behest of a woman.'

'Medusa,' says Kallas, unusually joining in the flippant, unnecessary discussion. 'She was commonly portrayed in art, decapitated by Perseus. Although, given she was a gorgon, maybe she doesn't count.'

'Yeah, I don't think she does,' I toss in.

Stevens nods in agreement, and that short, unnecessary conversation dies away. I wonder if the artists of today, or tomorrow, will start painting Rhona Campbell's head, but that seems unlikely, and I don't bother voicing that thought.

'There's a hefty lump at the back of the head,' says

Stevens, deciding that after a couple of minutes of staring in horrified awe, it really is time to crack on. 'And you can see the mark on the forehead, which I think is more likely from hitting a countertop or the edge of a table, something like that, on the way down. So, I'd say we have her being attacked from behind, likely knocked unconscious, and that then allowed her killer the time to sever the head. The deed itself was done slowly, with a steak knife. I mean –'

'A regular steak knife you'd eat dinner with, or –'

'A regular steak knife you'd eat dinner with,' she says, nodding. 'That's why I'm calling the process slow, because doing this with a steak knife is not a,' and she makes a swift chopping movement. 'Possibly a different, larger knife was used to finish the job. I'd say the use of the steak knife also explains the blow to the head with which the attack started. They knocked her out, so that when they cut with the steak knife, they'd have had plenty of time. No need to get into a struggle. Perhaps the killer wouldn't have been a match for Miss Campbell, or perhaps he or she just sought simplicity for its own sake... You haven't identified yet where the murder took place?'

'We haven't had the chance to look around the premises,' says Kallas. 'We will instigate a search shortly, once the back-up force arrives.'

'She was likely not killed on the premises in any case,' I say. 'No one seems to have seen her this evening. And her killer, in order to put on the little show they were aiming for, would've then only had to have brought the head in a bag. Might have been heavy, but no one's paying particular attention to some guy with a bag, are they?'

Kallas nods. 'I agree. We will, of course, look nevertheless, although obviously there will be a better chance of finding something once daylight comes.'

'We should get someone round to her house this evening,' I say. 'Might well be she was killed at home.'

'Yes,' says Kallas.

As ever, when in the presence of a decapitated head, silence comes quickly, threatening to take hold. We stand, the three of us, and stare into the lifeless, green eyes.

An Unreliable Narrative

iv

We feel a closing of the loop, we feel this period of our life is coming to an end.

Do we think that Jeremy's next? Yes, Jeremy is next. Jeremy let us down. It's time for Jeremy to get what's coming to him. Jeremy saw the severed head, obviously. He was in the room. But did he really see it for what it was? The threat to him? We doubt it. Why should he have done? At whom is any threat aimed?

He'll know soon enough. His head's on the block. In one sense this is about Jeremy for who he is, and in another, it's not. Stop us if we get too philosophical. But one can also look at this, look at Jeremy, as the representation of something. Yes, Jeremy is a metaphor.

We laugh at that.

You ever wonder what separates one thing from another? The Mona Lisa from any of Ghirlandaio's women. *Citizen Kane* from every other old, black and white movie. The song with five hundred million downloads and the song with none. The number one bestseller and the number eight million on the Amazon chart.

We wonder. We've given it some thought. We wrote about it in the article we sent to twenty-seven newspapers and magazines. Two of them said we sounded like we had a chip on our shoulder, the other twenty-five did not bother to reply. That was because every one of those twenty-seven publications will have found themselves *looking in the mirror.*

We shall not take our revenge on them, however. Their unhappiness and insecurity is its own revenge. Revenge will be administered closer to hand.

We've stopped wondering if we're mad. We don't care anymore. We are in control of something at last, and that's been a long time coming.

    We like being in control.

19

I come deep inside Kadri at 05:23. She's lying back, moaning, eyes closed, face euphoric in the midst of orgasm, her back arched, her breasts almost flat against her chest, and I'm kneeling between her legs, fucking her so hard, hands tightly gripping her butt cheeks, elevating her thighs and hips off the bed.

Oh God, this is fucking glorious, and I never want it to end.

Finally, after the orgasm has pulsed through me, repeatedly, for half a minute, I collapse forward on top of her, and she wraps her arms around me, and we kiss, the desire still animalistic despite the explosion.

I never want to let her go.

* * *

The rest of the evening went as such an evening would go, short of taking some dramatic twist. But there was no confession, no discovery of someone with a bloody steak knife in their handbag, no one caught sneaking away from the premises at two in the morning.

Kallas made a brief, pointed speech to all in attendance. Since we'd decided that the decapitation of Rhona Campbell could not possibly have taken place in the kitchen, and had also identified the ancillary room where the head/haggis switcheroo took place, we decided that the kitchen itself was open for use. Food and drink was on offer to keep the restless natives in place. Kallas asked that no one go anywhere, pointing out that trying to disappear would, under the circumstances, have a suspicious feel about it. If they needed to go, make sure they'd cleared it with an officer beforehand.

The reinforcements arrived soon after. One sergeant, nine constables, no detectives. They were immediately split into two groups: half on interviewing attendees, half on searching the premises. Meanwhile, Constables Laird and Whitelaw went to

Rhona Campbell's house to see what they could see. What they saw was a scene of devastation. She had been attacked in her kitchen, the body had not been moved from there, the head severed in situ. The kitchen was a horror of blood.

The house was closed off, another officer was dispatched round there, and a pre-SOCO, rudimentary search of the premises undertaken. It will be another major point of interest for Saturday. By then, of course, it will no longer be our problem.

Out on the grounds of the distillery, one of the officers discovered a Nike holdall. Solid piece of kit, in good condition, more than capable of transporting a head. The blood on the inside of the bag told its own story.

The bag had been tossed aside, with no attempt to hide it, somewhere between the main building and the road that runs back east, towards the Port Askaig ferry, the road adjacent to the wall marking the grounds of the Kilcraig distillery estate. And directly opposite, there is a farm track leading into some trees. We decided the bag was likely dumped as the killer made their way to the back wall, to jump over and collect their car, parked out of sight in the trees, up the farm track.

It is curious how they knew chef McDonald would definitely play his part, but then more than likely, if they were doing their nefarious job properly, they would have had more than one plan in place. Kill the woman off-site, bring her head to the party, take the first opportunity that came along to present the head to the public. If the haggis-switch hadn't come off, they'd have found something else.

Long before the end of the evening, Caleb Henderson was strutting around as though under the impression he was in charge. Nevertheless, everything happened as and when Kallas wanted it to, and she was happy to let Henderson think he was controlling operations. The place had been cleared of guests by two a.m., by which time all the kitchen staff had been interviewed and sent home. We were writing up notes as we went, and by three o'clock we were as on top of everything as we could have been. Montgomery had confirmed that he would be arriving on the island at ten, due to get to the distillery around twenty past. Bringing men and equipment and cars too multitudinous for a helicopter. Or perhaps he's just scared of flying.

Kadri and I left the distillery at three-thirty-two, to head back to the guest house. We'd already said to Janusz we would breakfast at seven again. Three hours sleep awaited, although we both knew that there wouldn't be much sleep to be had. We got back to her room, we showered together, and then we fucked, and every second since, from the minute we drove away in the same car from the distillery, tossing the investigation aside for a few hours and giving ourselves to the moment, has been absolutely glorious.

* * *

06:21

We sit at the small table in Kadri's room, a glass of water and a coffee each. There will be no sleep. Currently, at least, neither of us need it. We're both buzzing. I feel it myself, and I can see it in her eyes. Perhaps by the time we collapse and sleep becomes unavoidable, we'll be off the case. I certainly will be.

While I still hate that prick Montgomery, having got used to the fact that he's coming here, I'm rather looking forward to the look on his stupid, old, ugly, fat fuck of a face. At least, and here I'm a little surprised, to be honest, given how much of a suck-up he obviously is, he hasn't been promoted to Chief Constable of All The Multiverses. Or even just regular superintendent. Can't be as good as he thinks he is.

With the passing of the sex, and the glorious feel of the moment, the sadness returns. The inevitability of the end, and that this is something that will possibly never happen again. Even if, by chance, we're both still here this evening, even if we can do this one more time, or two more times, or however many more times, it will end soon enough, and she will be gone.

'Why are you going back to Estonia now?' I ask, even though I'm pretty sure I'd made the decision that I wasn't going to say anything. But that's your brain right there, folks, just takes charge sometimes whether you want it to or not.

I get the regretful eyes across the table, she seems to be conjuring the answer from wherever she has it locked away, and then she nods to herself. Time to give the unnecessary and inappropriate love interest the story.

'It began with Anders. He has wanted to go home for a long time. But now, with the war in Ukraine, and the increased threat on the border of Estonia, he wishes to go home and re-join the Estonian Defence Force. Not as a full-time recruit, but he did his national service previously, and he wishes to make himself available once more.' A pause, I can tell she has more to say, so I leave her to it. She lifts her coffee cup, takes a drink, sets the cup back on the table. A deep breath, composing herself. I'm always so amazed she feels the same way about me as I do about her, I have to remind myself how difficult this is for her.

'And he is right. We must fight. You may think we are crazy going back to somewhere that is threatened, but if war comes to the Baltic states, then war has come to the world. Nowhere will be safe. Anders and I belong in Estonia, and that is where we must go. I do not wish to sound overly-dramatic, but our country needs us.'

'What about your children?' I say, then I instantly feel bad even asking the question, and I can't help myself adding, 'Sorry,' because I don't want to sound like some busy-body, judgemental old fuck questioning the young 'uns parenting choices.

'You do not need to apologise. They are young, but they understand the situation. They are brave girls. Julianna says that if a Russian solder gets hit by a bullet in the head, it does not matter whether it has been fired by an army marksman with thirty years' experience in the field, or a ten-year-old girl, the effect will be the same.' She swallows. I fucking love these people. 'My mother is glad that we are returning, but will insist on taking the children away at the first sign of war. Anders and I will stay and fight. I do not mean to trivialise it. We may likely die.'

'Women and children have fled Ukraine in their millions,' I say. I have a not unfamiliar feeling of being out of my depth.

'Yes. I do not question anyone else in any circumstance. But if war comes to Estonia, then war has come to NATO and war has come to the European Union. To where will we flee? Where will be safe? If war comes to us, then it comes to all, and we must play our part.'

Jesus, she is fucking bold.

Weirdly, I feel like I could cry. Now, come on, sergeant, keep it the fuck together. She's talking about her and her husband holding off an army of three hundred thousand angry men armed with AK-74s (even if most of the weapons don't work, it's still pretty terrifying), and I'm getting all emotional listening to her talk about it.

Equally weirdly, and this has come from nowhere, it's the

best I've felt about her returning home since I heard it was happening. Fuck me, it's so romantically noble. To go and fight for the cause. Fucking hell. There is not a cause on earth that would make me cross the road to fight for it. I'd watch that fight and shrug and think, asshole, and then head back to the fridge.

'I love you.'

There I said it. And I didn't even give it any thought beforehand, the words just appeared from nowhere.

She stares sadly across the table. I'm not looking at her like some lovesick fool hoping she says it too. Doesn't matter either way, does it?

Our hands reach out across the table, our fingers entwine, our eyes are locked. There's no point in talking about whether this is the last time we'll get this kind of moment together, as it's too early to say. And there's no sense in pointless lines about whether we'll ever see each other again, but more than likely, there is zero chance. I mean, I could nip over to Tallinn, book a room, and invite her round on her lunch hour every day for a week. But I'm not going to do that. This is what it is. The end. Whether it's now, or tonight or tomorrow or in a few days' time, but this is it.

She squeezes my fingers, and I can finally see her face relax. Here it comes. The withdrawal from the abyss, the attempt to not leave this moment with its lingering sense of hopelessness and loss.

'You will have Eileen, at least,' she says. 'And I will have Anders. And... we will always have this place.'

'I don't think I've got Eileen in quite the same way as you have Anders,' I say, with an unavoidable rueful smile.

'I think you do, if you wanted to.'

She squeezes my fingers again, and then pulls away, taking another drink. Taps her phone, checks the time, and I can see her reluctantly accept that there is a day to be getting on with. Showers to be had, breakfast to be eaten, plans put in place for the first couple of hours of the day at least, and back to the distillery.

'What d'you mean?' I ask.

She smiles curiously, her head dipped a little to the side.

'You do not know?'

'Eileen barely talks to me these days. What should I know?'

'You have known a lot of women, Tom, without really

knowing women.'

That doesn't help. I kind of shrug in reply.

'Eileen is in love with you. She may not want to be, she may not enjoy the experience, but that is how it is.'

I take some coffee, shake my head.

'Oh, no, you're mixing me up with... well, I don't know who. I don't think Eileen's in love with anyone, but if she is, it ain't me.'

'You should talk to her.'

'I should ask her if she loves me? I think I know what she'll say.'

'Despite your determination to pretend to be otherwise, you are a sensitive and caring man. You can work out how to have the conversation.'

'We're forgetting here the fact that Eileen's a lesbian. That's a thing. That's just how it is.'

Kadri finishes her coffee, takes a sip of water, and gets to her feet.

'I should have a shower, and get dressed. You will return to your room and do the same, and we shall meet shortly at breakfast.'

I down my coffee, and push my chair back. I guess that's the end of the conversation on Eileen, with me none the wiser.

She kisses me softly, her hand touching my face, and then she steps away.

'Love knows no boundaries,' she says. 'Look at us.'

Another soft kiss, she smiles sadly, and then she walks to the bathroom and closes the door.

20

Breakfast is like the day after the thing. I don't know, the Cup Final or the coronation or the end of the universe. It's less than an hour later, but it feels like we had the conversation we've been meaning to have for a long time, said everything that had to be said. Sure, it might not have been much, but anything else would be superfluous, and Estonians – or, at least, this Estonian – does not do superfluous.

As we eat, we kind of plan what we're going to do when we get to the distillery, but really, it's more about seeing the lay of the land when we get there. There are people we'll want to speak to, but it's not as though it's going to take much coordination.

We end up looking at the news and reading the front pages of the newspapers. Unfortunately our story arrived early enough in the evening – by some way – to make this morning's front pages. And there was never any possibility of us, the authorities, keeping some kind of lid on it until we had an idea of what was happening. At least five of the guests posted pictures of the decapitated head online before we got the lid back in place. I was half-expecting one of these damned toilet rags to have a picture of me standing beside the head, staring at it like a tube, my face caught in a moment of wonder, or caught looking as though I'm smiling. Weirdly, I was overlooked in favour of my glamorous assistant, who is now, at seven in the morning, not particularly happy to discover she's on the front page of the Sun.

'I do not like that,' she says.

'Well, you know the phrase tomorrow's chip paper?'

She nods, while she takes a spoonful of yogurt.

'It's not even that anymore, the news cycle moves so much more quickly.'

'I will not miss the media of this country,' she says.

'I may come with you for that exact reason,' I say, and I smile, and she relaxes a little. 'We should stop looking at this stuff. I mean, they describe you as a shocked copper, when clearly the look on your face is one of classic Scandinavian cool.' She laughs now, and I, of course, want to drink in that laugh for the rest of my life, and I try to think of some other gag but it will just be a rehash, so I leave it there and rest on my laurels, and at the same time reach across the table and turn her phone off.

'Stop looking, Kadri, it's not important.'

'You are right.'

And the rest of breakfast is largely conducted in silence, but this is a new silence, born of an understanding of the way things have to be.

I don't think of what she said about Eileen, but one day I will.

* * *

We stand outside the distillery in dawn's grey light. Snow covers the landscape, no more than an inch or two deep, but for now, picture perfect. There's a bit of chop to the sea today, and I like the thought that Montgomery and his crew might have a rough crossing. I instantly think of how I will pay for my mean-spiritedness when realising that he's very likely to send me packing today, and I'll have to suffer the chop of the waves on the way home.

Behind us is the area where the cars were parked, largely clear, as it didn't snow much after the time everyone was leaving. But our backs are turned on that, and we look upon the silent majesty of a snow-covered, island morning.

'It's beautiful,' she says.

I nod. Nothing to add. It is beautiful. I want to hold her hand, but I know I can't. I also need to focus on work, and stop thinking like one of those nineteenth-century hack poets I regularly mock.

The moment was never going to last, and then it's snapped with the sound of a car, and then a white Porsche Macan arrives from behind, parks quickly, and Bethany Wright emerges, closes the door, takes in the morning, and approaches across the car park.

'Good morning,' she says.

She seems flat. I had barely given her any thought, and realise that she wasn't in attendance last night. I also, just now, recall her great interest in the decapitated head story. But then, I cannot read too much into that. Most people are going to be fascinated by the tale of a decapitated head in a fridge, especially when there was sex involved. Although, just to reiterate, the sex did not involve the fridge-based decapitated head.

'Good morning,' says Kallas.

'I heard what happened,' says Bethany Wright.

'You weren't here last night?' I say.

She looks at the two of us, troubled, and then turns away, back to the view over the distillery, the rise of the marquee behind, the hills and the run of the snowy slopes down to the beach and the sea.

'No. I mean, obviously I should've been. We all should. But, I just couldn't. I realise... I know when we spoke, there was... I don't know, it feels like I was drunk or something. It's hard to explain. I wasn't drinking, but I... God, I don't know where my head was. But it's really hit me this week, and what's even worse...' and she makes a gesture towards the buildings, encompassing everything about that place. 'No one seemed, like, particularly bothered. John was murdered, and it was just something that happened. And then I thought, maybe I'd be the same if I hadn't been the one to find the body. I mean, I feel like I was the same. And my head was just like, God, all over the place, you know? I couldn't stand the thought of coming here last night, I just couldn't.'

'No one called you?' asks Kallas, getting the question in before I do.

Bethany Wright takes a deep breath, nodding to herself, still not looking at us.

'I mean, it's not like I'm head of security. Not that we have an actual head of security, but there are three of us, right. I was just the poor bastard who happened to be on duty last Saturday. And last night, I just couldn't stand it. I knew everyone would be posting to Instagram and whatever, and there were at least three of the usual crowd around here who'd been badgering me to come, telling me how good it would be for me, so I just turned my phone off.' A pause, and then she turns to look at us. 'God, you do not know what that was like. The relief. No phone. It was wonderful. Didn't look at it all evening, and I read a book. It was like, God, I don't know, the nineteen-fifties or something. Just a quiet evening in. Two glasses of wine, made dinner in fifteen minutes from some Jamie Oliver book mum got me for Christmas like ten years ago that's sat in the kitchen unlooked at all this time. God, it was so nice. What a perfect evening. And I didn't even think about turning my phone back on when I went to bed.'

The end of the Elysian evening is signalled by the haunted look on her face, as her delight in it goes. 'I woke up at four a.m. with that... the same dream I told you about on Thursday. The same dream I've had every night since.' She doesn't say it, but makes a gesture to mimic the descent of the dead John Henderson, knife in his throat, from the ceiling of her bedroom.

'No chance of getting back to sleep after that. All the lights on, turned on the radio, finally opened my phone at about five, and boom. All kinds of shit hitting the fan. Oh my fucking God, I am so glad I missed that. But my phone had exploded, and it seemed I was missed.' She pauses, she puffs out her cheeks, she kind of nods to herself to signal the end of the narrative, then she adds, 'I called Agnes already, got the full rundown. And here we are, back to address the horror.'

She makes a *there you go* gesture, and looks between the two of us, then says to Kallas, 'I saw you on the front page of the Sun.'

'Have you spoken to Caleb yet?' I ask.

'Nope, just Agnes. She'll be in shortly. Sounds like a bit of an evening.'

'How well did you know Rhona Campbell?' asks Kallas.

Bethany Wright takes her time, staring at the ground. There's the sound of another car approaching. Another two cars. The day getting underway.

'Not very. She was, you know, the distillers, they're the high-priced talent of the whisky industry, right? They're the Ronaldos and the Brad Pitts. They're the ones you try to steal off someone else. I'm just someone doing a job. I mean, until last week, what did it amount to? Making sure no one broke into the gift shop and stole a place mat?'

'You never heard of any threat being made against the distillery?'

'Nope. That wasn't what having the security was about. This was just standard procedure, you know. More about the insurance than anything else. You get a break-in at a place like this, and you don't have a night guard, the insurance company's just going to tell you to do one, right?'

Caleb Henderson's car pulls into a marked bay, engine off, and he's straight out of the car and approaching us. Bethany

Wright does not appear to exist in his world, and she takes a step away, accepting that the head of her company has relegated her to the cheap seats by his mere presence.

She is still seen by some of us, however.

'Any progress?' asks Henderson.

He has a wonderful air about him. If his demeanour was a Paco Rabanne fragrance for men, it would be known as *Fucked Off*. You can see the ad, starring Johnny Depp.

'We only just arrived, and Miss Wright aside, we have yet to speak to anyone,' says Kallas.

You can see Henderson about to ask *who the fuck is Miss Wright*, and then he notices the security detail to his left, grudgingly acknowledges her, then returns to ignoring her existence.

'I've been up all night. Getting calls from all over. Investors were wary after last week, but holy Jesus, now the shit is hitting the fan. I want this matter solved *today*. If this hasn't been cleared up by Monday when business gets going again, we are completely fucked.'

He looks angrily between the two of us, like the future of his company depends solely on Kallas and I. That it will be our fault if matters are not quickly concluded. I guess, regardless of the solution, things do currently rest in our hands. Not for long, though, cowboy.

'We will do everything we can,' says Kallas, not being drawn into his snarky willy-waving.

'That's what I'm worried about,' he says, then he scowls. 'Thank God Montgomery will be here soon. Something might happen with this godawful investigation at last.'

He looks between us again, waiting to see if either of us is going to rise to the bait, and when we don't, he angrily shakes his head, and then turns away, walking quickly towards the main building.

We watch him, the three of us – with me silently hoping he slips on the snow – until he's opened the door, entered, and slammed it behind him. And then Bethany Wright turns towards us and says, 'Well, that wasn't very friendly, was it?'

21

Last call to Dr Stevens. Presumably once the suits arrive from Edinburgh, we will be removed from this particular duty. I will be, at any rate. The jury has to be out on Kallas. He'd be wise to keep her on, but then we know, from experience, that Montgomery is a Class-A asshole, so we can only presume he'll do the wrong thing in virtually every circumstance.

Hmm. Let's say this Montgomery eejit kicks me off, but goes against all predictions, sees sense, and doesn't kick Kadri off. The dude can't stop me being on the island. Sure, I might have to move out the guest house that's being paid for by the police, but I could find somewhere else, and just hang around for a few days. It's not like I don't have a tonne of holiday to take, and Hawkins isn't expecting me in next week anyway.

That's not a bad plan. I wonder if Kadri will go for it. While wallowing in the romantic bliss of the whole thing as I am, I have to remember that she's currently cheating on her husband. That's a thing. I mean, not that I'm judging, but then one of the reasons I'm not judging, is that I cheated on all three of my wives, and the last one I was only married to for a month, so that was some going. Surprisingly the cheating was not one of the things that contributed to that marriage's early demise.

The corpse of Rhona Campbell is laid out on the table, head placed at the top of the neck, like the most grotesque two-piece Lego set at Hamleys. Skin cold and blue, the eyes finally closed. Very orderly in the pubic area. I guess that's a Brazilian of some sort. Not at all relevant, one should note, just fleshing out the detail.

'You guys are getting booted off the case?' says Stevens. 'Ouch.'

'Right?' I say, nodding.

'I do not think we are being kicked off,' says Kallas, taking the question seriously. 'It is understandable, given the public reaction, that HQ feels the need to escalate matters, and to be seen to be escalating matters. It was apparent, as soon as Ms

Campbell turned up dead, that the investigation would likely be taken out of our hands.'

'Hmm,' says Stevens nodding. 'Too bad. You know this guy who's coming in?'

Kallas makes a small gesture, deferring to me.

'Sure,' I say, 'from a while back. Similar type of situation. A couple of murders, our team wasn't getting anywhere, Montgomery got brought in from Edinburgh.' A pause, and then, 'It didn't go well.'

'He didn't solve the crime?'

'Ultimately, we solved the crime, he did nothing. He seemed to take the credit for it at the end, though.'

She smiles.

'We all know that type.'

'You know, he's the kind of guy who knows people. Maybe he did something once that got him his reputation. And I mean, *maybe*, I have no idea. It might just be that he knows people from university or from six years of private school rodgering ...'

Stevens is smiling, but I get the grown-up look from the boss, and I nod. 'Yeah, OK, I'll... let's move on.'

'There are people who just land on their feet every time,' says Stevens, not constrained by a glance from Kallas. 'Doesn't matter how goddam terrible they are at everything they do, they keep getting promoted and promoted.' A pause, then she says, 'Liz Truss, right?'

No disagreement from me.

'And Johnson, of course,' she tags on.

I'm trying to keep my mouth shut, having been silently ordered to by the boss, but now that we're on to slagging off Tories, it's my duty as a member of society to join in.

'Most of that lot,' I say. 'But you know who, more than most? Frost.'

'Oh my God, yes!'

'I mean, how did that happen? How did *he* get to be a thing?'

'God, I hate that guy,' says Stevens. 'His entire career arc is the tawdry awfulness of British politics in a nutshell.'

Kallas coughs quietly. A perfect interruption.

'I may observe that it is human nature, and consequently the nature of politics everywhere. In Scotland, in Estonia, just as much as anywhere else. Perhaps, however, we could concentrate on the case before us. I would like to get as much detail as possible into the report that we will hand over to DCI Montgomery on his arrival.'

Stevens looks a little chastened, having allowed her prejudices to run wild, but I have to stop myself smiling.

'I apologise, inspector.'

'That is OK. Now that you have the entire corpse at your disposal is there anything further that you can tell us, or do you believe the murder to have unfolded as you first surmised?'

Stevens is nodding along with the question, placing the uncalled for Tory party evisceration behind us – where it does not belong, I should say.

'There's bruising on her left big toe, and that is the only additional interesting fresh mark on her body. That could mean, of course, that she had time to face her attacker head on, and she managed to kick out. That does not tie in, however, with her knockout blow from behind. I wonder perhaps if she spasmed upon being attacked, perhaps her foot struck a table leg.'

'Or there were two people involved in her death,' I say. 'She lashes out at the one in front, while the one behind delivers the knockout blow.'

We stare at the deceased while we all think this through, picturing the scene in her kitchen. Although, we have not yet established that the kitchen, where the beheading took place, was actually where she was initially attacked.

'That is plausible,' says Kallas, 'but I am not sure. There is something about a beheading, albeit this is only the second time we have come across it during an active investigation.'

'You've had a beheading before?'

Kallas does not answer, and I reluctantly feel the need to fill the gap and say, 'A double beheading, sadly.'

'Holy shit, where are you guys based? Westeros?'

'Nice. You were saying?' I say to Kallas, trying to get with the DI's vibe.

'A beheading in modern times, in these kinds of circumstances, does not feel like teamwork. In a ritualistic beheading, perhaps. For example, the Islamic State. That was very apparent. But here, if there is more than one person at work, then there is calculation and co-operation, there is purpose, and that purpose is not to invoke religious radicalism. In the circumstances in which we find ourselves, I believe beheading is something we would expect from the lone… wolf.'

'The psychopath.'

'Yes. A level of derangement is to be anticipated in the perpetrator.'

Silence returns, as we once again engage with the blue/grey corpse of the deceased. But there is not a lot of time to play with, and Kallas will not leave us standing here unnecessarily.

'Is there anything else that might be of use?' she asks, and Stevens shakes her head.

'As you can see, I'm only just getting started. Another couple of hours to go, but I don't think there's going to be much given up. I will see if there are any samples to be taken from the corpse, as we gleaned from the last one, although a quick check of the fingernails has revealed nothing. If this played out as we suspect, the quick blow from behind, then the chances of the killer leaving something of themselves behind becomes very remote.'

'Thank you very much for your time.'

Kallas gives me a quick glance, I shake my head, and then Stevens says, 'I'll message if anything else comes up,' and we're heading out of the small building, back towards Kallas's car.

'I know there is not much time before the DCI arrives, but I would like to write up a quick report with everything that we have so far. I will message it to him immediately, so that he has every detail prior to his arrival. Then perhaps we could have a coffee while we wait.'

'Sure.'

And then we're in the car, heading back towards the small police station.

22

'We need to know more about Rhona Campbell,' I say.

Turns out the coffee Kallas and I are having is a working coffee. I'd been hoping it might be us cementing our running away to Iceland plans, but she's far too focussed for that. She really does have exceptional compartmentalisation abilities. Me, not so much. I'm sitting here, in the distillery café, thinking about early this morning. The taste of her lips, the soft touch of her fingers as they ran down the length of my erection, the feel of sliding inside her. I mean, that's a great feeling with anyone, really, but obviously when you multiply it by heartbreaking, doomed romance, it's sensational.

The only thing that's making me concentrate is trying not to disappoint her, because if this was my investigation, I'd be so far into not giving a shit territory I'd be lost for good.

'Yes,' she says. 'There is potential that this is a business-related double murder, both killings aimed directly at the heart of the Kilcraig operation. But I do not see it that way. I believe we are looking for someone within the company, or at least, someone familiar with both victims, with a reason for killing them both, extreme though that is. But as we know from experience, it is the first murder that is the hurdle. Once murder has been committed and gotten away with, others can follow.'

'Yep.'

'So, we need to find a connection between Rhona Campbell and John Henderson. We are in a familiar position, however, in that there will be many who knew them both. Indeed, it could by chance end up being someone from one of the other companies who is committing the murder, but for personal reasons rather than business.'

'So you want to get on to Rhona Campbell now, or –'

She's shaking her head, so I ask the question with raised eyebrows, and she says, 'There is no time, and I do not expect, and neither does the DCI expect, that we should do any more investigative work before his arrival.'

She checks her watch. I do the same. His arrival, sadly, is imminent. I'd kind of lost the time there, and now the end of the affair, such as it has been, comes barrelling in like the most fuck-awful tsunami since Fukushima.

We are both gripped by the same thought, and we stare sadly across the table for a moment, before reaching for our coffee cups and hiding behind them. There's no one else here, bar the woman busying herself behind the counter. The visitors centre is closed, naturally, even though they'd probably do some pretty good business today, such is the state of the world, but the café is being kept open for the few employees that are in, and the large, about to be even bigger, police presence.

The site has been tooth-combed in daylight, there have been no new significant discoveries, and when a report is put together on all that's been unearthed, I'm not sure we're going to be here to see it.

'We probably shouldn't be talking about work, then,' I say.

'It is good to have ideas on how to progress the investigation. I do not know DCI Montgomery, and I should not pre-judge, regardless of your dim experience. I will prepare, and then he can decide whether he wishes for us to remain on the case.'

I smile, because I can't help it, at the incorrigible worker.

'We're not booking flights to Iceland, then?' I say, and I hate the words as soon as they're out there. Let it go, sergeant, you asshole. This thing is done, and there's nothing anyone can do about it.

She smiles sadly, a last look across the table, and then it all comes to an end.

A cacophony of noise outside. Three cars arriving at a clip, then a fourth and a fifth, and the fucking A-Team are in town.

Kallas and I share a glance across the table, and then she gets to her feet and walks to the door to go and meet the incoming storm. I, knowing what's coming and not being the authority figure in this investigation, choose to stay where I am. Tempted, in fact, to grab myself one of those small bottles of wine they have in the fridge. Not to drink it, you understand, just to have it sitting on the table to wind the fucker up.

Again, the presence of my Estonian pal saves me from myself.

The cavalry disembark from their expensive cars, five vehicles worth of crack Edinburgh investigative talent. The island doesn't stand a chance. And fuck me, Montgomery, the only one I recognise, has been at the fish suppers since we last met. Oh my God. And look, I'm not fat shaming, I'm really not…

Wait.

Yep, all right, maybe I'm fat shaming. But holy fuck, you know with this kind of crapulent wanker, there will be nothing medical about it, it will just be a life of fat fucker lunches with other fat fuckers, more than likely at the public expense. This is probably the first time he's been out in the field since back in the Crows day. Ha, maybe he's being punished for something. Maybe, like Darling sent to the trenches in *Blackadder Goes Fourth*, he doesn't actually want to do it, but someone in charge thought they were doing him a favour.

He dwarves Kallas as they stand and talk. A short exchange, and then she indicates the café, or more likely, the office space we've been allocated which is along a corridor behind here, and then they turn, and start heading in this direction.

Here we go. I contemplate sitting down, but decide this situation would be better handled standing up in my big boy trousers. Have a final thought, that perhaps the fucker won't even remember me anyway, and that this moment will pass in seconds. He is the kind to forget. Or perhaps to pretend to forget, because he doesn't want to revisit our history. After all, our previous experience did indicate that he was shit, and for all that my methods are so far the other side of questionable, they're pretty much in the same boat as those Californian psychiatrists in the sixties who thought it was a good idea to lock a bunch of hardened criminals in a room together, naked, on acid, for a long period, without food, it was me and my lot who solved the fucking crime.

He marches into the canteen, nods at me as he approaches, but is clearly not intending to stop for coffee, then he's heading to the door on the other side, on the way to the office.

And then he stops.

He turns back to me. He stares curiously. A couple of his team have followed him in – the others are unpacking the cars, and standing around outside – maybe they're getting all their weaponry in order – and they stand and wait behind.

'Hutton?'

'Sir,' I say.

I extend my hand, because that's who I am. He reluctantly takes it, and my fingers wrap around his pudgy flesh, and it may be me who's feeling a level of distaste at having had to touch this guy, but unsurprisingly it's him who's looking at me as though I've just crawled out from the primordial swamp.

'Sgt Hutton,' he says again.

'Sir.'

I'd have something to say if Kallas wasn't here, but I can't reflect badly on her. That would be dumb.

'The Plague of Crows.'

'Sir.'

Curiosity plays out across his face. He turns and shares it with his guys, and then with Kallas.

'I'm not sure I can believe you're still on the force.'

I have nothing to say to that. He's not the only one.

'Not even sure that I can believe you're still alive.'

Now he's being rude.

'And you're on this case?'

'Sgt Hutton and I have worked together for several years now,' says Kallas, leaping to my defence. 'I will show you to the operations room we have established,' and she indicates the door.

Montgomery continues to stare strangely at me, but it might take a while for the full horror of my presence here to hit him, and so I just nod, and he stares blankly, and then he turns and follows Kallas from the room.

* * *

'Just, no. No. It is quite clear from these notes you've sent through, inspector. You have been here a few days, you have obviously been immersed in this case, and we all know that in such circumstances it can be very difficult to retain objectivity, and very easy to lose sight of some of the basics.

'The targeting here, the targeting of the mash tun, the very start of the whisky-making process, while taking out the head of marketing, coupled with the killing of the head distiller, clearly indicates an attempt to cripple the business. The markets are reeling, the stock of this company is metaphorically tanking, and when the market re-opens on Monday, the actual stock will actually tank. As someone who was previously an outsider to this investigation, it is very clear that this is a case of industrial espionage, masquerading as some, I don't know, some deranged serial killer bullshit.'

Kallas and I stare blankly at him. He gets a few nods from his crew. I'm not sure there's much point in either of us questioning him, but some of his own people could do it. Maybe they're too in awe of his shit. Maybe they all agree with him. Fuck it, maybe he's right. I mean, I'm prejudiced against the arsehole, but perhaps he's talking more sense than I'd like him to be.

'We hardly need to be locked into this though, do we?' I say. 'We have the capacity now to come at this from all angles. The crimes may be grotesque, but the scope of the investigation, the potential players involved, are limited. We have the two rival distilleries, and we have people involved in the lives of both victims, which largely brings in people who work here at Kilcraig.'

I'm getting the *crawled out from the swamp* look, which would usually be enough in itself to encourage me to talk even more than normal for spite, but in this case, I do believe I'm talking sense, so he's going to have to do more than look at me funny to get me to shut up.

'As the inspector noted,' I continue, 'we've been checking everyone on and off the island, and so far there's nothing to arouse our suspicions, but the number of officers we have here now allows for far greater scrutiny of that. Sure, there's always the notion that someone slips over on a small craft from Jura. That would be easy enough. Base themselves over there, come over under the cover of darkness, or indeed in daylight, under cover of some other sort of story. There are options, but the amount of people we now have at our disposal allows us the scope to track them all.'

I finish. Montgomery continues to stare at me, his face blank. None of his crew elect to nod diligently along with me in agreement. Getting a very distinct us-and-them vibe.

'May I be blunt with the sergeant?' says Montgomery, switching his look to Kallas. Oh, you can just see the hint of a flinch in his eyes when he turns towards her. That's a thing of beauty.

Kallas does not respond. He swallows, reassembles himself, and turns back to me. A moment, engaging me allows him to reconnect with his inner douchebag, and then he gets into it.

'I'm curious, sergeant. What exactly did you mean by *we*? And *us*?'

Us-and-them, just like I said. I don't think he's actually looking for an answer. He's certainly not getting one, at any rate.

'There is no *we*. There is no *us*. This is not your case. As far as this case is concerned, you are no more. You have ceased to be. You have expired and gone to meet your maker.'

Uh-oh, Monty-Python-quoting-wanker alert. Get their words out of your filthy mouth, you twat.

A couple of his goons laugh. Jesus, how tribal is this shit?

'I didn't even want you in here now, sergeant, but the inspector suggested it might be beneficial. A little brutal of you to prove her wrong, but hardly surprising.' He pauses to let his superiority and weak-minded triumph percolate for a while, and then he decides to grandstand some more. 'I will not ask you to leave the meeting on the off-chance some other matter comes up that has usefully crossed your path, but otherwise, I would ask that you just keep schtum.'

I get the look, like he's expecting me to say something in reply to that, but I think we're done for the day. I usually don't find it too hard to switch off from a case, and switching off from this one, decapitated heads or not, can start right now.

'Well, I will take your silence as acquiescence. Right, where were we?'

* * *

The meeting continues. The Edinburgh boys decide that what's required is a major investigative assault on the other two distilleries, Glendun and Ardbreck. They all seem to be in agreement. Teams are assembled, duties are divvied up, a detective sergeant is put in charge of each of the two teams. The DCI will stay back at Control – this room we are in is now known as Control – to coordinate, and to speak to staff at Kilcraig.

The meeting is wrapping up. I've already got my marching orders. That shaky peg my jacket was on has fallen from the wall. It is not clear what will become of Kallas's place in the bunfight, though I suspect she will be jettisoned on the same fast train out of here as me. Montgomery appears to have a little more respect for her, however, and is unwilling to publicly defenestrate her the way he thinks he did me.

He's looking around the room, eyebrows raised, searching for any final comments or suggestions. I wish I had one. And I mean, either a killer, nominally sensible suggestion, or else something unbelievably stupid and trivial just to take the piss. Mind's a blank, however.

'We good?' he asks, and the sycophants nod in unison, like robotic hellhounds in Hitler's bunker, and then Montgomery looks at Kallas, says, 'Can we have a quick word, inspector, thanks?' and then he's giving the room a general wave of dismissal, when there's a knock at the door.

Caleb Henderson has arrived. I'm expecting some gruff bark from the guy, some look of contempt that we're all just sitting around on our arses talking rather than doing, but he looks at the head of the class, sees Montgomery, and breaks into a huge smile.

'Allan,' he says, 'terrific you're here at last.'

And he's walking forward and the two men actually embrace. I mean, it's hard to get too close to any part of Montgomery other than his gigantic paunch, but they give embracing their best shot.

'You solved the problem of who ate all the fucking pies, then,' says Henderson, and he guffaws, Montgomery laughing along with him.

The old boys' reunion continues, as all the clowns start to make their way.

Kallas and I have just turned to each other, each with a sceptically raised eyebrow, when I get an unexpected hand on my shoulder.

'Hey, sorry about the boss,' says one of Montgomery's female officers, her voice low. 'He can be a bit of an arse, but he's usually pretty good at getting his guy, you know.'

'That's OK,' I say.

She smiles, and moves on. I get another look of support from one of the men, and then they've filed out. And I need to join them.

'I'll see you in a few minutes,' I say, and Kallas nods, and I'm heading out of the room, part of a pack of which I am no part.

23

I smell a rat. A big, fat fucker of a rat. I have no idea how this all fits together, however, because the rat, that stench that pervades this investigation, is centred around a knife in the throat and a decapitation.

Decapitations are serious fucking business, by the way. I don't believe for a minute that someone does it for some nefarious business end, or political end. As Kallas said, these days decapitations tend to be the preserve of the religious zealot or the psychopath. Yeah, I know, look it up, there'll be others. You'll probably find this Tory government has reintroduced decapitations for asylum seekers or something.

But here's what stinks. Supposedly the first officer from the mainland got ejected from the case because the boss here, Caleb Henderson, was troubled by her politics. Politics was claimed to be a large part of the problem. Except, since we got here, the only mention of politics we've come across, is when we've asked about it. If we hadn't mentioned it, we'd never have known it had been an issue. So was that officer, DI Watkin, was she really so jaundiced that she tramped in here with her giant size-15 SNP boots on and started claiming the whole thing was about political persecution?

And then along comes another murder, and it turns out old Caleb gets one of his mates in. Very suspicious, particularly since it seems he was looking to get him here in the first place.

I sit on a bench near the low wall around the distillery grounds, looking through my phone. Looking at the careers of Caleb Henderson and DCI Montgomery, to see where the connection lies. And it doesn't take long. They both studied politics and history at Edinburgh, graduating in the same year.

I wonder how many other connections they have.

Still, is it corrupt, exactly? Is it odd? His brother is murdered, one of his senior employees is murdered, wouldn't it be natural that he wanted to get a senior officer with whom he's familiar in on the case? Makes sense. You're going to want someone you trust, and he presumably didn't know Watkin, and he certainly didn't know Kallas or me.

Still, I don't like it, and so, while I wait for Kadri, I look through the lives of these two men, such as they are available on the Internet, and when I'm done with that, I go to the life of Rhona Campbell. And though there's not too much about the murdered distiller, the papers have obviously had their hounds picking at the bones of her life, and this gives me a few rabbit holes to disappear down.

I'm lost in one of them when Kallas sits down beside me, and I look up, turn off my phone, and slip it into my coat pocket.

'How'd it go?' I ask.

She's staring straight ahead, down over the snowy slope to the sea. There's a cold wind, and her face looks pale, her lips with a winter's chill.

'I do not think it went particularly well,' she says. 'I reiterated the position that you had put during the meeting, and I should apologise for not doing so earlier, and then –'

'It's fine.'

'I should have said something, but it would have created awkwardness, and I chose in the moment to say something in private. Nevertheless, he was not receptive. He is intent on carrying out his plan as he outlined in there.'

She turns and looks at me now, no more than a couple of feet away. Stay calm, sergeant. We're in public. Don't do anything dumb. She has a life to protect, unlike you, you ruinous asshole.

'Our part in the case is finished,' she says. 'We will go home.'

'I'm not going until tomorrow.'

'You are not?'

'I mean, it's nominally a free country. He can kick me off the case all he likes, but he can't actually kick me off the island. I'm staying another night at the guest house. I'll pay for it myself, I've messaged Hawkins and informed her I'll be back at work on Monday.'

Those sad beautiful eyes stare at me for a short time, and then she turns away.

'I cannot stay,' she says. 'I am sorry.'

'I know you can't. You have to tell Anders your work's done, and there's no reason for you to stay another night.' I look at my watch. 'Barely after eleven-thirty. It's going to sound a bit thin if you say you can't get a boat.'

Rats. I'm being magnanimous 'n all, but really I was hoping she'd find the latent adulterer inside to sneak that extra night away. She is, despite everything, better than that.

A gull flies past, its mournful cry a fitting serenade to the end of the affair.

Fuck me, listen to yourself. You need to get your head out of your arse, laddie, because that's the size of it. The two of you are having an affair. She's a married mother of three, and she's having sex with someone she shouldn't. There's nothing romantic, there are no serenades, no one's feeling sorry for either of you. She's cheating on her husband, and you're a cunt, that's it.

'I will not get a ferry until late afternoon,' she says.

I give her a quick glance to see if she's saying that because she's thinking what I'm thinking, and although her face is completely impassive, I can see that it is.

Well, that sounds like a plan. Our actions may be questionable, but I'm all for raising more questions if given the opportunity.

'When are you actually leaving?' I say. 'I mean, for Estonia?'

'I finish work next Friday. We have three more days, and then our things are being moved, then we are beginning the drive.'

The clutch at normal conversation.

'Through Germany and Poland, up through the Baltics?'

'We will stop the first night in the south of England. We take the ferry to Belgium, then stop in northern Germany. Then we travel through Denmark and stop the third night in Sweden, and on the fourth, take the boat from Stockholm to Tallinn.'

'Sounds like an adventure,' I say, mundanely.

'We have made this drive before.'

She leaves it at that without further comment. I guess, right now, neither of us really cares about the drive across northern Europe. We turn and look at each other. Now that the late afternoon ferry has been brought into play, there's not much else on our minds. This is what happens when one is taken by sex and opportunity.

'I will go back to the guest house, check out and pack,' she says. 'You will be in your room?'

I go for the restrained nod, rather than the *Oh, fucking yes!*

143

that would be more appropriate.

We turn away and look back out to sea. Another gull flies past. Maybe it's the same gull. In the distance, the sad ululation of another of his clan.

* * *

I thrust my cock deep into her mouth. Rock hard, soaking wet, desperate. Her tongue is all over me, she licks and sucks and bites me, as desperate as I am. Fucking like it's the last time. God, I'm so close to exploding. I just want to come, and keep on coming, I want the feeling to last all afternoon.

I make the conscious effort to slow down. To stop pushing, to relax into the absolute glory of this. She's lying on the bed beside me, and now she goes with the flow, also slowing, making herself pause, and then she runs her tongue down the length of my erection, sucks on the base, and then glides back up its soaking length, taking the swollen head into her mouth.

Oh my fucking God, that is the most perfect feeling. I gently run one hand through her hair, and let the other softly caress her back. Time is lost. We are both moaning softly. I run my hands down to the curves of her backside, and she shifts to get a little closer to me, and then I run my hands round, and slip my fingers into her soaking pussy, and she gasps, my cock still in her mouth. She kneels beside me, the movements of her tongue on my cock becoming more urgent, and then I'm fucking her with my fingers, and I take her breasts into my other hand.

'Oh, God,' she says, and she's getting taken away, and she lifts her head and she looks at me, and Jesus, I love that look on her face, the one that says she's going to come soon, and that she absolutely fucking loves it. And then she moves quickly, swings her knee over my body so that she's kneeling over me, and then she lowers her pussy onto my mouth, and my tongue goes straight for her clitoris, and she's grinding herself into me, gripping the headrest, moaning and crying out, and coming loudly and wonderfully on my face.

24

How many cases have I been kicked off in my life? Unlike Sinatra and his regrets, way more than too few to mention. Closer to a fuck-tonne.

Sometimes I do something about it, sometimes I walk away. But it seems that even when I walk, I get dragged back in anyway, whether I want to or not. This case is weird, exceptional even, in that I've not been ejected because of incompetence, drunkenness, or insubordination. This one appears to be about internal politics. Perhaps. It's hard to tell.

Either way, as has happened before, I can't let it go. There's an itch to be scratched.

Kadri leaves to get the boat. Giving herself plenty of time. I feel like, with this last scratching of that particular itch, guilt has come over her. Perhaps it unusually transfers a little to me too. The parting, when it comes, is not as final as I was thinking it might be. She says she will try to visit some evening this week after work. I, of course, will be at home and waiting for her, happy enough, even if it's just for a cup of tea.

So, there's something subdued in it, a softening to the heart-wrenching sadness. She leaves, I kiss her goodbye. I stand at the window of my room, wondering why it is I've decided to stay another night when it will be dark soon enough, and it's not as though there are a million and one things to do on this island on a January evening. Then I accept that I stayed another night because I'm not quite ready to let this one go.

That's a weird sense of duty I have: subservient to my sex and alcohol drive, but the overlord to any other innate sense of self. Perhaps it's just because there's nothing else I want to do. This is my life. Sex, alcohol and work. Certainly explains why I haven't yet quit this lousy job and fallen on my pension sword.

I get hold of DI Niamh Watkin at her office. We speak on Teams. I have no idea if there's any working relationship between Watkin and Montgomery, and whether this could get back to Montgomery within minutes. In which case, there'll be a knock on the door, and I wouldn't put it past the fat fuck bringing a charge of tampering with an investigation.

'Sgt Hutton,' she says, 'how are you?'

'Pretty good, thanks. Thanks for taking the time.'

'Believe me, a welcome respite from this week's serial stalker. How can I help you?'

Serial stalker. God, some people are just assholes.

'So, I'm on Islay, and I don't know if you heard, we had a...' I cut myself off, as she's nodding. There's no way she's not going to have heard. 'Anyway, this isn't related to last night. I'm just trying to dig a little, still trying to understand the background to the whole thing. Would you mind if I enquired about you being asked to leave the investigation?'

She purses her lips a little, stares silently into the computer for a moment – she's sitting in an open-plan, the busy life of the station going on behind her – then says, 'What would you like to know? I mean, I'm not sure there's much to say about it. I came back talking very defensively, I must admit. Telling anyone who asked that getting removed from the case was nothing to do with me, all down to politics. And I'm pretty sure that's still the case, but I'm a little more chilled about it. I'll be honest and say I was relieved that DI Kallas didn't swoop in and solve the damn thing on the first day. That is, inexcusably, about my ego, but I guess we are what we are.' Well, this is a start. She's a sharer. As long as she doesn't get onto her relationship status.

'So,' I say, 'the explanation given for us being sent out, was that there was a political undercurrent to the investigation.'

She stares blankly through the ether, waiting for more.

'There was obviously a troubled relationship between the brothers, and part of that related to independence. The surviving brother, Caleb, is the unionist, and he claimed that you brought your nationalist politics with you, consequently prejudicing the investigation. He lobbied Edinburgh to get you removed.'

'Have you got a question, Sergeant?' she asks, her demeanour changing slightly, now that I've brought independence to the table.

'The weird thing is that since we got here the only time independence has been mentioned, is when we've mentioned it. No one's talking about this. Just so we're open, all cards on the table and everything, I don't care either way. Soon as I hear someone talking about it in absolute terms, I just switch off and wait for them to stop talking. So, you know, I turned up thinking, watch what the fuck you're saying,' and then I hold my hand up and she dismissively waves away the apology, 'and yet, nothing. You wouldn't even have known the possibility of independence was a thing.'

Her face has gone deadpan, but there's something going on with her eyes. Well, there's a look. I leave her a gap because there's something coming.

'Mind if swear?' she says shortly, and I answer with a laugh, and an on-you-go gesture. 'What the actual fuck?'

'You don't look happy.'

'No, I bloody well am not. This is such a crock of shit.'

'How did it play out when you were here?'

She looks curiously at me, although I think she's just trying to decide where I'm coming from, and whether she should try to extort more information from me before she gives up any herself.

'I'm not sure where this is going, sergeant,' she says, 'but what do I care? This whole thing has pissed me off. I got sent over there on Sunday. Obviously the first person I spoke to was Caleb Henderson. I have to say, he didn't look too pleased to see me. I was unimpressed. I heard about the very public arguments he'd had with his brother about independence, so I raised that. In the course of the discussion it emerged that on that matter at least I would've agreed with his brother. I didn't think it was that big a deal. I was not so unprofessional to let the discussion with Henderson become argumentative. Indeed, I'm not sure it even got as far as being a discussion. And then,' and she snaps her fingers, 'when I spoke to him again on Monday, we talk quite a lot more about the subject, but it's all him. It was weird. I was thinking, don't you want me to find out who killed your brother? Why *the fuck* do you want to talk about independence *with me*? Then I get up on Tuesday morning and there's a message waiting for me to call Edinburgh. I call, they tell me they've had complaints from this fucking guy at the centre of the investigation that I was being unprofessional, and that my politics were skewering the process. To be honest, the words *what the fuck* do not get anywhere near expressing how pissed off I was about that. I try to speak to Mr Henderson, he makes himself unavailable. I come home. I go and speak to my boss. He has no idea why I was pulled, but he says he hears rumours it was all office politics, and nothing to do with me. The matter will be omitted from my record, he says, and my participation, and the reasons for its shortness of duration, will basically be swept under the carpet. Go back to work and act like it never happened.' She shakes her head, looking as pissed off as you're going to look after that kind of bullshit, then she says, 'Your turn.'

Well, she's certainly shared, and I have to play my cards and accept that she's telling the truth and that I can trust her. What, after all, is the worst that can happen?

I give myself a sideways glance. We're literally involved in a case where someone just got decapitated.

'The inspector and I just got kicked off the case,' I say. 'Nominally because we haven't made any progress, but the guy who showed up, our replacement, appears to be mates with Mr Henderson.'

'Ha! Well, fuck me backwards,' says Watkin. 'Would you look at that? Has this replacement got a name?'

Continuing down the *what's the worst that can happen* road, I jump straight in. 'DCI Montgomery.'

'Well, fuck me backwards again,' she says, head shaking. 'And Henderson and Montgomery know each other. Literally no one is surprised.'

'Why'd you say that?'

'Cut from the same cloth, I guess.'

We stare at each other for a moment, always a little awkward, regardless of who you're talking to, when you're online. I mean, conversation really needs to be ongoing or that shit gets weird pretty quickly. I do have to address why we're here, though. What was I expecting from this?

'So, how come you and your boss got invited in?' asks Watkin, obviously feeling the need to fill the gap more quickly that I did.

'My inspector is Estonian, and so was brought in as a neutral. That was the story.'

'They brought in someone from Estonia? Holy shit, that's a bit excessive.'

'She's lived in Scotland for fifteen years, been in the police service the entire time.'

'Well, there you are, who knew? So why d'you think you're getting bumped for Montgomery now?'

I really have no answer to that, and she nods long before I get around to saying anything.

'Yeah, yeah, that's why you're calling. Your inspector ask

---

you to do this?'

'She's on her way already. Doesn't know I'm sticking my nose in.'

'Well, look at you, Sergeant Hutton, a busybody. I mean, I don't know this inspector of yours, and Montgomery is more someone I've heard tell of than actually know, but you? Everyone knows about Sergeant Hutton. Great sex video, by the way.'

I break the fourth wall and turn and give the camera a look. The camera gives me a look back and says, 'What the fuck d'you expect? If there was an online video of a fellow female officer having sex in a garden, you'd watch the shit out of that fucker.'

Choice, but not inaccurate, words from the camera.

'Is there someone in the room with you?' she asks, and I turn back and say, 'Just my imaginary audience,' and she smiles and says, 'I think your audience for that clip has probably been pretty large.'

* * *

I asked DI Watkin to make an enquiry or two about why DI Kallas came to be sent to the island, when obviously Henderson had been angling for Montgomery all along. She said she doesn't want to stir up too much shit, which is fair enough, because why should she care, but she's obviously wary enough to be concerned that somewhere down the line there are going to be consequences to her being removed from an investigation, the already murky reasons becoming murkier with time. She said she'd ask around, but that I shouldn't hold my breath.

'What would you do with the information, anyway?' she asked, a question to which I had no answer.

So, here we are. Late Saturday afternoon, a fading light, evening on its way. Sitting in my car, looking at the lights and the closed curtains of a small, white crofting house a little out of town.

What's the plan, rogue investigative genius? Can't go to any of the distilleries, because my presence will be obvious, Montgomery will get to hear about it, and I'm screwed. So, I have to conduct an investigation into three distilleries without visiting any of them, and without speaking to anyone. I was thinking an evening looking at the Internet awaited.

Then I thought, fuck it, Charlize Theron! What about Charlize? She asked me out to dinner last night. I don't know how serious an invitation that was, but we got on all right, and maybe there'll be enough of a connection there that I can bring her in on my side. Speak to her, and request at the same time that she tell no one.

Always the possibility she's involved, in some way, in what's going on here. I use her as a confidante, and it turns out she's handy with a steak knife. That really would be curtains for my police career, but then, as I regularly point out to the audience, fuck my police career.

And so, I'm waiting outside Charlize's house. No need to wait, but I'm just giving it a minute or two. There's only the one car parked in the driveway, but it's not out of the question that one of Montgomery's lot walked here, so this is me hesitating before I leap over the edge, full on into a covert, shadow investigation. This entire fucking thing is practically a *Mission Impossible* movie.

Come on. You didn't choose to spend the extra night in this place so you could sit on your fat arse. And after the late night, the early morning, and the sex, followed by three or four hours' work and even more sex, I'm pretty tired. Sit here too long, I'll be fast asleep and some officer will be chapping on my window checking I haven't committed suicide.

Out the car, breathe in the glorious chill of a cold island evening, then cross the road and knock. Take a step back, hands into pockets and wait. Can see my breath. Will be glad to get back inside, assuming I get let in.

An outside light is turned on, a moment, and then the door opens.

'Sergeant!' says Charlize Theron, looking way more pleased to see me that most women ever look. 'Thought there was a new team in town?'

'They haven't spoken to you yet?'

'Yeah, they have, so yeah, I know there's a new team in town. I guess I meant, I thought you left.'

'Unfinished business,' I say, and she smiles, intrigued by the idea, and then steps back.

'Come on in, then. Maybe I can help you finish it.'

25

'They sourced the best damned sherry and bourbon casks, and their distilling equipment looks like it's off the Star Ship Enterprise. They paid three times the normal rate for the land they built on because of the burn running through it. And you heard about Jeremy?'

'My inspector spoke to him. Henderson said he's a wizard copywriter.'

'He certainly is. Except, he used to be Ardbreck's wizard copywriter, then along came the Hendersons, with all the money in the world, and took him away. They've been killing us ever since.'

'You have sight of where their money's coming from?'

We're sitting at the kitchen table. She's just poured three glasses of whisky, intent on giving me an introduction. I said it was OK, I didn't really want educated in whisky, and she *talked me into it*. Yep, we alcoholics always need a lot of talking into alcohol.

'Of course not,' she says. 'And anyway, it's not like it's some football league with a salary cap or financial fair-play regulations. It's the new wild west of business. They can, of course, do what they want.'

'How d'you mean it's the wild west?'

'Whisky's expanding off the charts.'

'Everyone says.'

'When the bubble starts growing, and that growth is exponential, nothing can keep up. Regular business, and regular business practices and rules and standards get left behind. Sure, there are plenty of genuine fish in the sea, but then there are always a tonne of sharks looking to feast on the fish.' She taps one of the glasses on the rim and says, 'We'll start with this one. Eight-year-old Highland malt. Matured in bourbon barrels. Take your time, let yourself get used to the aroma, let your nose become accustomed to the alcohol.' I accept that this conversation, the more interesting part of the conversation, is going to be conducted to the accompaniment of my whisky education, then as I lift the glass, she adds, 'Are you used to any spirits?' and I manage not to burst out laughing, or break down into pathetic sobbing, though I do say, 'I've drunk Poland dry of vodka,' and she smiles curiously, probably wondering how I'm so youthful and attractive if I've had that much alcohol.

'Tell me about the wild west,' I say, because I really am here to learn something, rather than to spend the evening drinking. No matter how low key I try to be, it won't be long before Montgomery finds out I'm sticking my nose in.

'Cask investments,' she says. 'You must have heard of that, or at least, had an ad appear on social media promising amazing returns?'

'I must've missed that episode of social media. Tell me.'

'Taste,' she says, and she takes a sip. I follow. Yep, that's whisky all right,

'What are you getting?' she asks.

I cough, and say, 'A harsh and bestial brutality on the tongue, and a feeling of ferocious raw torture on the throat. Is that what it says on the label?'

She looks deadpan across the table.

'No vanilla, then?'

'Not on this occasion.'

'That's what one often gets for a whisky which has been aged in a bourbon cask.'

'Of course. Tell me about cask investments.'

'That's where ordinary folk are encouraged to invest in a cask of whisky, which is currently sitting at a distillery, or in a warehouse, happily ageing. The implication is, you buy this for five thousand pounds, a couple of years from now, or ten tears from now or whatever, it'll be worth twenty thousand.'

'It's not about drinking it?'

'It's no more about drinking it, than investing in gold is about wearing a pair of earrings.'

'So, what's the catch?'

She finishes off the taster glass of whisky number one, encourages me to do the same, smiles at the look on my face, and says, 'The catch is there's money involved, and where there's money, there will be scammers. Didn't they teach you that at police school?'

'Funny. Go on.'

'You're not buying gold from the Bank of England here.

You're buying a cask of whisky at a distillery. You have to make sure the paperwork is in order, the cask certificate, the transfer of ownership, the *double-signed* delivery order. Very easy to bamboozle the amateur. You should be able to come and put your eyes on it. But where there's potential for fuckery, where there are so many start-ups and whatever, how do you know they're not showing the same damn barrel to ten different people? Given the long lead-in time at the beginning of any distillery, how do we know, for example, that the clowns at Kilcraig aren't in league with a cask investment company? In fact, perhaps they have their own cask investment company. They put all this effort into their amazing new still. All this money up front. The new kid on the block, the next big thing. Buy into it while you still have the chance! People think, well fuck me, this is fantastic. They queue up. The price rockets, and these fuckers haven't even produced yet. I mean, that's where we are, we're in absolute tulip fever territory. I genuinely saw one of Kilcraig's casks go for just over three hundred thousand last week. Before Henderson's corpse turned up in the mash, I might add.'

'That's not true,' I say, without any exclamation.

'Last year a cask of 1975 Ardbeg sold for sixteen million.'

'Ardbeg's a thing,' I say. I mean, I've heard of it, so there's that.

'Sure, it's a thing. But that's what marketing is. It's taking something that no one knows anything about and saying, *this is a thing*. And it's cheaper than that thing over there, although one day, *boom!*, it's going to be worth millions. And these guys have created this whole amazing experience, everything about them looks sleek and expensive and extraordinary. But you know what, it likely paid for itself with a couple of casks in the last month. Try this.'

She indicates the next glass. I dutifully lift it, swirl it around the glass, stick my nose in, play the game, even if my heart isn't it, then take a taste, wince slightly, swallow, and say the first thing that comes into my head.

'Chocolate cake.'

'You're being funny, sergeant?'

'Yes.'

'This is a Speyside, aged in port barrels. The ageing process thereby lends it a sweetness. Most frequently people would say they get an orangeness, and sometimes chocolate cake.'

'I'm a natural,' I say. 'Keep talking.'

'They've created a monster, and people are already overpaying for the product.'

'You said yourself last night it was fabulous.'

'I did.'

'And?'

She stares across the table, then finally gives a small shake of the head. She indicates the third glass. 'This is from the island.'

'You said last night their whisky was fabulous.'

'I shouldn't say anything. I could be a million miles off, and then I'm open to all sorts of shit.'

'You're talking to an officer who's gone completely rogue. When Montgomery finds out I'm still here, he's going to lose his fucking rag. And Montgomery, I will say, though I really shouldn't, is working on the premise that this is most likely a plot from either your distillery or Glendun, to ruin Kilcraig.'

'Really? I mean… what? Aren't there still about fifty options on the table?'

'The one you're talking about, where these murders stem from financial shenanigans at Kilcraig, is most definitely not on the table. He ain't entertaining any of that.'

'Fuck me.'

'So, what were you going to say?'

She takes a breath, her right index finger rhythmically jabbing the table.

'I was going to say I was drinking that Kilcraig last night, and I was thinking, fuck me this is good. Like, this is *too* good. Wait, this is *three years*? *Three*? How the fuck did they get this level of flavour and complexity after three years in a fucking barrel?'

'You think maybe it wasn't their three-year-old whisky?'

She stares coldly across the table, though she's not mad at me, and then she nods.

'What was it, then?'

'Oh, I don't know. Wasn't too peaty, so it could've been from the north of the island. You know, it had that mossy, seaweedy feel. Some nuts.'

'Yeah, I got all of that,' I chip in.

'Could've been a Bunnahabnain, you know, maybe with a little something else added to bastardize it, to change the flavour profile enough. But, you know, for all the big launch and everything, you may not have noticed, but there was specifically no one from any of the big distilleries in attendance. If that was all genuine and above board, wouldn't they have been celebrating themselves to *everyone*? Seemed a little odd, I thought.'

'So, you think the whole thing is faked?'

'I don't know what to think.'

'Except, it doesn't really explain the murders. I mean, I'm not saying Henderson isn't dodgy, but why would he kill his brother? And, even more to the point, why kill his distiller?'

As I put the question, an answer comes into my head, and I start nodding to myself.

'That makes sense,' I say, and she smiles.

'Go on.'

'Maybe the distiller's not in on it. I mean, they poached her from elsewhere too, right?'

'God, aye. Getting Rhona was like Messi signing for PSG.'

'So they get this famous distilling artist in, that's all part of the sales pitch, all part of the brand. In order to be bringing in huge investments for their product, it's really going to have to mature more than seven years. Ten, twelve, eighteen?'

'Sure.'

'They lie. They serve this faked drink, knowing that the word will get around, but the entire evening is then disrupted. The distiller herself is dead, her head on a platter. What you're drinking here is one of her last ever creations. Everything about this evening becomes mythical in the whisky business. And at the top of that myth, is the extraordinary taste of this three-year-old whisky.'

She's staring a little wide-eyes across the table.

'Fuck me,' she says.

I kind of shrug.

'What d'you think?'

She continues to stare, then finally sort of shakes her head.

'I'm not sure. Sounds like the plot of a really shitty novel.'

'Hmm,' I say. 'I guess. And, to be honest, earlier today I was arguing with the new detective that the methods of murder were much more reminiscent of the works of a deranged serial killer, rather than some weirdly macabre, corporate scheme.'

'Try this last one,' she says, and she indicates the third glass.

I really don't want to, but I play along, swirling the liquid and putting my nose into the glass. The expected smokiness nevertheless slaps me across the face like a kipper in a Python sketch.

'Smoky,' I say, mundanely.

'Yes.'

'How can we go about proving any of that crazy idea I just put to you?' I say.

She lifts her own glass of island malt, and goes through the motions of what I'm supposed to be doing.

'Break into their distillery and steal a cask. Or, at least, break into a cask.'

'What would you do then?'

'What would I do then?'

'Yes.'

'I'd taste the whisky. Given a bit more space and a little more time, I'd work out what it is.'

'You'd be able to do that?'

'Might take a while. If you're looking to be detective of the month and solve this crime this evening, I'm afraid that's probably unlikely. But I have some contacts with the bigger distilleries on the island, I'm sure we could work something out. Not that the whisky would need to be from hereabouts, of course, but it would make the fakery more viable.'

We stare at each other across these six small taster glasses of whisky. I think this through. The distillery, the amount of our people that are there, the security that's now in place, the likelihood of being able to get in there and get what we need. The possibility – high – that it would be a risky business coupled with being a complete waste of time.

'I know what you're thinking,' says Charlize.

I nod. I know she knows what I'm thinking, as she's thinking the same thing.

'It's a tough get,' she says, 'and even if it turns out to be true and we can prove it… well, it would be good for the rest of us, there's that. It doesn't help you with your murder investigation.'

I lift the final taster glass and tip the remnants into my mouth. I stare at the table.

Here I am, putting myself in a familiar position. I have no direct route to follow because any reasonable and obvious direct route will be immediately apparent to Montgomery, and so I have to mince about in the margins. But it's worse, because it's not even clear what I should be doing.

Really, sergeant, you and the boss had three full days between you. What did you achieve in your three days? Nothing, and at the end of it, someone else died. Whatever the reasons for Montgomery being called in, maybe it's the right move. Your love interest has left, the beauty has gone out of the trip, go back to the guest house, eat dinner, drink some wine, go to bed, tomorrow take a walk along a deserted beach on the edge of forever, and then go home. Sit in every night waiting for Kadri to come over one last time, and hope she has longer than five minutes. That's your week.

I look up at her across the table. She raises her eyebrows questioningly. There's a smile playing flirtatiously on her lips.

Uh-oh. There's alcohol and an attractive woman.

Fuck off, Hutton. Just fuck off.

An Unreliable Narrative

v

There are more people here than there were supposed to be. We're not sure about that. But it's time to get away. We've been getting skittish. We don't like being skittish, do we? Let's take care of business, and then we can be gone.

Things have been getting a little out of hand. We enjoyed the thrill of the beheading, we won't deny that to anyone. Obviously, we enjoyed it a little *too* much. We do worry we'll have left a little too much of ourselves behind. Can't worry about that now, but this is what happens when you get carried away. Mistakes get made, and maybe the orgasm was a mistake. Certainly there was no need for the second one.

That makes us smile.

We came for Jeremy. We have to focus on that. We have contaminated Kilcraig's production line and killed their money guy; and we have eradicated with extreme prejudice their head distiller. Now, the mouthpiece, the third head of the marketing, corporate dragon.

Jeremy is a piece of shit, and will get what's coming to him, won't he?

Yes, he will.

And with Jeremy gone, with the three heads removed, Kilcraig will fall. We will be happy then.

And, what if it doesn't? What if people and business and the markets respond in an unexpected way? With sympathy, with fascination, with money? What if Kilcraig flourishes?

There is no accounting for *people*. Such grotesque, bloody arseholes. Believing the myths, creating monsters out of mediocrity.

If this does not work, we shall decide later. We shall play a long game. For now, however, we need to step away. Although not, of course, before Jeremy has fallen.

26

I walk back into the guest house to be greeted by our jolly host, Janusz. Except, he's no longer so jolly. I suspect that's because of last night's shitshow in fucktown. Kind of tough to look cheery when you've stared a decapitated head in the eye.

'You have had a long day,' he says.

Hmm, not so much. I mean, there was a fair bit of time in the middle spent shagging, my friend, so don't be feeling any sympathy for my day. I choose to ignore the line, rather than go into detail.

'Any chance of some food?' I ask.

'Yes, certainly. There will be limited choice, I am sorry, but –'

'That's OK, anything will do. Not looking for much.'

'The inspector will be joining you?'

'She left,' I say, then I look curiously at him because I know he knows this.

'You have not heard? The late afternoon ferry was cancelled. There will not be another one until tomorrow.'

'Oh. No, she hasn't said.'

I automatically take out my phone and check.

'Perhaps she drove to the airport and managed to get on the last flight.'

The idea that her ferry would've been cancelled and she wouldn't have used it as an excuse to spend another night with me immediately digs up the grave of my insecurity, spewing the soft, haunted remnants of self-hate across the floor, then I sensibly consider that she has her car with her, and of course she wouldn't have been so desperate to get back that she'd have made a dash to the airport.

'I'll call her,' I say. 'Thanks.'

'So, dinner for one?'

'I'm not sure. Give me a few minutes, and I'll let you know.'

He nods, I turn away, I make my way to my room. I

suddenly wonder if she's going to be there, waiting for me in bed.

She's not.

I call her. Her phone is turned off, or out of reach. Not the first time that's happened on the island. Still, curious that she hasn't tried to get in touch with me.

If this was a romantic drama that we'd suddenly stumbled our way into the middle of, then here's what would've happened. She would've decided to surprise me. She would've been going to tell me that she'd leave her husband and stay in Scotland. Perhaps she'd fight him for the kids, if that was what I wanted, and I'd say, of course, anything for you. She comes back to the guest house to find me gone. She thinks about who I'm likely to be speaking to, there aren't that many places to check, she drives around, she sees my car parked outside Charlize Theron's house. She walks up the garden path. She can see movement inside, and then she takes a secretive look through the window. And there I am, the sex addict, only a few hours after sleeping with the woman I supposedly love, banging Charlize on the kitchen table.

Kadri leaves. I realise what happened. I never see her again. That fateful kitchen table shag haunts me for the rest of my life, although I never know just how close I came to finding true happiness. The end.

Fortunately, this ain't no romantic drama. There are no real-life romantic dramas. Just crime stories and horror stories, and occasionally people undramatically getting by. I never fucked Charlize over the kitchen table. I don't even know if it was on, though I can't deny things had taken a turn. There were looks across the table. More alcohol had been offered. Sure, I was saying no, but there we were, me and Charlize Theron alone in a house on a Saturday evening, and I guess I was something different to do. And then my phone rang, a call from DI Watkin, and I excused myself and walked into the short hallway of the house to speak to her.

'You might be on to something,' she said.

'Go on.'

'And you one hundred per cent never heard this from me, Sergeant, OK?'

'You're good, don't worry.'

'Sergeant?'

'Really, we're good here. You sounded pissed off about

this earlier, I'm pissed off about this now. We're on the same team.'

I must've sounded convincing, although, to be honest, since she was *really* pissed off, she was always telling me.

'This guy Henderson, as we suspected, has political connections. He asked for DCI Montgomery straight from the off. Seems someone said, this is not a job for a DCI. We'll send DI Watkin. I arrive, and from the minute I drove off the damned boat, that guy was looking for ways to get rid of me. Didn't take him long. I, inevitably, heard about him and his brother fighting over independence. I started asking around about that, and he saw his opportunity.'

She paused, but she obviously wasn't finished. I stood in the hallway, one hand in my pocket. Like Alanis. I glanced back into the kitchen. Charlize was washing out the taster glasses. The spell had been broken. I felt the relief of it.

'I'm never going to get to the bottom of this part of it, and if I did, I likely wouldn't share it with you, but there's obviously a bit of infighting at HQ. I mean, it's Scotland after all, where would any of us be without petty internal squabbling, right? There's nothing in the world we can't fuck up.'

'So someone got you canned from the investigation with the intention of sending out Montgomery, but they lost the internal HQ power struggle, and someone else said, if you think independence is an issue, then we'll give you a complete independent. An Estonian who's about to move back to Estonia.'

'Exactly.'

'Fuck's sake.'

'Yeah, fuck's sake.'

'And then,' I continue, taking over the narrative, even though she was the one bringing it to me, 'there's a second murder, a bloody dramatic one at that, and now it's all over the news, crime story of the week, even the London papers are talking about it, and it's time for a DCI. Send in the clowns.'

'There we are.'

I stood for a moment staring at the carpet, thinking it through. The implications. Henderson wanted his pal sent out, and then a brutal second murder took place, a show murder, a murder for the news, a murder that will end up with its own show on Prime. A convenient murder. Very fucking convenient.

'What d'you think?' she says.

'I don't know,' I say. 'It's a fucking mess, and I'm going to have to go and stick my nose into it.'

She laughed.

'Well, that's really all I've got,' she said. 'Good luck. I won't offer any further service, I'm afraid you're on your own.'

'Roger that.'

I could feel her smiling down the phone, then she added, 'You already have something of a reputation, Sgt Hutton, I'm sure this will only add to it.'

'Thanks,' I said, with an eye-roll emoji tagged on at the end.

'Like I say, you heard nothing from me. That said, fair winds and following seas. I look forward to reading about you in the papers.'

We hung up. I returned to the kitchen. Charlize was still at the sink. The length of the call pretty much meant she'd given up on me. Which was good. I mean, I've fucked on a kitchen table, and it is not comfortable, sports fans. Sometimes, though, you just get carried away. Anyway, it didn't happen, and so Kadri did not walk up that garden path and have her heart broken by me being an asshole.

Which gives me a bad feeling. If this isn't a romantic drama, what if it's a horror movie? After all, we've already had a decapitation. That's pretty fucking horrific. Or maybe it's just a squalid little political drama, a proxy battle between competing sides of the nationalist debate in Edinburgh.

Not much gone seven o'clock, long since dark.

Maybe Kallas went back to the distillery to check in with Montgomery. Maybe they got talking. Maybe Montgomery decided he needed her on the case after all. I mean, he likely does need her on the case, because she's not a fucking idiot like he is.

Bugger it, I'm just going to have to go there and see the lay of the land. Nothing else for it. The drama is all taking place there, even if the murder of Rhona Campbell was offsite. It may be too early for the breaking and entering and stealing whisky plan that was hatched over the kitchen table, but I don't know if that was ever going to happen anyway.

I go to the bathroom. Pee. Wash my face. Look in the mirror. Fuck, I've been drinking, I should attempt to do something about that. Take a long drink of water, then gargle with Listerine until it hurts my tongue. Spit. Lean on the edges of the sink and stare into the mirror. One bloodshot eye. No idea how that happened, but I can feel it. I look tired.

What the fuck are you doing, Hutton? You're literally playing at being a detective. Your job here is done, and you're dicking around, sticking your nose in. Leave it alone, leave Kadri alone to do whatever it is she's doing. She'll be in touch soon enough.

All these thoughts – and more! – go through my head, staring at myself from a couple of feet, and then I turn round, leave the room, tell Janusz that I won't be needing dinner after all, and then I'm sitting in the car taking the short drive to the distillery.

* * *

The place looks as you'd think it would on a Saturday evening.

Closed.

There are a few more cars in the carpark, but no sign of the cavalry that arrived this afternoon. There are, at least, a couple of lights on in the building, though the foyer, which leads straight into the gift shop, is low lit, with no obvious human presence.

I contemplate walking round the building, choosing the best place to attempt a surreptitious entry, and then I make the more mundane decision of trying the front door to see if it's open, and we're good. Someone must be home, after all.

Into the building, closing the door silently behind me. The shelves are backlit in low light, a few bottles of whisky perfectly illuminated, casting a light brown glow across the room. This is exactly what Charlize was talking about. This is a damned nice looking gift shop, and I say that as someone who hates gift shops. Even I'd buy something in this place.

I go to the staff door at the rear, and it's also open. Voices down the corridor, a door open, a light on. Montgomery talking. I get the sense of her. Kadri is also here. She's not currently saying anything, but I can smell the Louis Vuitton she wears. Fuck, that smell whacks me over the head every time. Take a moment, then I hear her quiet, measured voice, and I walk forward, come to the door, knock and enter.

Just the two of them. Montgomery looks almost amused at my entrance, but in a very superior, condescending way. He's about to own the next five minutes, so he can afford to laugh. Kallas looks a little worried, a little surprised, her eyes widen.

'The ferry was cancelled?' I say.

'Yes.' I stare at her, eyes asking the question, but this is not the time to get into whatever it was that prevented her calling me.

'Sergeant,' says Montgomery. 'I didn't expect to see you again. Enlighten us.'

Put on the spot, what do I have?

'I'm here for another night, and I'd continued to work the case. I had a few thoughts –'

'You'd continued to work the case?'

I don't answer. His change of tone wasn't looking for an answer.

'You continued to work the case. Let's unpack that, shall we? I said I did not want you to work the case. Indeed, you were thrown off the case. You may not actually have been red carded, but the effect is the same. You're a player who's been red carded, who leaves the pitch, and then... you come back onto the pitch. Are we to commend your dedication to the cause, or are you to be further punished for insubordination?' Tone rising with his anger. Uh-oh. Good old Hutton, can't go an entire investigation without getting shouted at by some twat or other in authority. Nothing to be done now except stand here and wait for him to finish. I shall look forward to giving him my new theory that his old mate Henderson is guilty of massive investment fraud. That should play well. 'I don't remember how long ago it was, a few years ago I think, but I remember there was a bit of a buzz around the office one day. Everyone was laughing, and joking, and talking about the same thing. Word got around that an officer had been filmed having sex with a witness, an actual witness, and that film had been uploaded onto the Internet for all to see. Some officer that must be, I thought. I won't deny I looked at it for a laugh too, and... was I shocked it was you? If I was, the only surprise was that you were still on the force. And now, now, despite that incident, despite God knows what else in your career, you are somehow *still* on duty. You are *still* employed. You *still* get sent out on investigations.'

He's looking fake shocked, sharing his faux amazement with Kallas. She stares blankly back at him. In any case, he doesn't care that he gets no reply. His fake shock is so great it can bounce back off itself.

'And now you've got the balls to ... Jesus Christ, I don't know what. Come back here? Stick your nose in? Like my team and I can't handle it. Seriously? Seriously, sergeant? Well, I'll tell you what. You need to get out. I have no idea why anyone lets you anywhere near an investigation. You are a waste of police time, a waste of police space. A drunken, hopeless bum of an officer. You are not a resource, you are a counter-resource. You are an impediment. Everything you touch turns to shit. Quite possibly the worst officer on this entire miserable force, and given some of the people I've come across on my way up, that's saying something. You disgrace the uni –'

'Chief inspector,' says Kallas, quietly, cutting nicely across his bow.

He at least has respect for her – I mean, let's be honest, probably just because he fancies her, the prick – and he stares across the desk, gas at a momentary peep.

'I have worked with Detective Sergeant Hutton for several years. I will not argue that at times he has brought problems to the investigative table, but they are far outweighed by his insight and his diligence, the latter of which is on display this evening. He could be in the pub. Your characterisation of him would suggest that was where he would be found. And yet he is here, in the ops room, looking to see how he can help. I would ask that you afford him a little more respect.'

Gas at a peep is the wrong expression. She's shut him up, certainly, but he's still full of it. He wants to continue his denunciation of every aspect of my character – and let's be honest, he ain't actually wrong – but she's not going to let him, and he doesn't want to let rip at a junior female officer who's standing up for one of her own people. Bad optics.

They have some bullshit wrestle of wills across the desk, in which there's only ever going to be one winner, and then Kadri turns round to me.

'Had you unearthed any further information, sergeant?' she asks.

God, she's good. I mean, it's really only a couple of hours since we were loudly and wonderfully fucking, and this prick Montgomery would be exploding in pious outrage if he knew about it. But Kadri is as cool as you damn well like, by the way, and I need to match up.

Still, don't mention the politics at HQ that led to Montgomery being here in the first place. Don't mention the possibility that Henderson, at the very least, orchestrated the second murder.

Yet, the only things you have here are the possibility that Henderson is up to no good, one way or another. If he's not complicit in murder, then there's always the possibility the entire distillery is some cask investment scam. Although, of course, what's that based on? A conversation with someone from the opposition, the very people Montgomery will be targeting as the potential perpetrators of the crime.

'We're waiting, Sergeant,' says the fat fucker. 'We may not have all the principal players in the room, but still, if you have a Poirot moment in you, this is the time. Let's hear it. The inspector has put such confidence in you.'

Fuck it.

'I think the issues lie here at the distillery, and not with either of the other two. You're wasting your time there.'

He looks amused.

'Good to know. Go on.'

I hesitate, because really, what's the fucking point, this guy is not the audience for this. But then, he's not the only one in the audience, is he?

'I've been investigating the bigger picture around cask investment, and the way distilleries and investment firms interact. I think we need to take a closer look at how that's being run within Kilcraig, as their casks are already attracting the kind of sales that you'd expect from the well-known, well-established distilleries.'

'Really? And where are you getting your insight? Reading conspiracy theories on the Internet?'

I stare blankly across the table. No way I'm mentioning Charlize.

'Are you an acknowledged expert in whisky cask investment, sergeant?'

Enough dicking around. I find my balls from somewhere.

'No, but then I'm no pathologist, but I could still tell that Rhona Campbell was dead after someone cut her head off. You don't need to be an expert to see that the cask investment world is a wild west shitshow, and a couple of weeks ago a cask of Kilcraig sold for three hundred thousand. That doesn't happen with a new distillery.'

'Doesn't it? And you'd know?'

'So far, I've just done my checking on the Internet, because it's only been a couple of hours. There will be people to speak to, but probably not at this time on a Saturday evening. But it's absolutely something you should be looking into, because *it's not normal.* That kind of money usually goes on a Laphroig or an Ardbeg or a McCallan. A whatever. But this? Until last night, no one had even tasted it.'

'From what I hear, it's exceptional.'

'The people who paid three hundred thousand didn't know that.'

He holds my gaze now, as he lets the implications of what I've just said filter through the rotting fatberg of his head, he allows himself a quick scowl at Kallas – possibly wondering whether he can absolutely fucking explode at me in front of her – and then he turns the scowl on me.

'Would you be shocked, Sergeant, to find out that I've invested in a cask of Kilcraig?'

He dares me to be shocked. I, of course, couldn't be less fucking shocked if you told me Rees-Mogg was the ghost of a malevolent, Victorian rectologist.

'I'd wonder where you got the money on a DCI's salary,' I snark at him. I feel a familiar moment of career-defining anger approaching.

Montgomery slams his hand down on the desk, his face fizzing as he gets to his feet.

'I think you should probably leave, Sergeant,' says Kadri softly. 'If you return to the guest house, I will speak to you there when the DCI and I are done.'

Montgomery leans forward, still half-in half-out of his seat, like he's squatting above it about to take a shit. I glance at Kadri, almost get swallowed up by those gorgeous Scandiwegian eyes, then force myself to look back at the ugly troll on the other side of the desk.

'Is there anyone from Kilcraig here?' I ask, defying my partner.

'Sergeant,' she says, softly.

Montgomery barks out an ugly laugh.

'Jesus.'

'We need to be speaking to people here, at Kilcraig. Forget Ardbreck, forget Glendun.'

I get another extended glare, and then finally Montgomery seems to back down from the all-out, angry confrontation, and slumps back into his chair. That it wheels away under his weight and he falls on his arse, is sadly only the kind of thing I can dream about, and the chair comfortably holds all one hundred and sixty-seven of his giant kilograms.

'Who have you been speaking to, Sergeant?' he says. Something about his tone, like he knows something.

I don't answer. Kallas, momentarily, is forgotten, what with this part of the conversation being conducted in a bastardized mimicry of civility.

'Did you get all this from the glorious web, or has someone been putting ideas into that tiny, unimaginative mind of yours? How exactly is it you've been spending your day?'

Fuck it. Think Hutton! It's not like you not to have a ready-made, shit-stirring answer.

He moves forward, leaning into the argument.

'I understand you spent last night's dinner, prior to the incident of the distiller's head, at the Ardbreck table. More particularly, with their head distiller, who I'm given to understand is a very attractive woman.'

'This has nothing to do with it.'

'You have a reputation, sergeant. Follows you around like the smell of shit on a slurried field.'

'Oh, fuck off.'

'Sergeant!' Detective Inspector Kallas never raises her voice at home. 'You are no longer involved in the case. You should return to the guest house.'

'And the way I hear it,' says the fat fuck, 'you spent some of the afternoon in your room, and I don't think we have to look too far to see who that was with.'

Oh.

No, wait. He's not including Kallas in that. He means Charlize Theron. So, he's fucked it. But then, given the truth, I have to let him think I had sex with Charlize Theron. But, wait, what the fuck? He knows that I was having sex? Who the fuck told him that? Janusz? Really? Wouldn't he have known who I was sleeping with?

Either way, I'm fucked, and he knows it. Whatever this willy-waving contest was really about or wherever it was ever likely to go, he knows he's won.

'Now, be a good soldier, sergeant, and fuck off. Let the grown-ups finish here. Perhaps you can call your new confidante, although there is a lot of suspicion falling on her and her distillery, so you might want to be careful where you make your bed. The pathologist called a short while ago, and it seems that they found some unidentified female ejaculate on the body of Rhona Campbell. To put that in layman's terms so you don't have to Google it, it means she was killed by a woman who then likely masturbated over the corpse.' He holds my gaze, though he's certainly not finished. Too in love with himself, and with this moment. 'Whatever this story is, it's not some absurd cask investment money laundering scheme or major fraud, it's not about Kilcraig creating a mythical story around itself. It's about someone fucking with them, and that someone is a woman with a grudge against the distillery. So, all the women, all of them, from those other two establishments will be getting DNA tested, so you might want to hope that it doesn't turn out to be your new girlfriend.'

I still have nothing. I mean, fuck it. Just all kinds of fuck it. It was me who was in here earlier arguing with him that this was a psychopath, and now he's turning that shit back on me, while still, of course, putting the blame on the other two distilleries. The twisted, useless fuck.

He puts one elbow on the table, relaxes his hand so that he has a slightly bent wrist, then makes a shoo gesture.

'Go.'

It would likely be a bad career move to leap over the desk and put my fist through his face, and Jesus it's fucking tempting, but I can't. Just can't. Not for me, I have no more fucks left to give on that front, but for Kadri. There can't be anything here that's carried forward into some internal police inquiry. There can't be any questions asked.

I give her a quick glance, but I do not want to betray us, and so I turn away to the door.

Click.

The lights go out. The place is enveloped in darkness.

A moment, somewhere another loud click, and then a low hum, and low-level, emergency purple lighting comes on.

Somewhere, the rumour of footsteps.

27

'Who else is in the building?' I ask quickly.

'What the fuck is going on?' says Montgomery. He stands, pushing his chair back. It topples. Kallas stands, calmer, more restrained.

'Mr Henderson remains in his office,' she says. 'He is working with Jeremy Ludlow to firefight a strategy. The security guard is also in the building.'

'Bethany Wright or one of the oth –'

'Miss Wright, I believe.'

'Is this anything to do with you?' snaps Montgomery.

Through the dim, purple light I give this twat the look he deserves, but can't bring myself to leave it at that, and say, 'Really, fuck off. How the fuck could –'

'Did you see anyone else when you came in?' asks Kallas, determinedly persevering in the face of the bullshit dick-waggling competition.

I need to get with her programme. And if this is what we all likely think it is – the shit hitting the fan – I need to make sure Kadri isn't caught up in it.

'No. I mean, there are cars parked out there that I don't know, but presumably...'

'If there is someone here who shouldn't be, they will not have parked out front,' she says.

'We should get upstairs to Henderson's office,' I say.

'I'll do that,' says Montgomery. 'No need for us all to go. We should check the exits, in case someone tries to run. Inspector, you take the front exit through the gift shop, sergeant,' and he nearly chokes on giving me an instruction, with its implication that I'm back on board, 'you get the exits through the warehouse.'

He walks round the desk with a gnarly, 'Let's move,' then he's at the door, and pounding up the stairs.

'I don't trust him,' I say, as Kallas and I stand out in the corridor.

'He is not murdering anyone,' she says.

'There's more going on here than murder.'

'We are investigating the murders, Tom. We should do as he says. You take the warehouse. I believe you may find the security guard in that area.'

I hesitate, because I don't really want to split up. But that's me wanting to protect her, like she can't protect herself. We need to do our jobs.

'Arm yourself with something in there, will you?' I say. 'Pick up one of those seventy pound bottles of gin.'

She smiles, she touches my chest, says, 'I will be fine, Tom.'

She cannot bring herself to immediately withdraw her hand, and I lift my hand to it and entwine my fingers round hers. If this was a movie, I'd be shouting at us. *Get a fucking move on!*

A clumping on the stairs, we part quickly, and then Montgomery appears, carried downhill faster than Franz Klammer on the back of that fat fuck stomach of his.

He looks suspiciously between us, as though he's just caught us in the act, then he shakes his head.

'No one up there. Come on, let's split up, see who's around, and let's try to get the main electrics back up and running. This light is fucking weird.'

He moves quickly to the door into the main part of the distillery, then he turns, and with his back to the door as he pushes through, his phone already in his hand preparing to call his team back in, he says, 'Sergeant, outside, check if there's anyone around. Inspector, gift shop, other offices down here. Let's move, people.'

He turns, the door slams shut behind him. Time to crack the fuck on.

I touch her arm, throw a quick, 'Be careful,' in her direction, and then I'm past her and through the gift shop. The same lighting out here, the merchandise throwing strange shadows across the floor, and then outside into a cold night. Snow in the air, the ground already frozen hard.

I stand for a moment in the chill silence.

Hold my beath, and listen to the night.

There's nothing.

A snowflake falls. The purple lights of the shop behind blink slowly on and off, casting their eerie glow across the white of the carpark. I count the cars, snap the moment, and then move quickly to my right, aiming to run around the perimeter. Along the side gate, which is of course locked, but it's a low wall a few metres along from it down the side, and I'm up and over that and standing in amongst empty barrels, staring down the side of the building.

'Come on, sergeant,' I mutter, voice low, and then I'm off, running down the side of the distillery, an ill feeling growing all the time. Not about me, of course, and certainly not about any of those other comedians involved in this dumb case. Just Kadri, that's all. Of all the people involved in this, she's the one who shouldn't be here. She's the one who should currently be driving home, somewhere by the banks of Loch Lomond. She's become the kind of person bad things happen to: the accidental participant.

To the rear of the building, I stop for a moment and listen to the night. Still nothing, still quiet.

There's a large, empty area at the back, a double gate where delivery trucks can enter. More barrels stored back here. These fuckers must be expecting to make a fuck tonne of whisky.

A sliver of sound, a suggestion of movement. Something, somewhere.

Another sound from behind some barrels.

'Anyone there?' I say stupidly, and pointlessly to the night.

Stopped still, listening. Heart going now, despite all that crap I say about not caring for myself. Still tense, adrenalin still pumping.

'Ah, fuck it.'

Twitch of my head as I lean into the threat, angry at this stupid bullshit, hating that this has come to me walking around in the fucking dark like we're in some ridiculous horror movie.

Another sound.

I quicken my pace. Round the corner. A figure in black. An arm raised. The flash of a bottle in the night.

That's it.

28

The act of emerging from unconsciousness is much slower than they make you believe in the movies.

I lie here for a while, not knowing where I am, not knowing why I'm here. I just exist. I am warm, there is a sheet over me, I am not dead. After some time I become aware of a bandage on my head. I begin to notice my surroundings. White walls, other beds. It takes another amount of time, but I realise I'm in hospital.

Close my eyes, still too groggy to think this through. Why and how I got here. I could drift back off to sleep, but something tells me not to. There's something to be done. Someone I need to speak to. I need to remember what that is.

Slowly the distillery comes back to me. This is all about a distillery. Lying here, this bandage on my head. This splitting headache. Yes, I have a headache.

What was the last thing I saw?

Whisky barrels. A movement from amongst the barrels, a flash in the night.

There was someone. Who was the someone?

From nowhere the name Bethany Wright comes into my head, and I try to hang on to that and to picture the name and to picture the face that goes with the name, and finally things are beginning to come in to focus and I know who that is, and suddenly it all comes flooding back in a great wave, with the sure and certain knowledge that Bethany Wright is the one behind all of this.

She was alone in the distillery when the first murder took place. She would have been perfectly placed to plant the decapitated head. There was something about female ejaculate. Trust you to remember that, you sordid pig. And she was in the building, this evening, when we got hit.

Who the fuck is *we*?

It was her. That brief flash of the dark figure in the night. Bethany Wright, that makes perfect sense, even if I can't exactly

173

place her face in the moment.

I lift my head off the pillow, and a sharp pain bursts across my skull, but I don't feel dizzy and I don't immediately have to put my head back down. I try to sit up, but ultimately don't make it all the way. I rest for a moment, and look around the room.

Two empty beds, someone in the bed next to me. Long dark hair, a bandage across her forehead.

That's her. That's the guard. That's Bethany Wright.

Jesus, they left me in here with a fucking killer.

Look around, look for the bell, see the small orange button and stab at it. Try to force myself up and out of the bed, and this time I do fall back, my head thumping into the pillow, a 'Fuck it,' tossed out into the night.

Footsteps, the door swings open, a figure in white. I don't know this man.

'Sergeant Hutton, you're awake. How are you feeling?'

I look at the guy, trying to decide if he's familiar.

'Is there a nurse?' I say stupidly.

'I'm the nurse.' He smiles benevolently as he says it. 'You can call me Jamie. How's the head?'

'Where's em... are there any police?'

'They're all out and about. It's kind of kicking off out there.'

'What's happening?'

He smiles, making a small shrugging movement.

'I'm afraid that's above my pay grade. I just need to make sure you're OK. You probably need to rest for a while.'

'I should be getting back to them.'

'The inspector said that if you tried to move, I was to give you the biggest sedative in the hospital.'

I stare at him, brain still that second or two behind the curve, then manage, 'The inspector? Which one?'

'The, eh, the foreign one. I'm not sure what her name is, sorry.'

'She's all right?'

'She seemed to be. The only people who are hurt were you and Bethany there. She got an even worse bang on the head than you did, although you also banged your head when you fell.'

I look at him, and then turn to look at Bethany Wright. The security guard, in exactly the same position as me. Didn't I think a minute ago she was the killer?

'Is she going to be all right?'

'Should be. She's not in a coma or anything. She'll have a sore head when she properly wakes up. As, presumably, you do now.'

I stare at him, trying to think if there's anything else I should ask. My brow furrows, the nurse manages to stop himself laughing at me trying to put one coherent thought after another.

'Perhaps you should try to get –'

'Is my phone here?'

'Of course.'

He points to the small bedside table, and there it is. My phone. I mean, I'd already noticed it when I managed to lift my head.

'The inspector asked that you call her before doing anything, although she said she would prefer if you just slept.'

There's a cup and a small jug of water on the table. He sees me looking, pours a glass, and I now make the effort to ease myself up, and he helps prop the pillow behind me, then he places the water in my hands.

My head feels like it could explode. Close my eyes, take a moment. Are they sure I don't have, like, a severed skull, fluid leakage and my brain cleaved in half?

'OK, thanks, Jamie. We're good.'

'Can I get you anything else?'

'Phone, water, pillows… I'm covered.'

'Just buzz if you need me.'

He turns, he leaves, the door swings in the night.

I glance over at Bethany Wright, who still lies sleeping, then check the time, thinking it must be two in the morning. It's just after eight-thirty. Wow, that was a slow-ass hour. That was slower than watching Partick Thistle-Arbroath play out a nil-nil on a bleak Tuesday evening in February.

I make the call. Kadri answers before the phone's even started ringing.

An Unreliable Narrative

vi

Poor Jeremy. So trusting. So easy. We played like him like a fool. Led on by a pair of young, inviting tits. Ha!

29

Kallas wakes me when she arrives. She will want to have left me sleeping, but there was always the chance that she'd leave, I'd wake five minutes later and be calling her again. I feel better this second time that I wake, though my head still zings with pain, especially when I do something stupid, like move.

'You are feeling OK?'

'Sure,' I say. 'Shouldn't have walked into that bottle, huh?'

'Your head does not hurt?'

'Just a little. You know who hit me?'

'We do not. We are missing Jeremy Ludlow from the Kilcraig marketing department. Mr Henderson claims Jeremy received a message, he left the room. He waited for his return, and then the emergency lighting came on. When the DCI could not find them upstairs, it is because Henderson had gone looking for Jeremy. We found the security guard knocked unconscious in amongst the stills. We found you shortly afterwards.'

'You think this Jeremy character is who we're looking for, or that he's been taken, or, I don't know...' I try to think of something else that could have happened to him. 'Body dumped somewhere,' comes eventually.

'We do not know, nor do we have enough information to accurately speculate. It may be that he is in league with someone, because we must remember the evidence that suggested Rhona Campbell was murdered by a woman.'

'Of course.'

I let out a long sigh, then come back, once again, to Bethany Wright, and turn and look at her.

'Why do I keep thinking she's involved?'

'I do not know. But we are testing her DNA against that found on Campbell's corpse. We will hardly get that result returned to us this evening, but we will learn soon enough. This case, as you can imagine, is now exciting a lot of interest on the mainland. The DCI may not hold you in much regard, but the Chief Constable is certainly concerned that one of his officers has been injured in the line of duty.'

I can't help smiling at the thought of me being on the Chief's radar. He'll be getting all concerned, and making pronouncements and all sorts of shit, then someone will say, wait, Chief, you know it's *this* guy, right? And he'll be like, oh, fuck, can we find another officer who's been injured this weekend, there must be tonnes of them?

'You still have your smile,' she says, the smile reflected in her eyes, and then from nowhere I'm asking, 'Why didn't you call when your ferry got cancelled?'

She nods at me asking a reasonable question, even if it's not pertinent to the missing guy whose life, for all we know, might be in imminent danger.

'I am sorry, but I felt guilty. I have been feeling guilty since this afternoon.' She pauses, she nods to herself. 'I have been feeling guilty for the past three years, but after these few days, and particularly this afternoon, the guilt lay heavily upon me. It was because I did not want to leave you. When the boat was cancelled, my first thought was that I could come back and spend more time with you. My guilt grew. I determined that I should attempt to make myself useful in the investigation, before I gave myself back up to you.' A pause, and then, 'I am sorry that I did not call. I knew if I did... I would crack.'

Her voice nearly breaks on that last line. I stare impotently from my death bed. Sick bed. Whateverthefuck bed it is.

I want to reach out, but no matter that we're alone – well, alone with an unconscious woman – there can be no public displays of affection. She has too much to lose.

'You don't have to apologise. Your sense of duty is one of the things I love about you.'

I get that sad smile, and suddenly we lapse into one of our romantic silences, quickly punctuated by a sharp pain in my head, which has me wincing and her looking concerned.

'Should I get the nurse?'

'It's OK. He's already given me codeine. It's getting better.'

'It does not look like it.'

'That one was way less painful than half an hour ago.'

'That does not make me feel any better.'

'I'm fine, don't worry. Tell me where we're at?'

'We are going house-to-house looking for Jeremy Ludlow, or anyone with any idea of his whereabouts. I believe some people are finding it intrusive. DCI Montgomery is being heavy-handed, but I can do nothing about that. There is a helicopter due with another fifteen officers to aid in the investigation. I am not sure bludgeoning the investigation forcefully with more manpower is the way forward, but that is what is happening.'

'How is there a helicopter when the ferry was cancelled?'

'The ferry cancellation was not due to the weather. The ferry broke down. There cannot be a replacement until tomorrow afternoon. I believe this is not an uncommon occurrence.'

After another one of those long, silent stares, she says, 'I should leave you to get some sleep.'

'No.'

'I am sorry, Tom, but I should work. I cannot sit here, while other officers are being flown to the island.'

'That's not what I meant. I'm coming with you.'

'You cannot.'

'I know you're going to worry, and I know I should try to sleep off this pain, but you need to get back to work, and I'm too worried about you to let you do that without me there.'

She kind of smiles again, a sad, sweet smile.

'I survived the last hour and a half without you.'

'Despite my not being there, rather than because,' I say. 'I'm coming with you.'

'I think it was regardless of whether you were with me or not. We might also consider that you attract trouble a lot more than I do. This is who fate has decided you will be. An attracter of trouble. Perhaps I will be in more danger if I am by your side, than if you are here.'

'Well, in that case, don't you want me with you, so you can protect me?' I say, smiling now. Another stabbing pain in the head, but it's not quite so bad, and I manage to mask this one.

'You are safe here.'

I glance over at Bethany Wright, I look at the door.

'It's hardly a fortress. And that nurse guy doesn't look as though he could hold off a couple of Smurfs.'

She laughs at the word Smurfs. I mean, who doesn't? Fuck knows where it came from, it's not like I'm always talking about the flippin' Smurfs.

There's a sound, a stirring from the next bed along. A soft moan from Bethany Wright. Her eyes flicker, but do not open. Her mouth opens, she chews some air. Another moan, the moan becomes a groan.

30

Back in the original ops room, at the small local police station. Kallas and me and Constable Laird. It's her patch, but she's been completely shut out by the Edinburgh boots on the ground. Montgomery may have little time for a rogue, (but obviously brilliant) detective sergeant, but he's got absolutely none for a local constable. Not interested in anything she may have to contribute. Plus, he came here on holiday once a couple of years ago, and consequently thinks he's got all the local knowledge he needs.

So, here we are, kind of running that *Mission Impossible* shadow operation everyone was talking about earlier. Although, to be honest, it's an officially sanctioned shadow operation, as Montgomery accepted Kallas had to be involved since she was still on the island. Ever aware of anything negative reaching the press, such as *Insecure Fat Copper Sidelines Gorgeous Sidekick*. Or something.

Look, I write better newspaper headlines when I haven't been whacked over the head with a bottle of whisky. Every now and again I get a whiff of it from my hair. Not the first time, the rueful onlooker might note, that the DS reeks of booze.

We are sitting at a desk, all facing in the same direction, looking at the two whiteboards, now a mass of information. Laird has been sidelined since yesterday evening, but she's clearly kept up-to-date with all the developments. She's good.

'The best piece of evidence we have so far is what the killer left behind at the scene of Rhona Campbell's murder,' I say.

'The female ejaculate,' says Kallas, just to be sure that's what I meant. Look at me, mincing my words because I'm talking to two women. I really have had a bang on the head.

'The female ejaculate, yes,' I say. 'That's not getting there by any other means. It's a clear pointer. And if someone is mad enough for decapitation, it's hardly the weirdest thing to imagine they're going to be turned on by it.'

'Aye,' says Laird. 'That's always the thing that's surprised me the most as a police officer, throughout my career. The amount of weird sex stories that end up crossing the desk.'

She shakes her head at the thought, sadly choosing to save the details. Not entirely relevant, to be fair.

'So, what do we know about Jeremy disappearing?' I ask. 'He was with Henderson in the office, at the same time as we were downstairs with Montgomery?'

'Yes,' says Kallas. 'He told Henderson he was going to the bathroom, and did not return. This was only a minute before the lights went out. When he left, Henderson thought nothing of it. He admits he was distracted, even though the meeting with Jeremy was a one-to-one. He realised later that Jeremy had been looking at his phone, and had possibly been lured out by a message.'

'Going to see someone he didn't want to admit to,' suggests Laird.

'Possibly,' says Kallas, 'although if they were in the middle of a crisis meeting, he may well have thought Henderson would be unhappy about him seeing anyone, and therefore covered it up.'

'So it's someone who could lure him out,' I chip in, 'and we know it's a woman.'

I lift my eyebrows at the two of them, leaving the rest unsaid, and then Laird, getting my drift, makes a bit of a crude shagging gesture. Not quite Billy Crystal's, but from the same gesture family.

'I've never met this Jeremy guy,' I say. 'What do we know about him other than that he's some kind of writing genius?'

'He is not a writing genius,' says Kallas. 'But he is an interesting character. Young, very good looking, he can sell himself, certainly. Perhaps that is part of the mystique he has managed to create.'

'What d'you mean, he's not a writing genius? I thought that was the whole point of the guy. He exists to be, like, a brilliant writer. That's why he's here, that's why they poached him.'

'Yes,' says Kallas, 'it was. He told me something off the record. He said it was not relevant to the investigation, and while I pointed out that what was relevant was my decision, I did agree to keep it out of the evidence if I did not think it necessary. He is not a writing genius, but a coding genius. He created a programme to generate marketing material. It is similar to Google's ChatGTP, though entirely limited to marketing copy. He has not shared this with anyone else. He says the concept is not unique, but his own program is. This is what he uses.'

'Wait,' I say. 'He's got this genius programme, which presumably can spew out marketing drivel at, like, ten thousand words an hour, and he works for *this* lot? Why doesn't he get a job at Rolex or Shell or something?'

'He works for Kilcraig because he wants to live on Islay. He also has an online presence, and remotely writes freelance. Mr Henderson does not know about this.'

'Wow, nice going. Why'd he tell you?'

Her brow furrows a little, she looks at Laird, she looks back at me.

'I believe he might have been trying to sleep with me,' she says, with all her finest, Estonian roboticism.

Well, get a load of that prick, Jeremy. Laird makes a *fair enough* face.

'I did not mention it before, as I did not think it particularly relevant. I still do not, but given his disappearance, I thought it was time I said. Perhaps I should not have, as it is a distraction. I feel the most relevant thing about it was that he told me in an effort to sleep with me. This is who he is. He is young, he is attractive, he knows this, he likes women. We did not discuss this, but I feel he will be the type who has slept with many women on the island.'

We turn to Laird, who's nodding.

'Mandy, Lily's daughter, she had him, I know that much. They had a long weekend on Mull. Didn't sound like they left the room. Then he dumped her pretty much as soon as they drove off the ferry. Lily didn't sound as disapproving as I thought she might about her daughter getting hurt like that, then it turned out Lily...' and she finishes the sentence with a pair of widened eyes and a nod to the wise.

Some fucking guy, this Jeremy character.

'Tell us about Mandy and her mum,' I say.

'How d'you mean?'

I look at Kallas, I look at Laird, I make a small apologetic gesture to them both, as though I shouldn't be mentioning this, then say, 'The inspector is attractive. We can understand Jeremy making a move. The fact that he slept with both Mandy *and* her mum, kind of implies he'll go after anyone, unless...'

'Right,' says Laird, 'I get you. You're on the right track. I mean, they're decent. They're both nice looking women. I mean, I'm as straight as a pencil, but I've said it often enough in the past, if I had to do a woman, Mandy's mum's top of the list.' A pause, and then she tosses in, 'She does Pilates,' as though that explains everything.

'We are coming at this from a very roundabout perspective,' says Kallas, trying to keep the discussion on track, and likely knowing how easily I'd be distracted by the idea of two women in their early fifties having sex, 'but we know that Jeremy was called out of an important meeting, we know he has a thing for attractive women, we know has likely been abducted or killed by a woman.'

'D'you know of any women at Kilcraig,' I say, 'or, at either Glendun or Ardbreck, that Jeremy had sex with? Or had a thing, any kind of romantic thing with.'

'I'm not in the loop, sorry,' says Laird. 'I just knew about Mandy and her mum because they both told me about it.'

Wow, Mandy and her mum are sharers. Under other circumstances, I'd likely be volunteering to go and interview Mandy's mum.

'We need to consider players in the narrative who might have been of interest to Jeremy,' says Kallas. 'Age, if we are to consider Mandy's mother, who must be several years older than Jeremy, does not appear to be an issue.'

We look at the board. Charlize Theron leaps off the page at me. Jean Forsythe, possibly the best looking woman in the whole saga. And she was way more pissed off at Jeremy than one might expect from just a business matter, given that it wasn't even her business.

I try not to start with her, as she's so obvious.

'Helen Cairns and, whatshername, McGregor at Glendun. Lyn Samuels is not bad. I mean, she's got to be thirty years older than this guy, but if we think that doesn't matter.' Laird's making a bit of a *well I wouldn't shag her* face, and I find myself defensively say, 'I mean, she's no Gillian Anderson, but she's not bad, that's all.'

I scan the board. Might as well toss in the Ardbreck mob now, having done Glendun. Try and think of anyone else there other than Charlize who would be particularly attractive to him, but I don't think anyone ticks the box.

'Jean Forsythe,' I say. 'She's pretty hot. Not sure if there are others. Here, I'd say the lassie in the gift shop, and there was someone on the shop floor. Hmm… Sandy, I think that was her name. And Bethany Wright, but we seem to be ruling her out because she also got put in hospital.'

Weirdly, at the mention of hospital, I suddenly get a stab of pain in my head, like my brain was thinking, *fuck, of course, I'm hurting here*. Caught off guard, I wince, and I get a concerned look from Kallas, which I wave away.

'It's passed,' I say, even though it's left a lingering discomfort, and a sudden feeling of nausea.

I look back at the board. The others view me warily for a moment, and then they follow my look.

'The widow, I guess,' I say. 'She's around the same age, her husband was playing the field, she may well have thought, if he's shagging around, why shouldn't I?'

'That would seem like its own revenge,' says Laird. 'Why kill him?'

'We can't know what was really happening in their marriage,' I say, with a small accompanying shrug.

'She is slight,' says Kallas.

'She is. Lifting the corpse into the mash tun would've been hard, but not entirely out of the question. The killer caught Rhona Campbell off guard, and her corpse was not moved. And whoever this is, got Jeremy to come to them.'

We all look at the photograph of the widow.

'She has motive, and she fits the bill,' I say. 'D'you know if they took a DNA sample?'

'They didn't,' says Laird. 'DCI Montgomery did not consider Caleb Henderson's sister-in-law a likely suspect.'

'This guy is such a di –' I begin, then the words get cut off as there's another swipe of pain across the bows, and I openly and obviously wince. Once again, the nausea rises, and this time there's nothing I can do about it.

I stand, the pain and need to vomit written on my face, and say, 'Bucket!' because it's the only thing I can think to do, and fortunately Laird is down and up and round with the bucket in a second, and it's in my hands just in time, and I turn my back as I throw up.

———

31

Back where I was an hour ago. A beautiful night outside, cold and crisp, a light, fresh fall of snow.

The nurse has seen me into bed, confined until morning at least, and Kadri is now standing over me. Right at this minute, nausea and pain free. The nurse, nevertheless, just gave me a sedative. Sleep will come.

I don't want it to. There's a killer out there, the ugly feeling in my gut isn't just because of the head knock, and I'm worried about Kadri.

She reads my mind, she squeezes my hand.

'I will be fine. You should rest, I will return to check on you later. Hopefully you will sleep until morning.'

'Where are you going now?'

She holds my look, I get the feeling she wants to ask me something, a work something, but is holding back.

'I can talk about work for two minutes,' I say, 'it's OK. What's up?'

'Where did your questions about Kilcraig running a cask investment scam come from?'

I have to think about it for a moment, brain in sludge, then I nod.

'Charlize Theron,' I say.

She stares at me for a while, then finally says, 'You are not thinking straight. I should let you sleep.'

'What? Oh, yeah, sorry. Jean Forsythe. I meant Jean Forsythe, at Ardbreck.'

'And you said Charlize Theron, because she reminds you of that actress.'

'Yeah.'

'I do not see that. It was Jean Forsythe who put that idea in your head?'

'Pretty much. I... I feel like I came up with some of the explanation, but she was leading me on. And... there was something else...' Close my eyes, try to think.

'It is OK, Tom, you sh –'

'She was really pissed off at Jeremy,' I say. 'That was it. She hated the Hendersons, she was annoyed at Jeremy, she was pushing the narrative that all this might be an internal squabble, plus... the other thing.' A pause, she gives me the space. 'She's gorgeous,' I say. 'I mean, not as gorgeous as you.'

I look at her. What did I just say?

'You do not have to say that, Tom.'

She glances sideways at the sleeping Bethany Wright. Something suspicious about that woman. What is it about Bethany Wright?

I start to turn my head, but it hurts, so I don't get very far.

'I will speak to Jean Forsythe,' says Kallas.

'Don't go alone...'

'I will speak to DCI Montgomery first. I should coordinate with him.'

'OK, just watch him. Watch that guy. He's an asshole...'

The words drift away. She takes a step closer. My eyes are closing. I see her take a glance to her left, then she leans forward and kisses me quickly on the cheek. Another hand squeeze, and then she turns and is gone.

The door closes. I am alone with Bethany Wright. I wonder if she's really been asleep all this time. I turn to look at her, but nothing happens. I'm too tired. My head doesn't move at all, even though some part of my brain is telling it to. I try just to glance over, but I can't see anything.

Is there a movement from the bottom of her bed? A stirring of her feet?

My eyes close, my brain shuts down. That's all.

* * *

I wake sometime later to a harsh slap across the cheek, and the words, 'Wakey, wakey, sunshine!'

32

The waking process is slow. I get a glass of water in the face. Just the water, not the glass.

Rub my face, start to come to, look to my left. No phone on the table. The orange button. I think about the orange button.

'I wouldn't bother, the nurse is... incapacitated.'

Where's that voice coming from? There's no one standing by the bed. Those other two unoccupied beds remain empty. I look to my right. Bethany Wright, still in position. She's lying back, but her eyes are open. Staring at the ceiling.

I watch her for a moment, but she doesn't seem to realise I'm here. I look away, back around the room, to the door, resolutely shut.

'Who just threw water in my face?' I ask.

No one answers. I rub my face, realise that it's dry. There was no water. I touch my cheek. What was that? Was there a slap? It still feels like there was a slap, but that was a while ago. It feels like that was a while ago.

'Has there been anyone in here?' I ask.

I turn to Bethany Wright as I say it, so that she knows I'm talking to her. There's still pain with the movement. Maybe I didn't actually say that last question out loud. People tend not to hear you when you just think things.

Right now, I'm not entirely sure what it is I'm thinking.

She turns to look at me at last.

'Nope. Just you and me,' she says.

'Did you slap me?'

Mind beginning to clear. How long have I been asleep?

'Sure. I thought it was time we should talk.'

We stare at each other for a short time, and then she swings her legs off the bed and sits up.

'Why did you lie back down...? I mean, after you slapped me. If it was you who slapped me.'

'That was ten minutes ago. I could tell you were slowly coming out of yourself, so I thought I'd wait. Three a.m., your girlfriend's already been in to check up on you. There's no rush.'

She sort of low laughs to herself, then adds, 'There's a little bit of a rush, I suppose. I mean, we need to get off the island before, you know, the break of day.'

'How are you going to do that?'

'We're sorted. We have a boat to cross to Jura, we have a car over there, we have a boat at the other end. That one's liable to be a bit more of an *event*, but there's still plenty of time.'

I'm staring at her, not entirely sure I'm following everything. What does this feel like? Being a bit drunk, maybe. Drunk-tired. Words and sounds and things happening, all just a little out of reach.

'My girlfriend?' is all I can think to say.

She smiles.

'What?'

'You said my girlfriend. I don't have a girlfriend.'

'If that's what you think.'

'Is she OK?'

'Your not girlfriend? Sure, she's fine. Why wouldn't she be?'

'You're doing all this at three a.m.? You won't... you're not going to get off the island.'

'Plans have been in place for days,' says Bethany Wright. 'You don't start this kind of adventure without, you know, everything already in place. It's like cooking. You don't stick the pasta on, and then start making the bolognaise, do you? You have to be ready to lock 'n load.'

I sit back and close my eyes again. How did I know there was something off about Bethany Wright being here?

Oh.

'You hit me,' I say. I don't look at her. 'I can see it now.' Things come back so slowly.

'Yeah, I did. I mean, you being here, that wasn't part of the plan. It really wasn't. I don't think I hit you that hard, it was the, you know, you smacked your head when you hit the ground. I heard it.' A pause, and then she says, 'Ouch.'

I turn and look at her again. She has the look of someone completely in control of a situation. She knows what's going on, while I have absolutely no clue whatsoever. That's where we are.

'She was so tender,' says Bethany Wright. 'I mean, your

girlfriend. When she came to see you a while ago. She gave you this lovely soft kiss on the lips. I heard her whisper *I love you.* It was *so* romantic. I take it she didn't get that wedding ring from you?'

'Leave her alone,' I say.

She laughs.

'I said, we're not touching her. We have no beef with the inspector.'

'You... you what... you incapacitated the nurse? What does that mean? What did the nurse do?'

'Reasonable point,' says Bethany Wright. 'He was an add-on. Hadn't intended that one. But you know, I was going to have to walk out of here, and that was going to be a problem, so there was that, and then there was the thing where he grabbed my tits because he thought I was unconscious. That kind of thing, that kind of casual sexual assault, is not OK. And if he did it to me... The man's a nurse, people have to trust nurses. I'm not saying he deserved to *die*, but... well, maybe he's dead, I'm not sure. Like I say, incapacitated. That'll do.'

Another look between us. As my mind starts to clear, my look is getting harsher, and I need to relax. I need to feign the aura of barely hanging on to consciousness. She's just sitting looking at me, making no effort to subdue me, tie me down, take me out. Anything, really. So she's relying on my near debilitation. Soon as she sees that that might not be the case – and just because my head's clearing, doesn't mean it won't be – she's going to have to act. God knows when I'll be ready for a fight.

'What are you waiting for?' I ask. 'I mean... I don't know why you're here.'

I look away again, brow furrowed. Close my eyes.

'A call,' she says. 'Just waiting for a call.'

I leave it a moment. Eyes still shut. Don't speak, not yet.

The clock ticks.

Who's making that call? I can't ask, can't sound too switched on, too interested.

'Why did you wake me up? I don't... I'm not sure why you did that.'

'Just kind of curious what you know, what you might've said to your girlfriend. You seemed pretty whacked though, so I think we're safe.'

A gap. I don't look at her.

'Sadly…,' she says, and now I turn and stare through partially open eyes.

'Sadly what?'

'Sadly now that we've had this chat…,' and from the corner of my eye I see her run a finger across her throat. 'I mean, I'm the cover. Don't get me wrong, I haven't killed anyone. Well, maybe Norris out there, but that fucker shouldn't have felt my tits. I mean, that ought to be an easy enough rule by which to live your life, right? Don't grab tits unless you've got, like, actual permission.'

'Yeah,' I say. I mean, she's not wrong.

'Anyway, as I was saying, now that you're awake and I'm busted, you're going to have to join the pile. The corpse pile. I should probably apologise, particularly since it was me who chose to wake you up.'

Well, if she's going to kill me anyway, is there any point in faking a near-comatose state?

'Who are you covering for?' I ask, turning towards her.

I don't actually have to fake being tired and feeling like shit, that's coming fairly naturally.

She laughs.

'Yeah, let's just leave it at that, sergeant.'

She taps her phone, checks the time, says, 'Come on,' in a slightly exasperated way.

'How d'you know no one else is going to come here this evening?' I ask.

Bethany Wright looks at me. I can see the slight hardening in the face, the straightening of the shoulders. Uh-oh. It's coming.

'The only person who cares about you has been and gone,' she says. 'And the only person who cares about me is coming to pick me up shortly, and take me to that boat I was talking about. And then I shall disappear, and people will be torn. Either I'm a victim, and my body has been dumped somewhere, or else I'm the perpetrator. Time will pass, and then evidence will come to light that yes, it was me all along. Bethany Wright, now vanished into thin air. *Poof!*' She snaps her fingers.

'So, who are you the cover for?'

She stares at me from no more than four feet away, sitting on the edge of the bed, straightening all the time, getting ready to move.

'I think we're done, sergeant,' she says, and the whimsy

has completely left her voice.

She acts now, quickly, her movements lithe. Grabs the pillow from her bed, comes across, and as I'm lifting my arms, she swings a punch down into the middle of my face. And then the pillow is over my mouth, pressed down hard, and she's climbing up onto the bed to sit on top of me.

I try to move, but my legs are trapped, stupidly trapped, sheets tucked in tightly around them. My hands are still free, I start lashing out at what I can, aimless, pointless, bare knuckle swipes, barely making contact with anything.

Can't get a breath. Sucking in pillow. Writhing horribly, bucking as much as I can, but she's strong, Bethany Wright, and I'd likely struggle at the best of times. Hurt and drugged, I'm hopeless. Breath going, the familiar head pain coming from nowhere, zinging through my brain. I scream silently into the pillow, struggling to make one last effort.

My hands try to find her throat. I push a thumb into her open mouth, and she bites down hard. I jerk massively at the searing pain, upper body heaving, screaming in impotent, abject silence. Fuck! Fuck it! Her teeth clamped on my thumb, I yank harshly to the side, her head comes with me. I can feel the shift in balance. Thrust powerfully upwards, and she topples off, and then blind with fury and pain and rage I'm up, out the bed.

Not seeing properly. Not thinking at all. Everything feels fucked. She's regaining her feet as I crash out of bed, on top of her. She falls back, and then we're down on the floor in a thumping heap. Beds move, a light falls. A clatter of sound. An ugly grunt, me or her, not sure, then we're on the ground, her face in front of me, mouth bloody and gasping, and I do all I can think to do, my hands to her throat. Fuck! All I can see is blood. Can't feel my thumb, but the pain shoots through me at the pressure, and she's squirming and gasping and kicking frantically and lashing out, punches on the side of my head, and I keep the pressure on her throat, right thumb pressing in, left hand a balled fist, pushing against her flesh. A chaos of noise and blood. Her eyes are popping. I don't know what's happening anymore. There's just sound and fury, a desperate fight for life. This is all I've got. Unmoveable, here until I'm here no more. If I let go of her throat, I'm dead. So I can't.

Suddenly there's quiet, bar the sound of me gasping. I don't know how long it lasts. I can't let go. I don't want to let go. The gasp becomes a stupid sob from somewhere. Again pain

191

shoots through my head. And then I remember my thumb. My left hand is just a bloody mess. Can't see my thumb in all that.

A phone pings.

At last I straighten up. Head all over the place, and yet somehow, in the middle of it, a driving focus. This thing is coming to an end. See it through, get it over with, then I can lie down. Then I can go to sleep.

Fuck, it'll be so nice to go to sleep.

I get up off her, my knee in her belly, and there's nothing from her. She's dead. I killed her.

Fuck her.

I lift her phone. There's the text.

I'll be there in ten. x

And there's the killer's name right there. Well, fuck me.

Right, ten minutes. Where's that focus you were talking about a second ago?

I put the phone in front of Bethany Wright's bloody dead face. It works. Check the text stream to see the kind of reply Wright would send to such a short message, and I send back the thumbs up emoji, all that's required.

Can't sit down. Need to act. If I sit down, I'm asleep in seconds. Maybe I'm dead. My head isn't right. The fuck was I thinking ever getting out of bed in the first place?

Ten minutes. Won't be enough time for Kadri, or anyone else, to get here. It's on me. You know she has an exit route off the island, so you need to act.

Find my phone, and send three quick texts. Kadri, Laird and Montgomery. **Hospital ASAP**. That'll do. Need to keep going. Can't afford to stop and chat.

The phone rings instantly, and I don't even look at it. It will be Kadri. I will be distracted. There's no time.

Need to stem the bleeding in my left hand. Remove a pillow slip, wrap it around the hand. Then I'm standing in the still of the night looking down on the aftermath of the fight. Everything thrown asunder, Bethany Wright dead in the middle of it.

She's going to expect Wright to be waiting outside, and there's no way she's going to come in looking for her. If Wright is not outside, the killer will drive on. I need to get her out there.

I walk out of the ward, up a short corridor. Open a door. Another small ward, this one empty. Next door, storage, nothing of use. I'm looking for a wheelchair.

Hesitate, turn back, grab some tape, roughly and quickly wrap it round the bloody bandage on my hand. Bite the tape, throw the rest aside. Into reception. Behind the counter, the incapacitated Norris. Oh, he's dead. *Incapacitated.* Fuck. Against a wall, two wheelchairs.

Grab one, open it out, push it back through to the ward. And now the struggle. Push the bed farther away, park the chair next to Bethany Wright's corpse, brake on. Lean over her, take a moment, set myself, ignoring the screams of pain in my head and from my hand, ignore the taste of vomit in my mouth. Did I throw up? Fuck, I don't know. Just get the fuck on with it.

Gritted teeth, grim ferocity, arms hooked beneath her armpits, I lift her, every muscle in my body straining and screaming, my head absolutely fucking pounding like it's going to explode. Dump her into the wheelchair.

How much time has gone?

Phone keeps ringing. I have both hers and mine in my pockets. I check it's not Bethany Wright's. It's not. I see the time. I have two minutes.

Stop off at the store cupboard. Rummage, tossing things aside. Grab two, three scalpels. Then back to the wheelchair, and out to the bus stop at the front of the hospital, pushing Wright before me at a stagger. Jesus, it's cold.

Can't leave her sitting in the chair, it'll look too odd. There's a bench beneath a Perspex shelter. Park the wheelchair next to it, brake on, brace myself again, and then hoist Wright's dead weight up out of the chair, and place her on the bench, slumped against the canopy.

Oh, fuck, vomit. Can't stop it. Lean to the side, and now the vomit spews forth in a great rush, all the liquid I took in after the last heave.

In the cold distance, the sound of a car approaching.

My hand still on Bethany Wright's shoulder, as though that's all that's keeping her upright. Let go, step away. Doesn't look natural, but I don't have time. At least she's there, sitting in the bus shelter, waiting for her partner.

Fold the wheelchair, every movement accompanied by wincing and groaning. Fuck, I need to lie down. I need someone to take my head off.

Oh. She's coming. That's who's coming. The woman who cuts people's heads off. Maybe I can get her to do it, that'll ease the pain.

Wheelchair behind the shelter, out of the way. I stand like a dumb idiot staring down the road. Headlights in the distance. The sound of the car getting closer.

In the clear night, somewhere far off, a police siren. Oh fuck. She can't hear that, not before she's stopped.

And what's the plan when she has stopped, genius? You're going to stand here, and she's going to think, oh, rats, looks like I'm captured?

Her headlights swing through the night. Just a few seconds to decide.

I run across the road. Stagger, not run. Vomit comes again, and I throw up on the way.

Duck down, low to a dry stone wall, behind the bare branches of a tree. Need a snow suit. From nowhere, I cackle at the thought. A fucking snow suit. Nothing I can do. Hope she's distracted, looking at the figure of Bethany Wright slumped in the bus shelter.

The car comes into view, fast round the last bend, and then slowing, and then stopping by the bus shelter. She hasn't seen me. A moment, the window of the Jaguar F-Pace lowered.

'Beth! Beth!'

Once again I get the fizz of adrenaline, and I'm up, across the road, and opening the car door. Finola Henderson turns, shocked, but I'm in and sitting down before she can react. Where's the fucking hand brake! Why are there no fucking hand brakes anymore?

She aims a huge slap, and connects brutally across my face. My head is so fucked already, I barely feel it. Scalpel out of my pocket, and I thrust it into her left leg. She screams, but I hold it there, leaning into it. Police siren getting louder. More than one. Come on, you fuckers!

I push against her, keeping the blade thrust into her thigh, getting between her and the steering wheel so she can't drive off. She's hitting my head, thumping it, screaming at me. Fuck you! Fuck!

Come on. Grinding the fucking blade into her leg. Fuck you! And she's screaming in pain, screaming fuck at me, her voice high-pitched and wailing, then I feel her teeth on the back of my head, and then on the back of my neck, and the sirens are everywhere now, from more than one direction, and my head is thumping and thumping and thumping, I can't feel anything anymore, can't think anything anymore, and then the sound of a car screeching to a halt, and footsteps and shouting, and then Henderson is screaming fuck, but not at me, and she's being dragged out of the car, and the scalpel blade rips through her flesh, and then she's gone, and I collapse into the seat, and the last thing I feel is the blade stabbing into my face as I fall forward on it, and that's the last pain, and my head explodes and I'm gone.

An Unreliable Narrative

vii

So they got us. They got us. That's OK. We have lawyers. The lawyers will do a good job, that's what daddy says. We'll be fine. People like us, we won't spend much time in prison, if there even is prison. And if there is prison, is it even that much of a prison?

Daddy says we can probably get out of the mariticide charge. John was such a philandering boor. He taunted us with it. He ruined our mental health. We have a case, that's what the lawyer said. Jury's go big on mental health. It is *so* in.

The lawyer did say it would've been good if we hadn't decapitated the whisky lady. Oh. Oh well, he's probably right. And Jeremy. We shouldn't have killed Jeremy. Turned out he wasn't even writing all that marketing bullshit. He was, like, literally getting a computer to do it. That's pretty funny. The guy was such a fraud. Anyway, dead now. Sucks to be him.

Still waiting to see if our art will become something now. Like, a thing. People are talking about it more on social media, but, you know, it could go either way. We read a discussion on it. This girl wrote, it's not like Hitler got to become famous as an artist. Conflating us with Hitler. That seems harsh. But kind of sexy at the same time.

That's the kind of thought our lawyer tells us we should keep to ourselves.

33

Eyes open. Waking up slowly. My brain feels heavy. Is that a thing? How can your brain…

Doesn't matter.

Close my eyes again, letting them rest. It's daylight. I wonder what time it is. It feels like I've been asleep for a long time.

I lie, unmoving, trying to feel my way into the day. I feel nice, though. Warm, comfortable. Safe.

Safe? Why does that matter?

I open my eyes again. Lie like that for a moment. Head propped on a pillow, not lying completely flat. Hands resting on top of the covers. A small bandage over my left hand. Something doesn't look right.

There's something in my arm, something else attached to my chest. There's equipment. Monitors. A drip. Must be in hospital. I know this because I'm a detective.

And just like that, with that glib thought, the story comes flooding in, a wave of recollection.

Footsteps, someone standing beside the bed, a hand on my arm. A voice. Something. Something about Tom. A woman's voice, but I can't place it. And then she's gone, walking quickly from the room.

I try to watch her go, but my eyes can't keep up.

There's a clock. 5:17.

Five-seventeen. In January. That's not right. Doesn't matter whether it's morning or evening, it should be dark. And it's broad daylight.

I can't think what that means. I stop thinking about it.

I wonder where Kadri is. That must have been her. She left when I woke up. Does that make sense? Wouldn't she have stayed?

More footsteps in the corridor, at a clip. The door opens, a woman in a white coat. And a nurse. And Eileen. I recognise Eileen.

'Tom?' says the woman in the white coat. The doctor. She must be a doctor. 'Tom, can you hear me?'

I open my mouth, trying to find the words.

'You're shouting,' I manage to say.

* * *

'It's really March?'

Eileen sitting beside the bed, holding a cup of tea, from which I'm intermittently taking a sip through a straw.

'The third.'

'March the third. That's... that seems like a long time.'

'Just over five weeks.'

'Jesus. And they brought me here by helicopter?'

'To the roof of the building.'

'Never been in a helicopter before.'

'Too bad you didn't get to enjoy it.'

I look out of the window. Can see the tops of buildings in Glasgow city centre. Dark now, as late afternoon has turned to night. Eileen has stayed with me, through the wakening up, and through all the checks. She sent a few texts, though she hasn't told me to whom. A few replies, a couple of them making her smile. No one else has appeared, though she's already said my kids will be in later.

'Were you aware of anything?' she asks. 'I mean, when you were in the coma, did you know anything of what was going on in the room?'

I try and think, but nothing comes to mind. Struggling with the idea that I've been unconscious for over five weeks. My brain can't compute that yet. Five weeks of my life kaput. What if those five weeks had been going to be best five weeks out of the lot?

I was going to see Kadri again. Fuck.

Something stops me asking about her straight away.

'No, I don't think so. Were you singing to me?' I ask, managing a weak smile.

'That would've finished you off,' she says, laughing. 'Talking of bad singing, I did play you Dylan every day. I mean, obviously I put it on and then left the room so I didn't have to listen to it, but it didn't seem to get through.'

I smile again, she smiles with me. She offers the tea, I take another small sip.

'So what happened to me?' I ask.

'Seems you caught the killers, and nearly died in the process. One of them's dead, the other in custody. She's singing like a canary. I hear she might be a little bit psychotic.'

'The artist?'

'Yeah, she's an artist. A failed artist they're calling her on the news, although given the subjectivity of art, I'm not sure how you fail at it. You either do it or you don't, I'd've thought.'

'You never saw her art,' I say. Still got the lines, obviously. 'What about the guy, the main guy. Henderson. Was he involved?'

'Not in murder, but it looks like he's getting investigated for fraud. Something to do with cask investments. I'm not in on any of that, I just saw a couple of reports floating around. The press don't have that side of it yet, they're too busy getting excited about the murders. They'll love it that you've woken up.'

'Terrific.'

'You do seem to end up in hospital an awful lot, don't you?'

'I try not to.'

'I'm not so sure. Feels like you're bit of a needy attention seeker.'

'Thanks,' I say, and I can't help myself laughing. Weirdly it doesn't hurt to laugh. I'm cleared to watch Frankie Boyle and old *Not The Nine O'Clock News* reruns.

'My thumb got bitten off,' I say, making a small gesture with my left hand. There's still a bandage around the stump.

'Yeah, you're such a show-off.'

'Fuck off. Why didn't they sew it back on? Isn't that a thing?'

'It wasn't severed cleanly enough. More kind of torn off with her teeth. I don't think they even tried to put it back on.'

'Maybe I can get a bionic replacement.'

'Sure, Tom, a bionic thumb, because that's a thing.'

We share a smile again, and then the conversation goes. There's more to ask, but I know enough for the moment. Pieced together with what I can remember, I know more than enough.

My eyes drift away, down the length of the bed. I start to think about Kadri. I allow myself. She's not here, she's not by my hospital bed in Glasgow. She is, presumably, long gone by now. I want to ask, but at the same time, I don't want to know.

When was the last time I saw her? We were at the police station, she drove me back to the hospital. She squeezed my fingers, she kissed me on the cheek.

That woman, Bethany Wright, she told me Kadri returned later. I remember her telling me that, I don't remember it actually happening. The touch of her lips on mine, the softly spoken words.

'Kadri left you a note,' says Eileen, reading my mind.

I turn back. Face blank.

Sure, *face blank*. I probably look like Tom when he sees one of those Tom & Jerry anthropomorphised, glamorous whorecats. Eileen holds forward a small envelope, and I take it from her and rest my hands back on the covers.

'Thanks.'

'I should leave you to read it. You should eat something, then get back to sleep.'

'I've been asleep for weeks.'

'Tom, you had a ruptured aneurysm *in your brain*. You nearly died. You look like shit. Get some more sleep, make sure you're awake enough in a couple of hours to talk to the kids.'

'Yes, boss.'

She stands, she looks down at me. Something comforting about it, about being with her, that wasn't there before I got my thumb bitten off and had my aneurysm.

'Will I see you tomorrow?' I ask.

Not sure I deserve to see her tomorrow, but the words are just there, with all their implicit neediness.

'Would you like to?'

I nod, she nods in return.

'I'm on duty eight until five. I'll be in after.'

'Thank you.'

Another long stare. I lift my hand. I want to reach out and touch her, but I haven't quite got the hang of sitting up and propelling myself forward just yet. She does the job for me, quickly leans forward, kisses me on the cheek, says, 'See you tomorrow,' with a forced briskness, and then she's gone.

Silence. Me and my note from Kadri.

She will be back in Estonia by now. Long since gone. I will presume, although I didn't ask, that she was on the receiving end of one of those texts Eileen just sent.

I never got to say goodbye. Maybe it's better this way. Fuck knows what I'd've said. Potential for it to have been toe-curlingly embarrassing, haunting me for the rest of my life? Very high. I'm too old for that dumb, romantic shit.

I lift the note, and stare down the bed at the small, cream envelope in my hands, all that's left of those wonderful, erotic and romantic couple of days in amongst the bloody carnage.

The door opens, a nurse enters. Early-thirties, southern European. Spanish perhaps.

'How are you feeling, Tom?'

I notice no one's calling me Detective Sergeant. Do they know something I don't?

'OK. You?'

'Oh, I am just fine. You would like to eat something?'

I nod.

'Good, your friend said she thought you might.'

She stands beside me, helping me sit up more, to be ready to accept dinner.

'She's been in every day,' says the nurse. 'She said to me one day that you would owe her dinner when you woke up, and I said, that man owes you a week in the Maldives,' and she laughs, and I can't help smiling along with her. 'OK, you are ready, I shall send along the chefs.' Another infectious laugh, then she turns and walks quickly from the room.

I stare at the door. The note in my hand from Kadri, and thinking about Eileen. Here every day for five weeks.

Would I have done that for her?

A weak smile comes to my face when I think of the answer.

I awkwardly slide the note beneath the pillow. Chances of me bursting into tears when I read it are pretty fucking high by the way, particularly in this raw state. No one wants to see that.

I'll read it later, when there's less chance of an interruption.

The door swings open again, and this time a dining trolley is pushed in, a small woman behind it, a smile on her face, the smell of lemon and thyme and sadness in the air.

I AM MULTITUDES

(DS Hutton Book 11)

Glasgow is in lockdown, as a vigilante killer threatens to run amok.

There have been a series of revenge attacks in the city against accused criminals never charged or brought to trial. The attacks are presented as being committed by a series of individuals, perhaps even a rogue band of justice warriors, working in tandem. However, the police quickly establish it's all the work of one person.

Many guises, many methods of revenge, terror and murder, but only one perpetrator. Soon enough, they will make themselves known, with a simple, but chilling, three-word slogan:

I am Multitudes.

Meanwhile, time, alcohol and a long career of floundering in a cesspool of his own indifference, have led DS Hutton to the end, with retirement now only a few weeks away. However, much though he would like to wind slowly down to a soporific conclusion, hidden in his own small corner of the city, once again Police Scotland puts that bat signal in the sky, and Hutton, along with every other detective within fifty miles, is called to action.

Soon enough the vigilante's attention is turned on him, and suddenly Hutton's retirement will seem a very long way off...

BUCHAN

(DI Buchan Book 1)

A mystery written in blood.

The head of a literary publishing house is murdered, and Detective Inspector Buchan and his team enter a world of writers and editors, of passion, jealousy and hate. Suspects are not in short supply, but before the investigation can really get going, there's a second murder, this one throwing up the existence of an unknown manuscript.

Now clues and motives and suspects abound, and the hunt is on for *Ladybird*, a book that no one knows anything about. There's a game being played, and Buchan needs to find out what it is before anyone else dies. For that is the only certainty: sooner or later, as rain sweeps across the rundown city, and the players drift in and out of suspicion, the killer will strike again.

BUCHAN is the first title in a major new Scottish detective series, featuring DI Buchan and his team from Glasgow's Serious Crime Unit.

PAINTED IN BLOOD

(DI Buchan Book 2)

Where every murder is a masterpiece.

A double murder, a public spectacle, a killer toying with the police. And then, from nowhere, a mysterious woman with a story to tell, a suspect handed to **DI Buchan** on a plate.

It's been a bad few months for Buchan and his team, little going right. They need a win. What they don't need is a murder victim, the naked corpse of the young woman posed on a park bench, erotically summoning viewers to the scene of her death. Then a week later, a second victim.

Out of nowhere, a woman finds Buchan in the Winter Moon, claiming the posing of the corpses was based on two paintings by a little known Spanish artist. And she brings ill news; there's a third painting in the series, and she herself will be the victim.

It is so unexpected, and so alien to everything they've investigated so far, suddenly it seems Buchan is carrying out an entirely new line of inquiry. However, as he gets closer to the heart of darkness, it becomes evident the two strands of the investigation are linked, the threat is imminent, and that the re-enactment of the third painting is close to being realised...

THE LONELY AND THE DEAD

(DI Buchan Book 3)

A killer sings the song of the dead.

A man hangs by the neck from a derelict pier on the Clyde, while a haunting melody plays on a loop. Not until the pathologist discovers that the victim was already unconscious before he was hung, do the police realise this wasn't suicide.

DI Buchan and his team are called. The victim was a composer, who'd been working on the soundtrack of a TV serial killer show. The show, plagued by arguments and ill luck, is in post-production. An uncomfortable air of angst and anger hangs over it. Wrath has been unleashed.

As the short, claustrophobic days of a cold, bleak January continue, another member of the production team dies, and a real-life serial killer has been let loose…

A LONG DAY'S JOURNEY INTO DEATH

(DI Buchan Book 4)

A regular day at the Serious Crime Unit quickly spirals out of control, when DI Buchan and his team are asked to investigate the case of a missing film director.

The story of Claire Avercamp has been in the news, but her life has been a tale of a wasted career, failed relationships, drugs, alcohol and bad decisions. She's been missing for over a week, presumed drunk, comatose or dead, but she's burned so many bridges, no one seems particularly concerned.

However, an old colleague of the chief inspector is personally involved, and brings new information. Avercamp had been working on a film about the theft of antique manuscripts. Despite all the evidence to the contrary, he thinks her disappearance is not an act of self-sabotage.

At first reluctant to get involved, Buchan quickly realises this is a high stakes game, and there are more players than anyone realised. Money is at play, lives are on the line, and deadly intrigue lurks around every twist and turn of a day that will stretch deep into the darkness of night…

By Douglas Lindsay

DI Buchan

Buchan
Painted In Blood
The Lonely And The Dead
A Long Day's Journey Into Death

The Barber, Barney Thomson

The Long Midnight of Barney Thomson
The Cutting Edge of Barney Thomson
A Prayer for Barney Thomson
The King Was in His Counting House
The Last Fish Supper
The Haunting of Barney Thomson
The Final Cut
Aye, Barney
Curse of The Clown

Other Barney Thomson

The Face of Death
The End of Days
Barney Thomson: Zombie Slayer
The Curse of Barney Thomson & Other Stories
Scenes from The Barbershop Floor

DCI Jericho

We Are the Hanged Man
We Are Death

Pereira & Bain

Cold Cuts
The Judas Flower

DI Westphall

Song of the Dead
Boy in the Well
The Art of Dying

DS Hutton

The Unburied Dead
A Plague of Crows
The Blood That Stains Your Hands
See That My Grave Is Kept Clean
In My Time of Dying
Implements of the Model Maker
Let Me Die In My Footsteps
Blood In My Eyes
The Deer's Cry
A Winter Night
I Am Multitudes

Stand Alone Novels

Lost in Juarez
Being For The Benefit Of Mr Kite!
A Room with No Natural Light
Ballad in Blue
These Are The Stories We Tell
Alice On The Shore

Other

Santa's Christmas Eve Blues
Cold September

Printed in Great Britain
by Amazon